ANORIA

A Family of Wizards Book I

Gorg Huff & Paula Goodlett

Cover designed by Laura Givens

Gorg Huff & Paula Goodlett
Visit our website at https://warspell.com/

Printed in the United States of America

This Printing: Feb 2021
1632, Inc.

eBook ISBN-13 978-1-953034-53-3
Trade Paperback ISBN-13 978-1-953034-54-0

CONTENTS

CHAPTER 1

Location: Boden House, Brookshire
Date: 10 Barra, 134 AF

As she ate her oatmeal, it seemed to Anoria that the morning had been surprisingly easy. Mistress Boden had stressed, again and again, that Ann must make a good appearance at school, so for once, Ann had stood still for hair brushing and sash tying. Anoria had had to rush her own preparations, though. She still had to make sure that Mark was dressed and ready for the day, even though he wouldn't be attending school for another year.

"Anoria." Mistress Boden sniffed. "I did tell you that you must control your hair, didn't I? I'll not have a member of my household looking like a ragamuffin. Go upstairs and braid it or something. Right now."

"Yes, Mistress," Anoria responded. There was no advantage in pointing out that she had been unable to braid her hair because Mark had decided to hide under his bed. Anoria left her half-eaten breakfast and went to the room she shared with Merry, the girl of all work. She braided her hair so tightly that she felt her eyes were going to pop out of her head, even though she knew that the dratted mess would escape from the braids before noon. It was just that kind of hair, mousey-brown and flyaway.

Mistress Boden called that it was time to catch the wagon, and Anoria had to run back down the stairs. Merry handed her a basket that contained lunch and whispered, "I put a slice of buttered bread and ham in there, since you didn't get to finish breakfast."

Anoria smiled thankfully and ran to catch the school wagon. Stocky Harold, at fourteen the oldest child going to school from this village, had taken pride of place beside the driver. There were twelve children in the big wagon bed before Anoria and Ann climbed in. Six-year-old Ann, still grumpy from getting up so early, fell asleep quickly, and Anoria ate her bread and ham, relishing every bite. None of the other children appeared to care. It was barely dawn, and most of them seemed to be a bit dazed at the earliness of the hour. Anoria had a little more than an hour to simply enjoy the quiet.

It was wonderful. This close to sunrise, the dew glistened where the rising sun stabbed lances of light through the branches of the trees. The road was flat, wide and white, wizard-made, so the wagon didn't jolt you around like a road made by shovel and pick. Early autumn flowers bloomed beside the road, and the leaves were just turning gold and red. It was colorful and peaceful, and most importantly to Anoria, it was quiet. Nobody was yelling or demanding attention, for once. The only sounds were the crunch of the wheels on the road and birds singing in the trees.

Location: Schoolhouse, Greenshire
Date: 10 Barra, 134 AF

They reached Greenshire with just enough time to use the outhouse before the teacher began ringing the bell to start school. All the children, now awake and refreshed, ran toward the schoolhouse. The teacher, a spare-looking woman of about thirty-five, stood in front of the door. "I'm Deaconess Margaret Willow. There are two meanings for Deaconess. The first is a student learning to become an intercessor of a particular god. The second, which I am, is someone who has been trained by the intercessors of a particular god in some of the mysteries of that god. I was trained at the Teachers College in New Landrow, the capital of Fornteroy Province, in the teaching mysteries. Now, line up by age, please," she said. "We shall have to do some tests and see how much each of you knows. Older children to the back, younger to the front please."

That plan didn't work out all that well. It was the start of the school year and most of the children had only a vague idea of the age of any children not of their household. Also, they were combining the schools from two towns. Each child surely knew if his brother was older or younger, but how old the boy from the next village was could not be more than a guess. So, following the teacher's orders, they guessed and often got it wrong. So after . . .

"I'm five!"

"I'm seven."

"No, you're not. You're six!"

"Am so! Well, almost."

"Not till next month!"

"I'm nine. How old are you?"

"I'm eight. You want to be friends?"

"Naw! You're a girl!"

"Well, you're mean, and I'd rather be a girl anyway," said with anger and a little leaking of tears.

The teacher had to start over, which didn't put that formidable woman in a good mood. "Five-year-olds come over here!" the teacher didn't quite shout. A little boy and two little girls approached with great trepidation. A third little girl had to be pushed off by what was probably an older brother.

The teacher called for the six-year-olds, and Anoria took Ann by the hand and led her over to the spot indicated. There were only three, including the boy who insisted that he was almost seven. They got put in with the five-year-olds, much to their evident disgust.

Seven- and eight-year-olds also got clumped together for a total of five.

Nine- and ten-year-olds totaled seven. Anoria, who was ten, a dark-haired girl, and five boys.

Eleven- and twelve-year-olds totaled five.

Thirteen- and fourteen-year-olds, seven more. Including Harold.

There were three fifteen-year-olds in the school, five sixteen-year-olds. Altogether, thirty-nine children from two villages.

* * *

The classroom took up most of the building. It was one large room with the teacher's desk opposite the door. Along the east wall were images of the major gods, and the west wall had a small bookshelf and several maps. A map of Whitehall County, and in the upper right corner of it a likeness of Count Whitehall, then a window. Next to that was a map of Fornteroy Province with a likeness of Duke Makrslans, the royal governor of the province. Another window, then a map of the kingdom with the likeness of the king inset into the right corner. Another window and a map of the whole world. This early in the fall, the shutters were open and the room was nice and bright. Small tables that two children could sit at were used as desks. Shorter tables were to the front of the classroom and taller ones were toward the back. Anoria quite understood the teacher's directions to line up by age.

Anoria, after a certain amount of jostling and movement, wound up a bit more than halfway back in the center of the classroom, next to a girl who had a mass of curly, black hair. The girl smiled shyly at Anoria, who smiled back. It would be nice to have a friend her own age, she thought. The girl looked very friendly and a bit lonely.

"I am Deaconess Margaret Willow," the teacher said. "I know some of you Brookshires from last year, but others of you are new here." The arrangement for the children of to be carted to Greenshire for schooling had just been made that summer. Unfortunately, that arrangement had doubled the size of the student body. "I shall learn your names and families shortly. Meanwhile, I have some questions to ask you which will allow me to place you at the proper level for learning. Take out your slates. The teacher held up a black slate in a wooden frame. "Down the left side of your slate, write the numbers 1 to 20. Like this." Deaconess Willow wrote numbers quickly with a piece of chalk on the slate, and held it up again for the students to see.

"We will now have a test on mathematics."

After asking her questions, Deaconess Willow collected the slates. "You may all take a book to read or play quietly while I check these. Quietly now. And do be very careful with the books. Our patron furnishes them and wouldn't be pleased to find them damaged."

The little bookshelf held almost fifty books. That wasn't as many as the orphanage school had, but was still a great many books to be in one place. There were storybooks for the littler children, to help them learn to read, and some adventure stories for the older children. There were also books on math and alchemy, and books about the gods.

The children who were interested in reading went to the bookshelf. Anoria found a book that at first confused her a bit. All the words were scrambled. Then she realized it was a puzzle book and began to work them out. It was difficult without her slate, which Deaconess Willow still had, but she managed. Joanna Cooper, the dark-haired girl, began reading a simple adventure story that Anoria felt was more appropriate for a younger child. Several of the children sat and fidgeted instead of reading.

Deaconess Willow was halfway through the stack of slates when Ann Boden got bored. "Anoria," Ann said sharply. "Anoria."

Anoria looked up from her puzzle book. "Yes, Ann."

"My shoe is untied," Ann said. "Come and tie it."

Anoria began to rise, when Deaconess Willow motioned her to sit down again. Deaconess Willow looked sternly at Ann. "What is your name, child?"

"Ann Boden, ma'am," Ann said, with a small quaver in her voice. She seemed to realize that she had spoken out of turn.

"You didn't attend school here last year, did you?" Deaconess Willow asked. When Ann shook her head, Deaconess Willow continued, "And what, Miss Boden, leads you to believe that you may interrupt my school with this kind of demand? I directed that you should all be quiet, did I not?"

Ann nodded, but defiantly said, "Anoria is our servant and is only here because she takes care of me on the wagon."

Deaconess Willow sniffed. She said, in a tone that brooked no argument, "In this school, Miss Boden, we are all servants to Zagrod. If you do not know, Zagrod is the god of knowledge and learning, and this schoolroom is his temple. I am a servant of Zagrod, you are, and Anoria is also. None of my students, within the confines of this school, is more or less than another. Get that straight, right now. I am in charge. When I tell you to be quiet, you will be quiet. Do you understand me?"

Ann's face flamed with embarrassment. "Yes, ma'am. But my shoe is untied."

Deaconess Willow glared a bit. "If you are unable to tie a shoe by yourself," she said, "you may ask Anoria to help you. At lunchtime."

As Ann bent to tie her own shoe, Anoria's heart sank a bit. Ann was bound to try and find a way to blame Anoria for her misstep, as Anoria had already learned. Joanna, who sat next to her, leaned over and patted her hand. Joanna whispered, "That will fix Miss Annie, won't it?"

Anoria shook her head and whispered back, "She'll just find a way to make her mother mad at me again."

Deaconess Willow looked up from the slates and said, "Did I give anyone permission to talk?"

The classroom grew quiet.

* * *

More of Deaconess Willow's tests followed. By lunchtime, the classroom had been rearranged quite drastically. Anoria, instead of being in the center of the room, was two-thirds of the way to the back, as was Joanna. Harold Boden was in the center of the room with children who were younger than himself and very unhappy about it. Ann was in the very front, with the youngest children.

When Deaconess Willow released them to go outside and have their lunch, Ann and Harold both grabbed their lunches from the basket and went to eat with children of their own age. Anoria found herself sitting alone under a tree in the schoolyard, until Joanna ran out and joined her.

"That Ann must be a problem to deal with," Joanna said.

"She's not so bad," Anoria replied. "She's just never been to school before and doesn't know the rules. She'll learn. I'll offer to give her some help with her letters. Maybe that way she won't be angry and make trouble with her mother about it."

"That ought to work, I think. Maybe she'll keep her mouth shut at home if you help her out," Joanna said. "Same goes for that Harold. He didn't do as well at the maths as you did. You could offer to help him with that."

"I'll try it," Anoria agreed. "Problems or not, it's still better than the Home was."

"The Home?"

"The Gent Foundling Home," Anoria explained. "That's where I came here from."

"You're an orphan?" Joanna asked.

"Ever since I was about a year old," Anoria said. "I lived at the Home for almost all my life."

"What happened?"

Joanna was very curious, Anoria thought. Most people didn't want to know about this sort of thing. "My parents died when a plague swept through Gent," Anoria said. "And I don't have any relatives that I know of. So it was the Home or nothing."

"That's got to be really hard."

"Well," Anoria temporized. "There was a really good school and I started going to it way back when I was really little. And then Master Boden came, looking for someone to help with the little ones on the wagon trip to school. So the school mistress recommended me, as soon as she found out I could go to school too." Anoria left out the part about often not having enough to eat. About overcrowded dorm rooms and clothing that was always worn and threadbare and never fit. Most of all, she left out the parts about not having a family or anyone that cared for you all that much.

The girls discussed their lives at length. Joanna was the eldest of two children, and her baby brother was only two. She lived just outside of Greenshire, close enough to walk to school. By the time Deaconess Willow rang the bell to resume class, they were fast friends.

On the wagon ride home, Anoria sacrificed her reading time to help Ann with her letters. Ann was very grateful, as she had found that several younger children knew them better than she did. She smiled at Anoria thankfully. Harold struggled a bit with his maths, but eventually finished the slate of problems he had been set to finish. Anoria checked them for him, and he only had to re-do two problems.

"Thanks," Harold muttered. "Arithmetic gives me fits, and I've got to learn it. Father insists. He says I can't be a factor without arithmetic." Both Greenshire and Brookshire were farming villages. Master Boden bought crops and sold seed and other goods in Brookshire. There was a similar factor in Greenshire, Henry Abel, who was a farmer with plenty of help on his farm.

"It's like a puzzle," Anoria said. "I like them almost as much as reading. Not quite as much, you understand, but almost."

Anoria finished her own problems quickly and had about a quarter of an hour to read before they arrived at Brookshire and she reverted to her role as servant to the family. She hadn't really told Joanna everything. When she wasn't at school or on the wagon, she had to work like any servant girl. Keeping a home was a lot of work, what with washing on the scrub boards, carrying water from the well, getting wood for the kitchen fireplace, sweeping, darning socks, patching clothing, and the hundreds of other chores it took to keep things neat and working. It was more work than a single person could reasonably do.

Different households handled the load in different ways. Some divided the chores up among the family, especially if there was a large family to share the work. Others hired temporary help from the neighbors. The Bodens, being both relatively wealthy and rather proud of the fact, hired a cook and a girl of all work. When that had proved not quite sufficient and the matter of the trip to school had come up, they had taken

Anoria in. At ten years old, Anoria was sort of an apprentice girl of all work and part-time tutor for the children.

This was both legal and quite respectable in the world shared by the Bodens and Anoria. It was a moderately poor world, though it didn't know it, and poverty and justice didn't fit together well. They assumed that if you took in a child, it was for the work that child could provide, not out of love. And there weren't enough people who could afford to take in children to begin with. Wealth was concentrated among the nobility and magic users. A fairly high-level wizard could do the work of hundreds of men and was paid in accordance with that ability. And high-level magic users were rare, so magic was expensive. Magic items were even more expensive, albeit worth the cost in many ways. You could, for instance, survive quite well without a breadkeeper. However, if you had one, the bread never spoiled and the breadkeeper would last forever.

The magic made life better than it would have been without it, but Anoria had found that it was a life of long hours and hard work. Which was still better than the foundling home in the city of Gent, where she had also had long hours and hard work but less to eat and worse clothing. And the occasional beating by bigger kids who wanted something you had or were just in a bad mood.

Location: Boden House, Brookshire
Date: 11 Barra, 134 AF

The next morning, when Ann tried to fidget under the hairbrush, Anoria began reciting the letters Ann had learned the day before. Ann knew very well that she was expected to do well in school, so she stood quietly and recited the letters with Anoria.

"Very good," Anoria told her. "Now run along. I've got to get Mark dressed."

For once, Mark was more than ready to get dressed and have his breakfast. Anoria had a rare few moments to herself and spent them braiding her hair into submission.

That set the pattern for the next few weeks. Anoria went over Ann's lessons with her as she dressed the smaller child, then chased Mark down to dress him. And when she could, she struggled with her hair. Then she got to go to school and see her friend Joanna.

Location: Schoolhouse, Greenshire
Date: 11 Barra, 134 AF

"Anoria! Anoria," Joanna called. "What are you doing?" Joanna had curly, black hair that appeared willing to do whatever was wanted with no more than a glance from a brush. Anoria, who still had to resort to braiding hers as tightly as she could, envied it a lot. She still felt like her eyes were going to pop out from the tension of her braids.

"Reading," Anoria answered. "It's another puzzle book. It has letter puzzles where the letters are all mixed up, number puzzles where you have to figure out the next in a series. And it's got shape puzzles."

"Oh, come on," Joanna said. "Let's go walk around the village square. You can read any old time."

Anoria closed the book with some regret. Joanna had become a good friend over the last months, but she wasn't as much of a student as Anoria. Joanna liked socializing much more than Anoria did. But she was a very friendly sort, and Anoria liked her. "All right. It looks like Harold and Ann are busy with games, so I have a few minutes. But what's so fascinating about the village square, Joanna? It looks the same today as it did yesterday."

"Come on, will you? Old Pruneface is in town. She's gone to the Chandlers." The Chandlers were a family, and a business in the small town where candles and soap were made and sold. They also sold the much more expensive glows which were made by magic.

"Who," Anoria asked, "is Old Pruneface? I've never heard anyone called that."

"That's because she hardly ever comes to town," Joanna answered, pulling Anoria to her feet. "She's my Great-Aunt Cordelia, Mama says. She was my Grandpa's sister. He died before I was born, so she must be about a hundred years old."

"You might want to check, you know," Anoria said. "I'll bet you've done the math wrong again." Joanna often had a problem with math. Anoria had been quite a help with that. Anoria still felt that maths were almost as good a puzzle as letters were.

"Never mind. Anyway, Old Pruneface is in town, so we've got something different to see," Joanna said. "And next week we'll be having the town picnic, so you and the Bodens will be here. You'll come see me, won't you? Clarence isn't much fun yet. He's only two, and he slobbers all the time."

"I will if I get a chance to get away from the children," Anoria answered. "You know they take up a whole lot of time. Mistress Boden yelled at me for reading the other day. While I was distracted, Eve—the little monster—got into the clabber and spilled it all over the pantry. I had to clean it up, even though I didn't spill it."

Anoria and Joanna stood quietly at the corner of the village square and watched all the activity. "Why do you call her Old Pruneface, Joanna? She doesn't look especially dried up to me." The woman, in fact, didn't look as old as Mistress Boden, as near as Anoria could tell. She had short dark hair and was very well dressed.

"Well," Joanna said, "She probably isn't. She's just kind of spooky. My mother is afraid of her, I think. She comes to visit sometimes and we all have to be on our best behavior and wear good clothes every day. And she turned someone into a pig once."

"How?" Anoria asked. "You're joking with me, aren't you? Trying to scare me, I'll bet."

Joanna shook her dark curls, "No, it's true. She's a wizard. And she's spooky. Always going on about places she's been and people she knows. And how much trouble it is to work up spells. I saw one once. She was writing something, and I snuck a look at it. It just looked like a bunch of scribbles to me. But, anyway, I'm glad of some of the things she's done. She fixed the road, and that's how come you can come to school."

"In that case, I'm very grateful to her," Anoria said. "And here comes the wagon. I've got to grab Ann and Harold and go." The wagon driver was an older man whose son had taken over the farming. He didn't like to wait if someone was late getting to the wagon.

Joanna's face fell a bit. "Oh, I suppose so. I wish you could just stay, though." There were a few girls near their age in Greenshire, but none of them were as close in age as Joanna and Anoria were.

"Me, too," Anoria agreed, turning back toward the school. "But right now, I have to make sure we all get on the wagon. I'll see you on first day."

The hour-long wagon ride was almost the only time Anoria had to read for her own pleasure. She became absorbed in her puzzle book almost immediately. When the wagon stopped in Brookshire, she was disappointed that the ride was over. Yet another sixth and seventh day loomed ahead of her. No school, nothing to enjoy. Just more taking care of children, washing dishes, collecting eggs, sweeping floors, darning socks, sewing up tears in the clothing and doing laundry.

CHAPTER 2

Location: Boden House, Brookshire
Date: 23 Barra, 134 AF

"Anoria, are you ready yet?" Mistress Boden called. "Honestly, a person would think that you just dawdled around to make me angry." Mistress Boden expected everyone in the household to keep to her schedule and got impatient when they didn't.

"Yes, ma'am," Anoria replied, rushing down the stairs. She was late because she'd had to brush Ann's hair and hadn't had time to deal with her own. As a result, her braids weren't as tight as they usually were. "I'm ready. I'm sorry. I had to . . ."

"Never mind," Mistress Boden said. "Let's just get into the wagon and go. I don't know why I ever agreed to attend this picnic, anyway. It would be so much easier just to stay home."

"Yes, ma'am," Anoria answered, hoping that Mistress Boden wouldn't change her mind at the last minute. But, Mistress Boden quite liked to peruse market stalls. . . . "I heard in Greenshire that there are going to be some new stalls open today. There might be some things you'd be interested in."

Anoria was relieved when the family finally got into the wagon. For this occasion, even the girl of all work, Merry, was allowed to attend. The cook, Jess, had whispered that she was going to enjoy the quiet house while everyone was gone. With Merry to share the chore of looking after Mark and Eve, maybe for once Anoria could get away from tending the children and spend some time with Joanna.

The younger children made the trip something of a nightmare. The older children, Harold and Ann, were used to the trip back and forth between Brookshire and Greenshire. Mark had just turned five, though, and hadn't started attending school yet. Eve, now three, just didn't want to settle down and climbed and crawled over everyone in the wagon bed. Finally, a cross look from Master Boden quieted her down, and the last half-hour was spent in relative peace.

Location: Town Square, Greenshire
Date: 23 Barra, 134 AF

They arrived in Greenshire and the family scattered. "Anoria, you take Eve. Merry, you take Mark," Mistress Boden directed. "We'll all meet here at the wagon for lunch. And don't the two of you let these children get into any trouble. I worry so about them."

Anoria and Merry exchanged looks as Mistress Boden swept away. Anoria and Merry sometimes wondered why Mistress Boden, if she was so worried about her children, so often avoided them. Merry shrugged, but before she could say anything, Mark took off running toward a group of boys his age. Merry ran after him, knowing that she would be in hot water if he escaped her care. Anoria, grateful that it was little Eve she had responsibility for, took the child's hand and began to walk toward the games for the smaller children.

"Anoria, wait up," Joanna called. "I'm coming too."

Joanna came up, holding her little brother's hand. "Well, at least we're only stuck with these two," she said. "They're not as bad as that Mark." Clarence had hair just as curly and dark as Joanna's was. He was a cheerful boy, chubby and happy to see all the people around him.

Anoria nodded agreement. "Poor Merry. He'll run her a merry chase, all right." Anoria giggled, then said, "Clarence and Eve might play together, and we'll have time to talk."

Anoria and Joanna chattered away, as Eve and Clarence got to know one another. The day passed pleasantly, although at one point Joanna's mother passed them and gave Anoria a raking glance.

"What was that about?" Anoria asked.

"Oh, nothing," Joanna answered.

Anoria looked at her friend and tilted her head a bit before asking, "Is she upset that we're friends? That's happened before, you know. One mother in Gent wouldn't let her daughter play with me because I'm an orphan. She said they didn't know where I was from and had to be careful."

"I don't think so," Joanna answered. Joanna didn't want to tell Anoria that her mother was unsure of their friendship, and for that very reason. "I don't think being an orphan is catching, like a cold."

Anoria's face was a little pale. "I certainly wish I hadn't caught it. But if that's the problem, I'll understand. Really, I will."

"Mama worries about what the neighbors think," Joanna said. "The people here in town know about Old Pruneface being our relation. And you know how they feel about wizards."

Wizards were both resented and feared, and not without reason. Aside from their wealth and their power, there were forms of magic that could be very dangerous to bystanders, and many wizards felt their abilities gave them license to do whatever they wanted. There were all sorts of stories about wizards killing people in gruesome ways or casting evil spells on them. And, finally, many of the intercessors didn't approve of magic without a god's involvement, so they either did little to discourage such stories or even condemned wizards themselves.

"So I don't have a lot of friends because of that," Joanna continued. "Mama will realize that, sooner or later. Besides, you're the best friend I've ever had. I told her that. Just give her a little time."

Anoria nodded, but her face was worried.

Joanna was a little worried as well. Her mother had made some nasty remarks about orphans and their disadvantages as friends. Joanna thought her mother was getting a little snooty lately. Great-Aunt Cordelia had improved the roads and endowed schools, and was even a baroness, but the villagers still remained suspicious of "that wizard Cordelia Cooper." Joanna was exposed to more taunting and teasing than other children of Greenshire. It was hard to make friends with someone who made spooky noises behind your back. So Joanna was lonely, even in the middle of the village.

* * *

A bit later it was time for lunch, and Anoria had to head for the wagon. Joanna came along, as her parents had headed in the direction of the food tables. The tables had been set up along one side of the village square, and the wagons were parked a bit farther in that direction. "Oh, look, Joanna, your parents are close to the wagon too. We'll get to eat lunch together."

The children were getting very hungry by this time. Joanna let go of Clarence's hand, and he toddled toward his mother. Mistress Debra Cooper, Joanna's mother, gave him a piece of candied orange peel to keep him quiet while Joanna introduced her to Anoria and Anoria introduced her to Mistress Boden. The two adults fell into conversation, while Joanna and Anoria began to get some lunch.

"Oh, no!" Mistress Cooper shouted. "He's choking! My baby is choking!"

Mistress Cooper and Mistress Boden were thrown into a tizzy, but Anoria had seen this at the foundling home. One of the intercessors of Barra was trained as a healer. After a baby had nearly choked to death waiting for him to get there, the intercessor had shown all the children how to handle a choking child. So she knew what to do. Mistress Cooper had picked up Clarence but clearly didn't. Anoria took him from Mistress Cooper.

"They showed us how to fix this at the Home." Anoria laid the little boy on the table. Then she pressed on his chest and belly. She had to be careful. If she pressed too hard, she could hurt the child, even break the bones in his chest. But if she didn't press hard enough, the food that was caught in little Clarence's throat wouldn't pop out.

Anoria pressed again, just a little harder. The orange peel flew out of the baby's mouth. Anoria was afraid she had pushed a little too hard and Clarence might have a bruise. He stopped choking and began to cry in fright. Handing Clarence back to Mistress Cooper, Anoria apologized and explained, "We had a baby almost choke to death at the Home."

* * *

Mistress Debra Cooper had almost snatched Clarence back from the little foundling, but she hadn't known what to do.

"He'll be all right now, Mistress," Anoria said. "The healer intercessor showed us."

"Why did you push on his belly like that?" Mistress Debra Cooper asked suspiciously.

"You're not supposed to stick your finger in their mouth. That will likely just shove the blockage deeper. Instead, you use the pressure of the air in their lungs to push it out. He may have a sore stomach after this," the girl said.

Mistress Gemma Boden was chattering about the natural rewards of respect for the gods and advantages received when one gave charity, as though it was Mistress Boden who had saved Clarence by taking in the girl. Not to be outdone, Debra suggested that Anoria deserved a reward.

"Oh, but the child was only doing what she was taught," Mistress Boden said, as though she was the one who had done the teaching. "I'm sure she doesn't expect a reward for that."

"Even so," Debra declared, "I shall provide one, with your permission. Next month there will be a village dance. Normally, Joanna and Anoria would be too young to attend, but perhaps this time we might make an exception. If you will let Anoria visit us for that event, she and Joanna will be allowed to attend the dance. And, Anoria, you shall stay in my spare room, if you like."

CHAPTER 3

Location: Schoolhouse, Greenshire
Date: 3 Cashi, 134 AF

Anoria grew more excited as the days between her and the dance passed. In truth, she wasn't that interested in the dance part of all this. Mostly the dances were a way for the older teenagers to meet prospective mates. What excited Anoria was the invitation to stay in a spare room. Anoria was a foundling in a world of class distinctions. To be treated as a real guest, not the next best thing to a servant, was special. She didn't remember life with her parents very much at all. Just a vague memory of being held and sung to, although she wasn't even sure of that. Her parents had been taken sick when she was very young. After they died, she was put in the Gent Home for Foundlings.

At the foundling home she had lived in a dormitory with a dozen other girls. At the Bodens, she lived with Merry, the girl of all work. Jess, the cook, had a room of her own because being a cook had more status than being a girl of all work. The Bodens did have a spare room, but that was reserved for guests, not for the likes of Anoria. It had not, in fact, been used at all since Anoria had been there and was kept locked except when being cleaned or dusted. To have such a room reserved for guests was itself a matter of status, a demonstration of wealth.

"I'm so looking forward to next week," Anoria told Joanna. "The Bodens have a spare room, you know. But it's only used a couple of times a year, when the factors come to buy the crops."

Joanna, a child of relatively young parents who were fairly wealthy by the village standards, didn't really understand what staying in a spare room meant to Anoria, but she did understand that it was somehow important to her. "I've always wanted a sister, Anoria," she said. "Someone to share the chores and someone I could talk to. You sound like Old Pruneface. She spends almost all her time alone, you know. If you aren't careful, you'll wind up just like her."

Anoria shook her head at Joanna. "You don't understand." Anoria didn't really know how to explain. She had been an orphan for as long as she could remember, and she couldn't remember ever being important to anyone. Most of her birthdays had come and gone without so much as a word. She didn't know it, but the word for what she was missing was "status." She'd never been anyone's guest. She was always their charity case or servant girl. To be a real guest—actually invited. To matter to someone—anyone—even for only a day or two. It made you a real person, rather than just the orphan girl. Anoria had no way to explain that to Joanna, who had always been someone who mattered to people. "Your family is rich, just like the Bodens, so you can't really. My parents died. I can't remember when I had a place I belonged. When you go home after school, what do you do?"

Joanna started counting on her fingers. "I do my homework."

She held up the next finger. "Then I spend some time helping Mama.

She held up another finger. "Then we eat supper."

One last finger went up. "Then I can play, right up till bedtime," Joanna finished. "What do you do? And why is it so terrible?"

"I get up at first light." Anoria started holding up her own fingers. "I get Ann and Mark ready for the day at school. If there is time after that, I eat breakfast. Then it's an hour to school, with all those grumpy children in the wagon. Then school. Then I wait for two hours for the wagon, while I watch Ann and try to keep her out of trouble. At the same time, it's the only chance I have to do homework or study. Then an hour back to Brookshire, which is the only time I have to read."

Anoria had to use her other hand, since she'd run out of fingers. "Then, it's time to get everyone fed, wash the dishes and get Ann and Eve ready for bed. About the only time I have to myself is a half hour between getting the girls ready for bed and going to bed myself. I really envy you."

"It sounds pretty bad," Joanna said.

"It isn't, not really," Anoria explained. "It's not hard or anything, and I get plenty to eat at the Bodens. It's a lot better than the Home was. There were so many children at the Home that you never got a minute's peace. There was always a chore to do or a little child to take care of. I just wish that I had a family of my own, like you do. And time to study. That sounds wonderful."

Location: Schoolhouse, Greenshire
Date: 14 Cashi, 134 AF

It was finally the day of Anoria's visit to Joanna and her family. Today Ann and Harold would take the wagon back to Brookshire by themselves, and Anoria would go to Joanna's house for sixth and seventh day. It felt like heaven to Anoria. Almost three days without responsibilities beyond a few little chores. No laundry, no dishwashing. "We'll feed the chickens," Joanna said. "And Clarence isn't any trouble, most of the time. Auntie Tess takes care of him, anyway."

"It all sounds great to me," Anoria agreed as they walked toward the farm. They turned down a lane, and Anoria saw a slate roof ahead of them. "Your house is even bigger than the Boden's."

"Old Pruneface did it," Joanna explained. "Years ago, back when Grandpa was still alive. Papa said she couldn't do the walls any smaller, not with the spell she had, so it's big. After she put up the walls, Papa cut the windows. Papa says that was a lot of work because the walls are stone a foot thick. Mama says that it felt creepy when she moved in. Too much empty space."

"You know, Joanna," Anoria said, "You really ought to be grateful for what you have. And it just isn't right to call someone Old Pruneface, especially when they aren't."

Joanna considered for a moment. "You might be right, Anoria. Papa says that things weren't nearly this good around here, not before Aunt Cordelia came back."

"Aunt Cordelia?"

"That's her real name. The Wizard Cordelia Cooper. Papa says that she's been a lot of help, really. She went adventuring when she was young, and when she came back she bought half the forest. Then she turned some people into pigs just because she could, Mama says."

Anoria shook her head at this. "Joanna, why would she have done that? There had to have been a reason, if she really did do that. Even in the stories, a wizard doesn't turn people into pigs unless they've offended her."

"Mama says so. Of course, Papa says it was a goat and it was only one time. I don't know. I just know I have to be really good when she's here. That part is really hard, and Mama is really, really nervous. Even Papa walks on eggshells when Aunt Cordelia is around."

Then they reached the house and ran inside. "Mama," Joanna shouted, "We're here."

* * *

It was a lovely meal. Mistress Cooper had made a roast of pork with vegetables. There was even a dessert called apple dumplings, which was covered in a spicy, sweet syrup. Mistress Cooper had pulled out all the stops for the evening. Anoria was amazed at the variety of food on the table and thought it was all delicious.

"There's something about food you grow yourself," Michael Cooper agreed. "Perhaps it's just the knowledge that it was your hands that brought it out of the earth that makes it a sacrament to Barra."

"It was wonderful, Master Cooper," Anoria said. "And Mistress Cooper, you're one of the best cooks I've ever seen."

Debra blushed a bit. A compliment, even from a ten-year-old, was still a compliment. "Thank you, Anoria. Now, what are you two girls going to do this evening? No chores, not for a guest, so you'll be able to run and play, if you like. At least until it gets dark."

"I want to take Anoria for a walk, Mother," Joanna said. "She's never been here before, and she doesn't really know what a farm is all about, since she was raised in the city. We'll go see everything, the pond and the woodlot, and the orchard. And we've got a horse that's going to give birth any day now, Anoria. We'll go see her too."

"Well, go along then," Debra said. "Come back before it's dark, though. Auntie Tess will take care of Clarence." Clarence was a bit grumpy, and Debra was beginning to worry that he had taken sick. Tess was staying in his room, caring for him.

The girls ran out, giggling. "Yes, ma'am," they shouted in unison. "We'll be back later," Joanna added. "I'm going to show Anoria everything."

After the girls ran out, Debra smiled at Michael. "She's a very polite child, isn't she?"

"Certainly seems to be," Michael agreed. He pushed his chair away from the table. "I'll be going to check on the mare, Debra. She's been restless all day."

"Fine, dear." Debra smiled. "I'll handle the rest."

Debra began to clear the table as Michael went outside. She had her hands full of dishes and dropped them all when Cordelia appeared in the center of the kitchen. Debra was sure the dishes would be broken, but Cordelia waved her hand. The dishes floated in the air. Debra was grateful the dishes were saved but got even more nervous.

"I'm sorry, Debra," Cordelia said. "I didn't mean to startle you."

Debra was always startled when Cordelia arrived unexpectedly. It was just plain rude to pop in without knocking, in Debra's opinion. But she couldn't say that out loud. Everyone was very careful to keep their opinions to themselves around Cordelia. Cordelia was a powerful wizard, after all, and there were all sorts of sayings about not offending wizards. Even minor wizards had their dangers, much less the powerful sort like Cordelia.

Debra knew she was red-faced and flustered. Cordelia had that effect on her, even when she was trying to be friendly. "It's quite all right, ma'am," she said. "I probably had too much in my hands, anyway."

"You might let me help," Cordelia offered.

Debra had trouble not shuddering. She didn't care for Cordelia's visits, not at all. She shook her head. "No, thank you, ma'am. You're a guest." So far that had been sufficient to deter Cordelia's attempts at assistance. For all Debra knew, if she accepted the offer, the dishes would wind up in the outhouse.

Cordelia shrugged. Debra wished, sometimes, that Cordelia would just stop visiting and go away. Cordelia, and Cordelia's reputation, had made the village a bit reserved around Debra's family.

"As you wish," Cordelia said. "I've just come back from a short trip and thought I'd stop in for a few days."

"Would you care for some supper?" Debra asked, waving at the table. She hadn't gotten around to clearing the food off it yet and there was quite a bit remaining.

"I'll serve myself, Debra. There's no need for you to wait on me. Is Michael here?"

"In the barn, ma'am. There's a mare about to foal. I'll go get him." Debra rushed out the back door. Michael was a lot more comfortable around his aunt than she was.

* * *

Shaking her head at the vagaries of people, Cordelia served herself some dinner and ate rapidly. She hadn't taken time for lunch and was a bit hungry.

When she finished, Debra and Michael still hadn't come back. Cordelia knew that Debra would delay returning as long as she could, so she went upstairs to the spare room. She began to unpack her things and settle into the room that was always hers when she visited.

* * *

"Michael," Debra said as she looked over the stall door, "She's here."

"Not yet, she isn't," Michael responded. Debra thought that was an odd comment, until she saw that Michael was seriously involved in the delivery of a filly.

"She's on her way, though. And I think the mare is going to gift us with twins, too. Give me a hand here."

Debra forgot about Cordelia in the excitement of the birth. It was the mare's first, and they had been worried about it for months. She entered the stall and began to assist Michael.

* * *

"What do you want to see next, Anoria?" Joanna asked as the two girls walked back toward the house. They'd seen the woodlot and the orchard. The apples were tiny and green, but the peaches were beginning to ripen and it had smelled wonderful.

"The spare room," Anoria answered.

Joanna shook her head at this. Maybe if Anoria saw the room she'd realize it was just a bedroom, and not anything special.

"We'll go there, then. Race you."

And the girls were off, running as hard as they could.

* * *

As time passed and Debra didn't return, Cordelia sneaked a quick scry on the barn. Even for Debra, this amount of neglect was unusual. She saw that Debra had a good reason. The mare was heaving, preparing to deliver another foal. Cordelia estimated that this could take a while, so she laid down for a brief nap. This trip had been harder on her than usual. Prince Tarsis had wanted combat spells and combat spells only. Cordelia, when she had been an adventuring wizard, had specialized in combat spells, but she was a bit out of practice. Still, Prince Tarsis had paid a very pretty penny to have her load his amulets.

Cordelia lay down and was asleep almost as soon as her head hit the pillow.

* * *

It was a bit of a distance between the orchard and the house, but the girls ran every bit of it. And when they arrived, they didn't stop as they knew they should have. Joanna was pretty sure she wouldn't get in trouble for running in the house when she had a guest. The girls ran up the stairs, through the door of the spare room, and threw themselves on the bed.

* * *

"Yaaagh!" Joanna screamed as she jumped toward the bed.

"Yipppeee!" Anoria screamed as she did the same.

"*Xan dlo* . . ." Cordelia began and then stopped abruptly. She was covered in curly girl hair, somehow. "What the devil do you think you're doing?" she shouted. "I nearly killed you!"

The miscreants scrambled out of the bed. When they had managed that, they stood in front of Cordelia, heads hanging. They were mussed and sweating from the run. Cordelia only knew one of them, her great-niece, Joanna.

"You brats!" Cordelia shouted. "One more syllable and you'd have been dead! What did you think you were doing?"

Joanna muttered, "Sorry, ma'am. We didn't know you were here."

The unfamiliar child had tears beginning to form and sniffed a bit. "I apologize, ma'am. We didn't intend to . . ."

Cordelia, terrified by the fact that she had only been a brief instant away from killing two innocent children, snapped. "Just be quiet. Be quiet, now."

Cordelia took a moment to try and calm herself. Her chest was heaving from the realization that she had nearly destroyed her own great-niece. She placed her hand over her heart, wondering if she was actually going to swoon. "Girls, are you supposed to run in the house?" she asked, sternly.

Joanna was sniffling now. "No, ma'am. I know better, I truly do."

The other girl stayed silent.

"You. Will. Both. Leave. This. Room," Cordelia said in her coldest voice. "You will go to your room. You will stay there until you are asked to come out. You will do it now."

Two trembling girls crept away, and Cordelia staggered to a chair. *My word,* she thought. *I nearly killed them. Two babies.*

Cordelia took a deep breath and tried to calm down. The thought that she might have killed the children had her more rattled than her first orc battle. She couldn't help the battle reflex, not after so many years as a wizard for hire. Those reflexes had kept her alive more than once.

She sat quietly for a while, trying to reconcile her wizard self and her family self. It was hard.

* * *

Anoria and Joanna crept silently to Joanna's room, nearly in tears. When the door closed behind them, Joanna sat down, holding back her sobs.

Anoria knew that they had come very close to death, but she tried very hard to comfort her friend. "Joanna, please. It's not so bad. We got away, after all. And she didn't turn us into pigs, either."

"You don't understand," Joanna whispered. "You just don't understand." With lips trembling, she explained, "Once a year, Papa goes to Gent. This year he was going to take me with him. I've never been even as far as Brookshire, Anoria. I so wanted to go. Now, when Auntie

Cordelia tells about this, I'll have to stay home again. I'll never get away from this farm, never!"

Anoria was a bit disconcerted at her friend's lack of concern about nearly having been killed. After learning about Cordelia, Anoria had done a bit of research at the school and knew that they'd had a narrow escape. True, the only books she had found were adventures, but the teacher had explained that yes, wizards could do those things. Joanna's emphasis on a lost treat seemed, well, silly, to Anoria.

Anoria patted Joanna's back. "There, there, I understand. I really do. Just try to be calm. Please, Joanna, don't cry."

"I won't," Joanna said. "And don't you worry about it. It's not your fault."

* * *

Anoria disagreed. It was clearly her fault. Joanna never would have run into the spare room and jumped on the bed if Anoria hadn't been with her. There was only one thing to do. She stood up.

"What are you doing," Joanna asked.

"I'm going to go talk to your aunt," Anoria said.

"Anoria . . . that's not a good idea. Aunt Cordelia told us to stay here."

"Yes, I know. But I need to explain," Anoria said firmly and turned to the door.

She stepped out of the bedroom and down the hall. In spite of all her will, her tap on the door sounded very timid.

There was no answer the first time, and she nearly went away. But she screwed up her courage and tapped again.

Cordelia said, "You may come in."

Her voice still sounded angry. Anoria shook a bit and poked her head around the door. "Ma'am, may I please speak to you?"

"You might tell me your name. I've never seen you before. I'm fairly sure you don't belong here."

Knees knocking, Anoria stepped around the door and performed her best attempt at a curtsey. She'd read about them, but didn't really understand what they were. "I'm very sorry, ma'am. My name is Anoria. And, no, I don't belong here. Or anywhere else, I suppose. But running into the room was my idea. Joanna didn't have anything to do with it."

"Anoria, don't say that," a voice hissed from the hallway. "She'll turn you into a frog."

Cordelia rolled her eyes. "Miss Joanna, you will come forward," she directed. Anoria thought she detected a bit of humor in that eye roll.

Joanna crept around the door also and bobbed an awkward sort-of curtsey toward Cordelia. "I'm sorry, ma'am."

"Now, ladies," Cordelia said. "Let's have the truth of it, right now. Miss Joanna, whose idea was it to run in and jump on the bed?"

Joanna hesitated a moment, and Anoria rushed in to say, "It was mine, ma'am. Joanna shouldn't have to take the blame when it was my idea."

Joanna started to deny Anoria's statement, but Anoria rushed on. "It's all my fault, ma'am. Please don't tell Mistress Cooper that Joanna did it. It's all my fault."

Cordelia seemed to become interested in the whole business. She questioned each girl carefully until the truth came out.

By the time Cordelia's form of questioning was over, both girls were exhausted. Cordelia now knew that the running had been mutual, that Joanna was afraid of losing her trip to the city, and also all about Anoria and her belief that staying in the spare room would be a great event. "Well, Anoria, I suppose I can understand how you felt and I'm even a little sorry about spoiling your holiday."

"Oh, no, ma'am, it's not spoiled," Anoria rushed to say. "Just being here in such a wonderful home is a treat. I'm happy to be here, spare room or not, really I am."

* * *

Cordelia was dealing with a rash of old memories. It had been a lot of years, but she recalled being the overlooked, oldest girl. She remembered the way she had been the one who had taken over the housework and chores when her mother died. She remembered how it had been expected of her, how no one had bothered to ask how she felt. There had been the assumption that she should be grateful that she had a place to belong, even as an unpaid servant to her family.

After her natural wizard powers had become the talk of the village, her family had been quick to apprentice her to a traveling wizard. People had begun making signs against magic in her direction and avoiding her. It was an uncomfortable time. She began to feel some sympathy for the little foundling, yet another girl child who wouldn't have many opportunities.

Now that Cordelia was over the scare caused by nearly killing the girls, she grew more interested in them. On an impulse, she summoned up a few treats and a pot of cocoa. This little feast appeared on the small table in the "oh so special" spare room, and she invited the girls to join her.

"What is this?" Joanna asked, sipping the rich, creamy drink. "It's wonderful."

"Coffee," Anoria answered. "I think. I read about it. It was in one of my puzzle books, and it took me a week to find that answer. The question was "a six-letter word for an expensive foreign drink." Tea sure didn't fit as the answer, so I had to look it up."

Cordelia's interest perked up. "It took you a week? Why so long?"

"I'd never heard of it, ma'am," Anoria answered. "No one had. I finally found the word in an adventure story, and the letters fit the puzzle. So I used them. I still didn't know what it was, not until just now. It is coffee, isn't it?" The child looked at her so earnestly that Cordelia couldn't help but be interested.

"I'm afraid not. This is cocoa. Which is also an expensive foreign drink but has only five letters. On the other hand, you probably wouldn't like coffee," Cordelia answered. "It's very bitter. Though I must say you showed some determination to finish that puzzle. A lot of people would have given up on it, once they had asked around." Very few people in the villages, in spite of their schooling, spent much time with abstract thought. They tended, quite rightly, to concentrate on their work.

Anoria shook her head and grinned. The grin made her look like a mischievous urchin. "I love puzzles. And I keep working on them until I solve them. Sometimes it takes a while, is all."

"Girls, what on earth are you doing, bothering Lady Cordelia?" Debra said from the doorway. "Honestly, you shouldn't be . . ."

Debra's face had its usual half-terrified look on it. Cordelia was a bit impatient with that look. She'd never done anything except try to be helpful, after all.

Cordelia cut her off abruptly. "Debra, the girls and I are having a very nice visit. And—" Cordelia gave Debra a telling glance. "It's quite nice to speak to someone in this household who doesn't fear that I'm going to do something terrible for no reason."

Debra looked a bit disconcerted for a moment. Cordelia decided that impatience wouldn't help the situation and asked, "Are the new foals in good health?"

"Yes, ma'am, they are," Debra said, face flushed with embarrassment. "I'm sorry I was so long in the barn. I haven't properly done my duty to a guest, I'm afraid."

"It's quite all right, Debra," Cordelia said. "In fact, I'm pleased I had the opportunity to get to know these young ladies. So much so that I'm going to issue them an invitation. Since I've inadvertently spoiled young Anoria's treat, I'd like to have the girls come visit me this summer. And for a month, young ladies, you shall both stay in my very sparest of spare rooms."

Location: Cooper Home, Greenshire
Date: 15 Cashi, 134 AF

Joanna was beginning to get a bit bored. Cordelia and Anoria shared a common interest, one Joanna had no use for. Puzzle solving was just something Joanna left to other people. She preferred to talk and play. Anoria and Cordelia were immersed in a conversation about magic and something called "Wizard's Mark," whatever that was. And there was something called "come to me," and Joanna was tired of hearing about it.

"Auntie Cordelia," Joanna said during a brief pause, "if you'll excuse me, please. I want to check in on Auntie Tess and Clarence. He's been a bit cranky lately."

Cordelia waved her hand and continued to explain the various uses of the Wizard's Mark thing. Joanna crept away and left Anoria and Cordelia to their very involved conversation. As she left, she heard Anoria ask, "I wonder why Wizard's Mark isn't used with other spells. It seems to me that it could be used for a lot of applications." Joanna hadn't understood the last half-hour of conversation.

CHAPTER 4

Location: Cordelia's Cabin, Greenwood, Whitehall County
Date: 17 Cashi, 134 AF

It had been an interesting few days, Cordelia thought as she popped back into her home. Anoria and her puzzle-solving ability were very intriguing to her.

In three months, the girls would come to visit. Plenty of time. Cordelia began looking around her home and suddenly realized that she didn't have a "spare" room. She had rooms aplenty, but none of them could properly be called "spare." She used them all, at one time or another. She had workrooms, living rooms, and a kitchen of sorts. Parlors, a bedroom, and, of course, the third floor had a few rooms too. But none of them could be called "spare."

Cordelia knew that she could just move some things and call a room her "spare" room, but that wasn't what she wanted. Everything in her home had a place. She didn't want to move things.

After considerable thought, Cordelia decided that what she really wanted to do was exactly what she had promised. She'd told Anoria and Joanna that they could stay in the "sparest of spare" rooms. Now she wanted one. A room that had never been used, not by anyone. A room that would be just, well, spare.

Cordelia was an exception among wizards in a number of ways. She was both a natural wizard and a book wizard, and she knew how to make magical amulets. More importantly, she was a magic researcher. Few wizards actually researched new spells. Mostly spells were traded for or fought for; spells were the wealth of wizards, just as land was the wealth of the nobility. You would think that knowing that a bit of research could provide a wizard a new spell, all the wizards in the world would be hidden away in laboratories constantly researching new spells.

It didn't work that way. First, because natural wizards took a very long time to make a new spell their own, and more than half the wizards in the world were natural wizards. Second, because the books and materials you needed to research new spells were outrageously expensive. Third, because most people—even most book wizards—didn't really have the knack of researching spells. There is a difference, after all, between being able to use a recipe and being able to make one up. Making one up takes a lot more knowledge of how the ingredients work together.

Cordelia had been tinkering with spells since she had learned book wizardry. After she retired from adventuring, it had become her main focus. She began tinkering with the Dimensional Mansion spell she had used so often in her adventuring days, but it wasn't quite right. The Dimensional Mansion would probably make the girls uncomfortable. It had too much room. The Cozy Cabin spell would work, but it had to be above ground and might be seen.

What a position: to be in need of a spare room and be totally without one. Hmmm, Cordelia thought. How can I do it?

Dimensional Mansion started out by enlarging the small model of the entry door into a full-size door. If she used a full-size door, she could eliminate that whole section of the spell. "Hmmm." No, that section was tied into the rest of the spell in several places. As she worked on the spell, Cordelia found herself rehearsing how she would explain it to Anoria.

The [A] in the door-expanding section was connected to the [B] in the dimensional expansion section, but it simply fed it power. That seemed to be what most of the connections between the door expansion and the rest of the spell did. No, not entirely. There was some control there too. Muttering happily, Cordelia set out to make a spare room that would suit the girls.

Over the course of the next three months, she had a false door placed in a hall. She developed a variant of Wizard's Mark that worked better to define the flow of magic and used that spell extensively on the false door, to aid in defining the interdimensional space that enclosed the spare room. What she finally ended up with was a relatively uncomplicated, easy spell that couldn't be developed by a wizard who didn't already know the Dimensional Mansion spell. However, once her new spell was developed, any wizard who had a reasonable amount of concentration could learn it. The spell was limited though, and only worked on the one door that was specially made for that spell.

Location: Schoolhouse, Greenshire
Date: 23 Cashi, 134 AF

While Cordelia was working out the Spare Room spell, Anoria and Joanna were dealing with the trials of ten-year-olds. School assignments. Deaconess Willow, having to teach students from six to sixteen, gave out assignments and called on older students to give reports to the rest of the class on what they had learned. This gave her time to help the younger ones or children who were having problems, while keeping half an ear on the reports in case the older scholar proved less scholarly than hoped. Anoria was assigned the geography of Whitehall County. Joanna was assigned to discuss the road that went from Greenshire to Brookshire and beyond.

Doing the research for the report hadn't been so bad, Anoria thought, as she was faced with the requirement to stand at the front of the room and talk.

"Whitehall County was given to the first Count Whitehall even before Amonrai was granted independence by the Kingdom Isles," Anoria started. "It is located on the east side of Fornteroy Province and, like most of Fornteroy Province, is mostly rolling hills and plains. There are five shires and one barony in the county. The count owns the rest of the county, which amounts to three-fifths of the land in the county. On that land, he has a fishing village at Lakeside, a hunting lodge, and several herding stations for sheep. He derives over half his income from the herds. There is a school in Copriceshire and one in Greenshire. Brookshire, to the east of Greenshire, doesn't have a school but a wagon brings us to school here in Greenshire by the wizard road. Farther east along a regular road is Herinshire, and northeast of that is Hillshire where the county administration is located. There the wizard road starts up again and goes to Lakeside, the count's fishing village and docks.

"Count Whitehall keeps a house in Hillshire and another at Lakeside and is an avid sport fisherman."

Anoria stopped because she was out of things to say, and was a bit worried that Deaconess Willow might be upset that she hadn't filled the fifteen minutes she was supposed to fill. One of the older children came to her rescue by asking a question.

"Where are the count's lands located?"

Anoria considered for a minute, then walked over to the map of Whitehall County and started pointing out the count's lands and all the sheep stations and grassland that had once been elfin forest. She spent the next ten minutes answering questions from the students, some of them reasonable, some of them silly. In some cases, she had to admit that she didn't know the answer. Finally her turn was over, and she headed back to her desk in relief. When Anoria sat down, Joanna snickered. Anoria told her, "You just wait until tomorrow. Your turn then."

One of the older boys was called up next and gave a talk on calculating volume.

Location: Schoolhouse, Greenshire
Date: 25 Cashi, 134 AF

Today was Joanna's turn, and she was to speak about her great-aunt and the making of the wizard road that connected the shires of Whitehall County.

Joanna, unlike Anoria, had hated the research. But she was more excited than frightened to be standing in front of the class as she started to tell the story of how her great-aunt had created the wizard road.

"At first, Count Whitehall didn't want Great-Aunt Cordelia to build the road around all the shires. He wanted a road from the Elentral River on the east side of the county to the Thorenga Lake on the northwest corner of the county. But a road that went straight from the river to the lake would mostly be in Dartomith County to the north of here. In fact, there was already a road like that. Well sort of; it's pretty twisty. Anyway, Count Dartomith collects the tolls on the wagons that go from the Elentral River to Lake Thorenga on that road, which is not what Count Whitehall wanted. He wanted the wagons to go through Whitehall County so he could collect the taxes. But he didn't have the money to have a good road built. That's what my papa said, anyway.

"My Great-Aunt Cordelia was already living in the county based on an informal agreement with the old Count Whitehall." Joanna giggled. "That is, Count Whitehall agreed not to bother her, and she agreed to stop turning people into goats and pigs and things." Papa said it was only the one girl turned into a goat, but it sounded better this way. Besides, Papa said that Aunt Cordelia threatened to turn the count into a rutabaga. Then she sobered, remembering what else her papa had said. About Aunt Cordelia being half crazy when she first came home—after whatever happened in the Orclands. So Old Count Whitehall was probably right not to press the issue. She didn't think mentioning any of that would be a good idea. "So anyway, Aunt Cordelia had been living here a few years when the old count died and the new count took over."

Joanna pointed at the picture of the present Count Whitehall which hung on the wall. "Count Whitehall decided that she owed him service since she was staying on his land." Many of the children nodded understanding. Taxes and rents were sometimes paid in money and sometimes in service, and since she was living on his land, she owed both. "The service the count wanted was for her to magic up a road that would go through Whitehall County so that the merchants would come this way. After some talking back and forth, Aunt Cordelia agreed to make the road."

"So why don't we have a road all the way from the river to the lake," asked Tommy Poll, without even raising his hand for permission. The teacher cleared her throat, and Tommy pinked a little but also looked stubborn.

"As I was about to explain," Joanna said even though she hadn't been, "you don't magic up a road all the way from the river to the lake in an afternoon. A spell to make the road doesn't make the whole road. It makes one little section of road, which is only about forty or fifty feet long. To get one mile of road, you have to cast that spell over a hundred times. That takes time and effort. Besides, the count and Aunt Cordelia got in an argument about where the road should go. From Lakeside to Hillshire is ten miles as the crow flies. But it's twelve miles and two bridges as the wizard road goes. That took over four years. Aunt Cordelia couldn't spend all her time making the road, either. From Hillshire, the count wanted the road to go straight to Copriceshire, but Aunt Cordelia used to live here in Greenshire when she was a little girl, so she wanted the road to go through Greenshire. The count said that if she was going to make the road go from Hillshire to Brookshire, she ought to make it go through all the other shires, too. But that would make it a much longer road. From what my papa says, they argued about where the road would go for almost a year. They were also arguing about how much land Count Whitehall would give Aunt Cordelia for building the road. Finally they agreed, and they marked it all out on the map, and Aunt Cordelia started the road. But she started at Copriceshire up by the Elentral River, and that section of the road got finished just about the time the War of the Servile Provinces started. So Aunt Cordelia stopped working on the rest of the road and went to serve in the king's army. While she was fighting in the war, the king made Greenwood, her barony, a king's barony, so her service was owed to the king, not the count.

"The count said that she still owed him since she had agreed to finish the road. And they argued about that and it even went before the king's bench. Well, it worked out that Aunt Cordelia is still supposed to finish the road but she only has to work on it when she has time. And that's up to her. So she works on the road whenever she has a mind to, and if she doesn't feel like it, she doesn't have to. About two years ago she finished the bit between Brookshire and here."

One of the students asked, "What about the trees?"

"What about the trees?" Joann asked.

"Well, the road goes straight. It doesn't go around the trees. Did they chop them all down?"

"I don't know," Joanna admitted.

That was only the first of half a dozen questions that Joanna didn't know the answer to. Deaconess Willow made her write down all the questions, and she was assigned to find out all the answers.

It turned out, as Joanna explained a week later, that the spell Aunt Cordelia used to make the road was actually two spells. The first spell shaped the land into a road shape and moved all the trees and plants out of the way; then the second spell turned that stretch of land into stone. That explained the major questions the other children had, except for one. Laurence Firebird kept asking just where Aunt Cordelia lived, but Joanna refused to tell him. She rather liked Laurence and didn't want him turned into a goat.

Location: Schoolhouse, Greenshire
Date: 27 Cashi, 134 AF

Between Joanna's two lectures, Laurence Firebird had to give a talk about the gods. While it was clear from the outset that the gods were not exactly Laurence's favorite subject, he did know quite a bit about the Amonrai and Centurium pantheon.

"When Amonrai was settled from Centraium and the Kingdom Isles, we brought our gods with us, the Centraium pantheon. The elves had their own pantheon, which focused mostly on forest gods and natural magic. The pantheon we brought from Centraium was more concerned with civilized things. Like wars, growing crops, healing, and knowledge. We also brought with us a god of the sea and gods of weather and trade. The most popular god among farmers is Barra, the goddess of the harvest, but next to Barra is Estormany, the goddess of weather, because it's real easy for weather to ruin your crops. Among the nobility and the soldiers, Noron, god of war and judge of princes, is very popular. Now, sailors also pay a lot of attention to Estormany, but they also follow Wovoro, the god of the sea.

"Pago, the god of natural magic from Centraium, is not considered a good god, because he approves of human sacrifice. Some people say that Narce, the elfin god of natural magic, is just another aspect of Pago, but the elves don't think so. Pago figures," Laurence continued, as he got into the story of Pago because it had a lot of gore in it, "that natural wizards and natural magic users are the only real people. That those without magic aren't proper people, and so it's as all right to sacrifice them as it is to sacrifice a bull or a goat."

Deaconess Willow made a warning sound, so Laurence got back to his planned report.

"Zagrod, on the other hand, according to the intercessors, doesn't approve of human sacrifice, so most people think of him as the good god of magic. But . . ." Laurence gave a covert look at Deaconess Willow, then continued, "but the gods don't see it that way. To the gods, not doing human sacrifice is like somebody deciding not to eat meat."

Another warning sound came from Deaconess Willow.

"But it's true," Laurence said.

Deaconess Willow sighed. "I know, Laurence. But we don't need to focus on that. How do the gods gain their sustenance, aside from human sacrifice?"

"Well," Laurence said, sounding disappointed, "through prayer, for one thing. And through symbolic sacrifices, like when we burn wheat for Barra. Or light a candle to Estormany. It takes an awful lot of candles, though, to equal a cow. And a lot of cows to equal a person."

"That's quite enough!" Deaconess Willow said. "Go back to your seat, Laurence."

CHAPTER 5

Location: Boden House, Brookshire
Date: 25 Banth, 135 AF

Debra looked around the sitting room. It was somewhat fancy for Debra's taste. Just a little too much brocade, a few too many porcelain figurines, and a bit crowded with expensive furniture. And yet it suited Gemma Boden. Once seated with tea and cakes, Debra explained Aunt Cordelia's offer.

"She what?" Mistress Boden asked, face flushed with anger. The anger, it was clear to Debra, was hiding a certain amount of fear. Gemma Boden, like Debra herself, didn't trust magic and magic users, and the story of Cordelia Cooper turning people into animals had expanded over the years. Besides which, Debra knew enough about magic from her unwanted association with her husband's Aunt Cordelia to realize that people's fear of magic was totally justified. Wizards were chancy to deal with and not, in general, respecters of those not skilled in magic.

"She invited Anoria and Joanna to visit her. This summer. For a month," Debra repeated, taking a sip from the delicate teacup. She glanced around the sitting room, trying to decide what to say next. "As far as I know, she's never had a visitor, not that I really know, you understand. I don't know why anyone would want to visit her, but the girls do. And it has to be said that Cordelia has always been very supportive of her family."

"Well, I'll just put a stop to this nonsense right now. Anoria is here in my house, and I have a responsibility to protect her from . . ." Gemma hesitated, clearly aware that Debra was related to Cordelia by marriage. "Anoria has work to do here. She has to assist in taking care of the children. What would I do if she were away that long? I'll tell her it's just impossible."

It was market day in Brookshire, and Debra had made a special trip just to talk to Gemma Boden. The trip had been much easier than it used to be, thanks to Cordelia's road. Debra missed Brookshire, which was where she had been born. It was a bit bigger than Greenshire. The market was a bit larger and had a few more things available. "Well, Gemma," Debra said, "you might want to reconsider."

Debra and Gemma had become quite friendly since the picnic. Instead of immediately flying off the handle, Gemma asked, "Why?"

"I'll agree that Cordelia is kind of spooky." Debra tried to hide her shiver. "Heaven knows, she makes me a little . . . nervous. But she's been quite a help to this area. You do know that she's the one who started the school and improved the roads, don't you?" Debra had thought that Cordelia would have forgotten the invitation by now, but Cordelia had come to check, unexpectedly. Permission needed to be confirmed.

"Of course," Gemma answered. "But I don't understand why she did that. There's something sinister about magicking up a road, especially when she doesn't charge a toll. There's some hidden cost that'll come due, mark my words. Wizards are chancy things, best avoided. I disapprove of magic. People shouldn't use it, and them that do should be avoided whenever possible." Debra glanced at the temple, and Gemma went on. "I don't mean intercessor's magic. Respectable people worship the gods, and when the gods give an intercessor spells it's a sign of favor, but arcane magic. . . . It's just unnatural."

"I quite agree," Debra answered. "Quite. Even so, Cordelia just isn't someone I'd want to offend. For one thing she is very wealthy and not ungenerous. You know she provided the dowries for my sisters-in-law. And if we let the girls go, well, Michael says you just never know. She provided the building for the school in Greenshire, and she provides the funds to pay the teacher."

Gemma considered for a moment.

Debra went in for the coup de grace. "A school in Brookshire itself would be very nice. If she built one here, your children wouldn't have to make the wagon trip every day."

Gemma sniffed a bit, but clearly began to see the advantage of the connection. "I'll consider it, then. I must speak to Master Boden about it, though."

Debra nodded. It had taken Michael quite a bit of talk to convince her that this was a good idea. Perhaps Master Boden would see this connection in a favorable light also.

Location: Cooper House, Greenshire
Date: 28 Banth, 135 AF

It was Auntie Tess who settled the argument. "Why don't I go visit the Bodens for the month Anoria is gone? I can help with the children," she volunteered. "I'd like to spend some time in Brookshire, anyway." Remembering the event that started it all she added, in a fair imitation of Anoria, "Perhaps she'll let me stay in the spare room."

"Tess, are you unhappy here at home?" Michael asked.

"Of course not," she answered. "But you never know. I might meet someone in Brookshire. I'd like a home of my own some day, and there's just no one around here that I'm interested in."

Michael nodded. Most of the young men of the village were married fairly young, and Tess, at twenty-eight, was in a somewhat hopeless situation. She was quite attractive but was almost too smart and sensible. There simply wasn't a suitable young man in the area, at least one who wasn't intimidated by Tess. "Are you sure? You'll be tending to more children, you know."

"And I'll be taking them for walks in the village. Looking around. Seeing who's who. It will be a break from the farm, at the very least." Tess seemed quite happy with the thought.

Tess herself proposed the face-saving compromise to Gemma Boden, who agreed, albeit a bit reluctantly. Tess wasn't a foundling who could be put to helping with the laundry and dishes. Still, she would take care of the children and help them with their studies. Anything that kept the children occupied and out of trouble would be an advantage. Tess would be able to handle young Harold, who was becoming a bit of a menace with his undisciplined ways.

Gemma Boden, who had been dreading the end of the school year, gradually started looking forward to having Tess' company.

Location: Schoolhouse, Greenshire
Date: 28 Banth, 135 AF

Behind the schoolhouse a small brook flowed in spring, summer, and fall. In winter it slept under a cloak of ice and snow. But spring was coming, and the ice was melting. The little brook was becoming the friendly abode of water-loving birds, squirrels, little fishes, pixies, and at night, the occasional will-o'-the-wisp. Pixies looked like little bitty elves no more than three inches tall, with translucent wings. They had large, for their size, eyes, and were, in part, magical by nature. They lived in nests in the trees and burrows under rocks and spent most of their time cavorting about and eating pollen from flowers. In winter they merged with the small trees and bushes that grew around the brook.

Because it was warmer, the children at the Greenshire school had taken to having their recess and lunch breaks outdoors again. Anoria and Joanna had a favorite place on a flat rock near the brook that ran behind the school. They usually ate their lunch on the rock while watching the younger children break as many rules as they could.

Anoria jerked her head back as a pixie shot between her face and the book she was reading. The pixie, showing either wisdom or good fortune, had chosen the right hiding place, for in hot pursuit came Ann and two other children of similar age. The pixie flew around Anoria's head and stuck out a tongue much too long for its three-inch body. Then it giggled like tinkling bells.

"You know you're not supposed to chase the pixies," Anoria said sternly.

"But I want one," Ann whined, then pouted at Anoria's look.

"You know what Deaconess Willow said," Anoria told her. "The pixies are part of the brook like the frogs and the snakes and the birds. But they are also magical and not to be bothered."

Anoria didn't know it—even Deaconess Willow didn't know it—but pixies had been created not very far from where the school sat. Many hundreds of years before, before the first human had set foot on Amonrai, an ancient elfin mage had created the first pixies out of magic moss, dragonflies, and hummingbirds. That mage had also used a touch of elfin blood to form their shape. They had entertained the mage's children for some years and then escaped into the forest. From their elfin blood, in addition to the shape of their bodies, they had gained the ability to merge into trees. So like elves, they could live much longer than their size suggested. A pixie that did not find a tree would die over the winter, but with the trees' help, they could live many seasons and lay many a pixie egg.

They lived off the nectar of flowers, pollen, mushrooms, and sometimes insects.

"I still want one," Ann whined again.

Anoria sighed. "I don't blame you, Ann. They're very pretty. But they wouldn't be happy caged up."

Deaconess Willow rang the bell and they trudged back into the school house.

CHAPTER 6

Location: Cooper House, Greenshire
Date: 22 Zagrod, 135 AF

After the last day of school, Joanna and Anoria waited for Cordelia's arrival at Joanna's home, giggling with anticipation. They were dressed in their best, which, in Anoria's case, was simple and plain.

"Are you ready to go to Greenwood with me, ladies?" Cordelia asked from the doorway. She was smiling at them.

"Oh, yes, ma'am." Anoria smiled back. "We're ready."

"Off we go, then. Pick up your bags and stand beside me." Cordelia put a hand on each girl's shoulder and mumbled something they couldn't quite understand.

Location: Cordelia's Cabin, Greenwood, Whitehall County
Date: 22 Zagrod, 135 AF

"Oh," Joanna breathed. "That didn't take any time at all, did it?"

"I should hope not," Cordelia said. "I can't tell you how often I've used that Translocation spell. I've very nearly got it memorized, in fact.

Although generally, it's not a good idea for book wizards to try to memorize spells."

"Why not?" Anoria wanted to know.

And they're off, thought Joanna, smiling at the two. Anoria hadn't stopped talking about that "Wizard's Mark" thing for months. Maybe now she would get over her curiosity.

Joanna cleared her throat and gently interrupted the conversation. "Umm, Auntie Cordelia, could we go in?"

Cordelia looked up from her conversation with Anoria and actually blushed a bit. "I'm being a terrible hostess, aren't I? Neglecting you like that."

"Of course you aren't." Joanna smiled. "I figured out months ago that the two of you are alike. Interested in solving puzzles, getting immersed in the difference between this and that. But we are standing here, and I'd like to see your home."

"I'm rather pleased with it, if the truth be known," Cordelia said. "Tell me, what do you think of it?" Aunt Cordelia grandly waved her hand at the little cottage sitting on a rocky hill.

Joanna looked at the small cottage that sat on a hill and above a cliff. Mostly she noticed the beautiful, large garden. She said, "It looks very nice." She couldn't quite keep the doubt out of her voice, though.

"It looks like a tiny cottage, Joanna. I know that. I planned it that way. I didn't want Greenwood to look like a baron's hall or a wizard's tower, because I value my privacy. Come along, let's go see it closer."

Cordelia and the girls walked through the garden and up the hill. Joanna stopped to sniff several of the flowers on the way. "Oh, Auntie, they're beautiful," she said with her eyes shining. "I've never seen such blooms. And they smell just wonderful."

Cordelia was very pleased at this. She liked fragrant flowers and had been working on the garden for a while now. "Most of the people around here are just too busy to grow flowers like this," Cordelia said. "And it's a pity. Not only do they smell wonderful, but they have qualities that come in handy. They do take some care though. Pruning, deadheading, that sort of thing."

"I would like to learn more about them," Joanna said. The flowers were every color of the rainbow. There were low hedges lining the separate beds, and in the distance, she saw an intricately designed herb bed. It had interlocking patterns of foliage in different colors. Pixies abounded, dancing between the flowers and the herbs, laughing like tinkling bells, swooping and swirling in mating dances.

"So you shall," Cordelia answered as they reached the door to the cottage. "So you shall."

Cordelia opened the door and ushered the girls and their bags inside. "I had to install this access especially for you two," she explained as she led them through the single room of the cottage to a small door. "Usually I just pop in and out, but you can't do that. After you leave, I'll remove this door again. Come along."

She led the way down a winding stair. Joanna noticed that the light had a warm golden color, and that it wasn't in the least dark. They went down quite a few steps before they arrived in what appeared to be the space Cordelia used for her leisure time.

"Well, what do you think?" Cordelia asked.

Anoria and Joanna stared about them with awe. The room was huge. The chairs and sofas were plush and expensive-looking. There were a number of carpets on the floor, which itself appeared to be made from a beautifully mottled and streaked stone. The wall to the outside was a huge expanse of what looked like glass from the inside, but hadn't shown at all on the outside.

"Oh my," Anoria breathed. "It's lovely."

Cordelia nodded with delight. "It is, I think. Just drop your bags. The servants will take care of them."

"Servants?" Joanna asked. "I thought you lived alone."

"Servants of a sort," Cordelia said. "I'll explain later. Let's go look around, if you'd like."

* * *

The tour took quite a bit of time, and the girls were amazed again and again. Finally they returned to the room Cordelia called "my parlor," and sat down to rest. Joanna started a bit when a meal floated in, but Cordelia smiled and explained, "They're called Servant spells, Joanna. I never much liked housework, I'll admit. The basic Valet spell was one of the first spells I learned. Back when I started learning natural wizardry."

"Oh, my," was about all Joanna could say, she was so impressed. "I wish I had one of those."

"Let's have lunch," Cordelia suggested. "Then I'll show you the sparest of spare rooms."

"I wondered where it might be," Anoria said. "You didn't call any room in the house a spare room. Work rooms, bedroom, all, but no spare room."

"That's because," Cordelia said as she poured cocoa for the girls and began serving lunch, "there wasn't one. Not when I asked you to visit."

Anoria looked curious, and Cordelia began to explain. The conversation grew more and more intricate, but eventually she said, "So, that's what I did. I made you a special room, one just for you two. It's never been lived in by so much as a spider."

That night, as Anoria and Joanna settled into their room, Anoria said, "It was a lot of trouble she went to. Imagine, inventing a whole new spell, just for us."

The spare room wasn't spare at all. It had two beds and matching chests at the foot of each one. Everything in it was girl-sized, as well. Anoria didn't have to stand on tiptoe to reach anything, which was quite a change for her.

"It certainly sounded like a lot of trouble to me," Joanna agreed. "Of course, I didn't understand most of what she said."

"You don't feel like we've neglected you, do you?" Anoria asked. She was unbraiding her hair at the moment. It always felt good to release the tight braids and let her hair loose.

"Not even a little bit. I started reading the book Cordelia gave me, the one about the flowers. You know, I really love those flowers. I wonder if they'll grow on the farm. It said in the book that you can make a perfume with the petals. I think I'd like to learn how."

Location: Cordelia's Cabin, Greenwood, Whitehall County

Date: 23 Zagrod, 135 AF

Anoria and Joanna sat at the table with its white linen cloth and the silverware, cups and plates all laid out with great precision. It seemed to Anoria that a servant had spent hours setting the table, but she assumed it was more of Lady Cordelia's magic. This was confirmed as a platter filled with scrambled eggs floated gently into the room to hover next to Lady Cordelia's left shoulder.

"Normally the guests would be served first, but I thought it might be easier for you girls if I showed you how the servants work." With that, she gestured with her left hand, and the platter floated down in front of Lady

Cordelia's plate and a bare four inches above it. Lady Cordelia spooned a serving of eggs onto her plate. Then the platter floated up and over to Anoria's left shoulder. Where it stopped and waited.

Anoria just looked at it. It didn't move. "Um," she said. "What do I do now?"

"Gesture with your left hand," Cordelia said, "indicating where you want the platter to place itself."

Anoria had to try it twice. The first time her gesture was a bit too large and the platter wound up too high. But the second time she got it right. Lucky Joanna, since she'd seen Anoria do it wrong, got it right at her first try.

They went through the same routine for the sausage, toast, and fruit. By the time the already-filled glasses came with the juice, Anoria was starving from the scents.

After they were served, Lady Cordelia asked, "What would you girls like to do today?"

Joanna said, "Aunt Cordelia, would it be all right for me to go out into the garden?"

"Of course, dear. Just a moment," Cordelia said. Then she waved her hands in an odd little gesture and mumbled some sounds that Joanna and Anoria weren't certain were words. "There you go, girls. You can go out after breakfast."

"What did you do?" Joanna wanted to know.

"I cast a simple spell of protection on you. You see, we're a bit out of town here," Cordelia said. "I put it on you to be safe. I don't usually have any trouble, but elves and will-o'-the-wisps do live out here.

"And what about you, Anoria? Do you want to go and look at the garden as well?"

"Actually, I would like to look at the library," Anoria said.

"Ah," said Cordelia. "The library is a much chancier place than the garden. Perhaps I should accompany you?"

* * *

Joanna's and Anoria's eyes got really, really big when Cordelia said that, and she couldn't help laughing. "A little knowledge can be a dangerous thing," Cordelia said, and took a bite of wintermelon to keep from laughing again.

They talked about the garden and the library for the rest of breakfast, with the occasional comment about boys and girls from school. When they were done, Cordelia said, "You go have fun in the garden, Joanna. I'll take Miss Anoria into the library."

* * *

The library had shelves that reached all the way to the ceiling and a big, comfortable chair. But just one. There was a long table that had open books and notes scattered atop it.

Anoria could tell that Cordelia didn't sit down much when she was working. Otherwise there would be at least one chair pulled up to the table.

"How does magic work?" Anoria asked.

"That sort of depends on what you mean," Cordelia said. "If you mean what does what, that I can tell you, but it's a long-time learning. If you mean why does it work that way, only the gods know, and even Zagrod isn't telling."

"I guess I mean how do you make a spell."

"By trial and altogether too much error. By experience and years of learning. Let me give you an example. When I was an apprentice, my teacher had me visualize a sphere of blue. The reason he had me do that, and I had to do it a lot, was because it's the first thing you do to perform the See Magic spell."

"What's the See Magic spell?"

"Well, it's awfully hard to do magic without being able to see what you're doing," Cordelia said. "The See Magic spell is the spell that lets someone who isn't a natural mage see how their thoughts, words, and gestures are affecting the magic. Once you perform the See Magic spell, you can see that visualizing the blue ball makes a shape in the flow of the magic. Visualizing a red ball makes a different shape, a different kind of ripple. And as you put more and more of these shapes and colors together, you eventually get to a point that they actually make spells that do things in the everyday world."

As Cordelia had been talking, Anoria had been concentrating very hard on visualizing a blue ball. But it was hard, because she was also trying to concentrate on what Cordelia was telling her. She didn't realize that Cordelia could see her efforts affecting the flow of magic. This was not unusual. Any time anyone thought about anything, it affected the flow of magic. Even animals affected the flow of magic. It's just that mostly those effects didn't produce any results.

They continued to talk about magic and how you puzzled out a spell. Cordelia explained that even for a natural wizard, the wizard's concentration and improved focusing of the magic was helped by the See Magic spell. "You see, when you're a natural wizard, you see magic all the time, and when you get old enough, you start doing magic by accident. That magic is only spells that are simple, but they can take a lot of power. It's easy for an untrained natural wizard to cause disasters because they don't know what they're doing with the magic. Anyway, when you grow up seeing magic all the time, it can be hard to tell when you're seeing magic or the mundane world. See Magic separates out the magic so that it's easier to tell the difference. Here, I'll show you."

Cordelia made a quick gesture and said something that was almost like a word but not quite. Suddenly everything was surrounded by color, and it was like Anoria was standing in the middle of a rushing river that flowed through everyone and everything. Nothing stopped it, but everything distorted it. Every move she made, everything she thought, everything Lady Cordelia did. The potted plant on a table distorted it in one way, the table in another, the book on the shelves, the floor, the walls. It was a world filled with colored flows rippling and eddying around and through her. Anoria found it amazingly distracting, because when she thought about the blue ball, a blue ball was not what appeared in the field. It was a strange kind of rippling, and as soon as she started to think about the rippling, it started to change.

Still, it was a most enjoyable morning, and Anoria was starving by lunch.

CHAPTER 7

Location: Cordelia's Cabin, Greenwood, Whitehall County
Date: 23 Zagrod, 135 AF

At lunch they talked more about the garden than about the magic, mostly because Joanna was a bit obsessed with the flowers called musk roses.

When they'd finished eating, they all went out so that Cordelia could explain to Joanna about the flowers' properties. But rather than taking the stairs, Cordelia simply put her hands on the girl's shoulders and pop! they were out in the garden.

Anoria could understand why Lady Cordelia called her mode of travel "popping." Pop, you were here. Pop, you were half a world away. It was amazing.

Meanwhile, in the garden there were musk roses, which were small, red flowers that weren't all that impressive to look at but put out a very strong scent. "Perfumers in the capital use these to make perfumes. They also use skunk weed."

"Ew," Joanna said, wrinkling her nose.

Cordelia laughed. "It's true! Apparently the skunk weed scent, in very small amounts, can add a lovely accent to perfumes. So you see, girls, sometimes things that don't appear to be very useful or pleasant can have hidden virtues. These," Cordelia said, pointing at another bed of flowers, "are moss lilies."

"They don't look mossy to me," Joanna said.

"They're called moss lilies because if you chop them up they make a really nice food for magic moss."

Joanna sidled a bit away from the moss lily bed, and Cordelia stifled another laugh. Truly, inviting the girls had been one of the best ideas she'd had in years.

Anoria asked, "Is magic moss the same as witch moss, Lady Cordelia?"

"Yes, it is. Witch moss is what peasants call it, because wood witches often live near the plants."

"Why's that?"

"Because the main thing that magic moss does is distort or change the shape of the magic field. You remember we talked about that this morning."

Anoria nodded, clearly thinking about the implications, and Cordelia waited to see if she would make the connection. Finally, Anoria's eyes lit up. "Does that mean you could grow a spell out of witch moss?"

"Magic moss," Cordelia corrected. "And yes. And no. Magic moss can be used in casting spells and especially in making magic items. And there are many spells that are more easily cast when there is a lot of magic moss nearby."

Meanwhile, Joanna was clearly getting uncomfortable with the conversation, so Cordelia pointed out a bed of yellow coneflowers. And they talked about flowers and their virtues, including the ones whose only virtue was that they were pretty. A few were actually poisonous, and some of the beds were kept magically warm so that more tropical flowers could be grown.

After they'd gotten about halfway to the edge of the garden, Joanna asked, "Do you take care of all these yourself, Aunt Cordelia? It's so big!"

"No. I have an arrangement with a wood elf. He takes care of it, mostly. When he's merged with his tree, the Servant spells take care of simple things like deadheading the spent blooms."

"Merged with his tree?" Anoria asked.

"It's their natural way of life," Cordelia said. "Elves do indeed live a very long time, but not generally all at once. More than half of their life spans are usually spent hibernating in a tree. Sometimes for a week. Sometimes for a hundred years. It depends on the elf. If he's been injured in body or soul, he might retreat into a tree for many years.

"Elagon was a forest elf who lost his wood in the Servile War. So I gave him a clump of trees up here when I bought this place. He should be coming out in a few days, and you'll get to meet him then."

* * *

That evening, as they sat in Cordelia's parlor after dinner and looked out the magic window into the night, they saw will-o'-the-wisps dancing in the moonlight.

"I'm sure you've been told to stay away from them," Cordelia said. "But they are fun to watch, aren't they?"

"They're beautiful," Joanna said. "I know they're supposed to be dangerous, but it's hard to see how."

"They're quite dangerous, and not without reason," Cordelia told her severely. "It's not often that it happens, but in general will-o'-the-wisps are forest ghosts. The spirits of elves who were murdered or died violently.

They have lost most of their intellect and have only the most extreme of their memories. If you know anything about elves, you can recognize their ceremonial dances in the dances of the will-o'-the-wisps. Wedding dances, funeral dances, that sort of thing. They know enough to realize that they have lost what they were, and they resent those who still have it. If you attract their attention, they will try to lead you to your death."

Location: Cordelia's Cabin, Greenwood, Whitehall County
Date: 29 Zagrod, 135 AF

That set the basic pattern for the next few days. Anoria and Cordelia spent time in the library every morning, while Joanna wandered the garden. Then they would all get together in the afternoon, either in the garden or in the house somewhere, studying or doing any of the myriad of little chores that needed to be done even in such a magical place.

They had been at Greenwood nearly a week when, "Mistress! Mistress! There's a stranger in the garden," sounded in Cordelia's ear.

"Oh, goodness," Cordelia said. "Come along, Anoria. I should have realized." Cordelia reached out, touched Anoria's arm, and popped them into the garden.

Elagon was nowhere in evidence, and Cordelia realized that she shouldn't have expected him to come out of hiding when a strange human was about. "It's all right, Elagon," Cordelia shouted. "It's just my niece, Joanna and her friend, Anoria. They are visiting for a few weeks, and Joanna loves the garden."

Cautiously, Elagon stepped from behind a tree. Cordelia watched as her gardener and the two young girls stared at each other with mutual trepidation. It was unlikely that either Joanna or Anoria had ever actually seen an elf. Elves were uncommon in the north, usually serfs or sharecroppers in the south, and wild and dangerous in the west. The girls would have heard nothing to go on but stories of wild elves committing atrocities on poor, innocent humans, while the opposite was closer to the truth. It tended to be humans committing the atrocities, starting with the simple fact that five hundred years ago all this continent had been elvish.

Elegon looked like he was expecting the two small girls to attack. The two small girls looked like they expected the same from him. Cordelia laughed. "Come now. We're all friends here. Elegon, the dark-haired girl is my grand-niece Joanna, and the blonde is her friend Anoria. Girls, this is Elegon." Cordelia waved Elegon closer and said, "Elegon, Joanna is very interested in our garden. Perhaps you could show her around."

* * *

Joanna looked at the elf, and he didn't seem that scary. He was taller than her but not much taller. He was very slim and wore a hat that seemed to be made out of the thin bark of a beech tree, but was shaped all in one piece as though it had grown that way. At the same time, his pants and shirt were all ragged and he wore no shoes.

"Tsk, tsk," Aunt Cordelia said. "Elegon, your clothes are about to fall apart. You're supposed to let me know when you need more."

"It's all right, mistress. They're warm enough."

Aunt Cordelia sighed. "I'll take care of it. Girls, tomorrow we'll be taking a trip."

The thought of a trip gave Joanna a little thrill.

***

"Where does Elegon come from?" Anoria asked.

"Is he one of the wild elves out of the west who chop up people to feed them to their trees?" Joanna jumped in with such a mixture of dread and glee that Cordelia wasn't sure whether the girl was afraid he might be a savage western elf or that she wanted him to be.

"No. He was born in Pangera two hundred years ago," Cordelia told her grand-niece repressively. "His parents were slaves on one of the big plantations there, and they planted his tree in the plantation's slave grove. He went into a tree for the first time when he was seven, but his tree wasn't ready so his tie to the grove wasn't as great as it normally would have been."

Anoria was apparently following the explanation, but Joanna was looking confused. So Cordelia explained a little more. "Elves without their trees have shorter life spans than humans do. They are normally grown up, physically anyway, at about ten years old. And without a tree they die of old age at about forty."

"But elves live forever," Joanna protested. "Everybody knows that."

"And like most things everybody knows, it isn't true," Cordelia said. "In fact, elves can live a very long time but not all at one time. That's where their trees come in. As I mentioned earlier, when elves get hurt or sick or just get old, they go into a tree and hibernate for weeks or years, sometimes decades. It depends on how injured they are. And when they come out, they are healed and in their prime. To do that, they need a tree big enough for them to fit into. That means that the tree has to be at least as big around as the elf is. But trees don't grow as fast as people. When Elegon was seven, he was just a little thing as people and elves go, but his tree—the one that had been planted at his birth—was barely four inches across. There was no way even a small elf child was going to fit in a tree that small, so when he was injured, they put him in a grownup tree, and he came out five years later cured, but not much taller than when he had gone in. Over the years, he went back into trees a dozen times, for from a few months to a few years. Then, when the Servile War happened, his grove was burned to the ground, and with it went most of his family because their owner had locked them in their trees to keep them from running off."

"You mean the owner murdered them?" Joanna asked.

"No. He just planned on locking them up while we were in the area, but we didn't know that, and it was policy to destroy the groves to force the elves out. The plan was to grow new groves after the war."

By now both girls were staring at Cordelia.

"That's right!" Cordelia nodded. "I used fireballs on the grove and burned it to ash." She looked down at her soup with no appetite at all and continued quietly. "I didn't know until later that the spell that the southern wizard had used to lock the elves in the trees had also hidden their presence. I've often wondered whether he knew it would have that effect. I doubt it, though. Anyway, we'll never know."

"Why not?" Johanna asked.

Cordelia looked around the fancy restaurant she had brought the girls to, with its glow lights, glittering glass, fine wooden sculptures, clean linen napkins, and silver and porcelain tea service, and all the other accoutrements of fine society. And she remembered another place. A private dining room in a mansion. A dining room quite as well appointed as this one, but choked with smoke and fire. And a man quite as well dressed as anyone here and—Cordelia imagined—quite as well mannered. The southerners were stickers about manners and etiquette, after all. A fine linen tablecloth atop the table and atop the cloth an elfin lad who looked much younger than he later turned out to be.

Above the elf, a knife raised for the stroke that would end the elf's life and provide power for the spell.

And she remembered the expression of utter shock on the face of that fine southern wizard as she appeared where she shouldn't have been able to appear in his warded dining room. She remembered the vital seconds while he tried to decide whether he had time to kill the elf and take his life force or needed to act now. She remembered the lightning bolt that sought out the silver knife in his hand and burned him to a crisp.

Then she was back with the two little girls hanging on the words of her story and took a deep breath. She wanted to shield them, to protect them from the evils of the world, but another part of her resented them. How dare they sit here in comfortable innocence, not having seen the things she had seen nor done the things she had done? And she didn't know how to answer Joanna's question.

Protect or prepare? Keep silent or explain?

Then she looked into Anoria's eyes and decided. "Because I killed him about a half an hour after I burned down the grove. He had kept Elegon out to use as a sacrifice, which is how I learned about him locking the elves into their trees.

"After that, Elegon followed the army around, working for his keep," Cordelia continued. "With his grove gone and his family with it, there was nothing to keep him on the plantation any more. When the war ended, I brought him home with me. I felt I owed him that much, anyway. And when Count Whitehall wanted his road and traded me the forest for it, I gave Elegon a grove. Elves have fairly delicate constitutions without their trees, you see. They don't heal as well as humans do, and they get sick easier."

Anoria said, "Perhaps it's because they can bond with the trees. After all, if you can heal yourself by joining with a tree, you don't really need to be able to get well on your own."

Cordelia's resentment of the girls eased a bit. Partly because Anoria came up with that reason on her own, without years of study. And partly because even if the child hadn't experienced the things Cordelia had, Anoria's life had not been without thorns. "That could be it," Cordelia said. "And now that we've finished lunch, let's get to that shopping I promised you."

* * *

Later it would be discovered that her parents found Joanna's newly discovered joy in shopping to be rather less than a blessing.

CHAPTER 8

Location: Cooper House, Greenshire
Date: 24 Pago, 135 AF

At the end of their month, the girls and Cordelia went back to the farm, along with quite a few items they had bought in various places. As well, Joanna had a large collection of roses to plant and several books on how to produce perfumes and salves.

"I shall miss you, Auntie Cordelia," Joanna said. "I shall miss you very much." It had been quite a wonderful month. It was filled with new experiences and luxury. Joanna had overcome her mother's aversion to Cordelia's presence and decided that she liked her great-aunt as well.

"Oh, I'll be in and out, just like always, girls."

"I will miss you too," Anoria said. "But it was a wonderful visit." And she would miss her, she knew. Lady Cordelia and her talk of magic interested her more than the best puzzle book she had ever tried. Magic seemed to be one giant puzzle, one that would take years to solve.

Debra Cooper was thrilled to see Joanna back safe and sound. As well as being back in her own person, rather than having been turned into a pig. Then she saw the new clothing and began to wonder if a pig might not have been a better option. A pig, after all, doesn't need a new dress every season and get upset when the other pigs tease her about her outfits. These outfits hadn't cost them anything, but what about next time?

Was a pig really worse than a clotheshorse?

Location: Boden House, Brookshire
Date: 25 Pago, 135 AF

Mistress Boden apparently thought that a clotheshorse was worse. Much worse. Debra Cooper could see it in her face as she dropped Anoria off at the Boden home. Somehow Debra doubted that Gemma Boden was all that concerned with buying replacements when Anoria outgrew her new outfits. Debra and Gemma said their hellos and goodbyes quickly. Neither one wanted Debra there for what would happen next.

* * *

As the carriage left the Boden property, Mistress Boden turned to Anoria and said, in a cold, hard voice: "We'll put these away for now, Anoria, they're much too fine for you to wear while doing laundry. And scrubbing pots."

"But Merry scrubs the pots," Anoria said, and she knew even as she said it that was the wrong thing to say.

"Merry is training as assistant cook now. And you are clearly getting above yourself, my girl. You're an orphan living on our charity, and you should show more respect."

Anoria suspected that Merry would be surprised to learn that she was training as assistant cook, but she had her tongue under control now. "Yes, ma'am," was all she said.

"And we'll put these away, as I said."

"Yes, ma'am."

"Go and start work."

"Yes, ma'am."

Anoria didn't trudge off to her work. She knew better than that. In Mistress Boden's present mood that would probably mean the strap. She had forgotten while she visited Lady Cordelia that she was just a piece of human trash that no one much wanted. She was someone who got her food and clothing from the charity of people of higher station. Perhaps it had been foolish to forget that while she stayed with Lady Cordelia and Joanna in the sparest of spare rooms and was treated as an honored guest. But, oh, it had been glorious while it lasted.

Location: Cordelia's Cabin, Greenwood, Whitehall County
Date: 14 Wovoro, 135 AF

For several weeks after the girls' visit, Cordelia couldn't settle into work. She tried studying but couldn't keep her attention on the book.

After a week of feeling somewhat irritated with herself, she left and went to visit friends. That was better, but she still felt unsettled. She continued to feel a bit on edge for the week she was away. Finally, she decided to return home.

That evening, back in her marvelous parlor, Cordelia found herself at loose ends. She puttered about, trying to find something interesting to do, and finally gave it up. After a long talk with herself, she realized she was lonely.

Perhaps, she thought, I should take an apprentice.

Cordelia had never taken on an apprentice. She had never wanted to. Never felt the need to either pass on her knowledge or to receive the fees and free labor that came with an apprentice. Now Cordelia realized that she wanted one. Not for the fee or the free labor. She wanted someone who she could teach magic and talk magic with, like she had with Anoria. In fact, she didn't want just any apprentice. She wanted Anoria. Anoria was quite suitable. The girl had a lot of untapped abilities. She liked puzzles and was willing to work at them for as long as it took to solve them. That determination boded well for her ability to learn wizardry.

Cordelia had learned to be a wizard the hard way. She had great power, but her knowledge would be wasted if she didn't pass it down. That had never mattered to her before. After all, she would be gone by then. But the visit had reminded her that the world would not end with her death. Anoria would still be here and so would Joanna and all the other people living and not yet born. Taking her knowledge with her to the grave would be a great waste. The more she thought about it, the more she didn't like the idea of waste.

Location: Boden House, Brookshire
Date: 14 Wovoro, 135 AF

Now that her wonderful visit was over, Anoria found herself quite busy with the Boden children, not to mention the laundry and pot scrubbing. Ann was curious about her visit and kept asking questions. Silly questions that were full of rumors and misinformation.

"Did she turn you into a frog?"

"Of course not, Ann. She's a very nice lady, not a mean, evil spook. She wouldn't do that not unless I made her angry and probably not even then."

"Does she live in a dungeon? I thought all wizards had to live in dungeons. With chains for the people they lock up."

Anoria sighed. "It is not a dungeon. It's a very nice cottage on top of a hill." Ann didn't need to know about the rest of it. First, because, well, it wasn't a dungeon but it was underground, and Ann was too young to understand the difference. She'd just give out wrong information, anyway.

"Would you go back there?"

"If she asked me to, I surely would. She's got one room that's full of books. And she had a big stack of paper and all colors of ink. I read a book about dwarves and a book about elves while I was there. Would you like to hear a story?" Anoria needed to distract Ann, as well as herself. Cordelia's home in the forest was perfect, as far as she was concerned. Full of quiet and books, with all the time a person needed to study.

Ann had one more question. "Would you want to be a wizard, if you could? I'm not sure I'd want to be that different from other people, would you?"

"I don't think I would enjoy people being afraid of me like some are of Lady Cordelia, Ann," Anoria admitted, thinking to herself that things were quite bad enough just being an orphan girl. "And it just wouldn't be possible for me to be a wizard. I've heard that it's the most expensive apprenticeship in the world. I'd never have that much money." Anoria would be glad when school started next week. She needed something to occupy her mind.

Location: Boden House, Brookshire
Date: 19 Wovoro, 135 AF

"But girls don't apprentice," Mistress Boden sputtered. "They don't." She had received Cordelia in her own parlor, which was cluttered with brica-brac. It might have been very fashionable, but Cordelia found it crowded and stuffy.

"Perhaps not here," Cordelia answered with what she considered great restraint. "But they do in many other places. I did, in fact. Would you deny the girl the opportunity to learn a well-paying trade, if one were offered? Say if the local seamstress offered to take her on?"

With an effort, Cordelia didn't grit her teeth. She had to be careful here. Once a family took in a child, legally they had all the rights of a parent, with considerably less responsibility to the child. If the Bodens took it into their heads to refuse permission, there was no legal way for Cordelia to force them.

"Harumph," Master Boden began. "We did think that she might someday become a nanny, Gemma. And Lady Cordelia is right. It's a very good opportunity for the child." Master Boden kept the records for the wool production of Brookshire as well as selling cloth he imported from Gent. He was a portly man with a red face, but he had very kind eyes. The eyes were a bit deceptive, in Cordelia's opinion.

It had taken Cordelia two days to convince Harold Boden, Senior, that it was indeed a very good opportunity. Only by informing him that no, she did not require an apprenticeship fee, was she able to convince him.

"What if Anoria would prefer to stay with us?" Gemma asked.

Cordelia wondered if Gemma Boden was jealous that the opportunity was coming to an orphan and not her own children, or if she was as afraid of wizards as many people were.

"I wouldn't want to force her to go if she wanted to stay."

"We'll call her in and ask," Cordelia said. "She's a very studious young girl and quite able to become a wizard, I know that. But it is true that not everyone has the desire. If she prefers to stay, she has only to say so."

* * *

It was wash day again. Anoria had just wrung out another of Jess' aprons and was laying it over the hedge to let the sun bleach it when Jess called from the kitchen. "Anoria, come in. Mistress Boden wants to see you in the parlor."

Mistress Boden rarely allowed any children into the parlor. Anoria wondered what this might be about as she dried her hands and brushed off her shirt a bit. All of her work clothes were getting a bit tight and ragged. Mistress Boden had complained about it just yesterday, wondering why Lady Cordelia hadn't bought her something useful, instead of the fancy and frilly clothing she'd brought back. They were going to make Anoria another shirt or two, she said. Perhaps Mistress Boden had started and wanted to check the fit. Worse, maybe she wanted Anoria to sew the seams. Anoria didn't really like to sew very much and hoped she wouldn't wind up with another chore to do.

Anoria rushed into the house, and Jess made a motion for her to be quiet. "Shh. There's a very fine lady in there with them. Act presentable. They want to see you."

"Why? I don't know any fine ladies."

"No idea. Just be on your best behavior. Act like a lady."

Anoria shrugged and complied as best she could. Not knowing what a lady was supposed to act like, she was guessing about how they behaved. She was also wondering who the fine lady could be. She walked to the parlor and tapped at the door.

"Come in." It was Master Boden's voice. Anoria grew a bit scared and wondered what she had done wrong this time. Still, there was nothing to do but face the music if she had.

She entered the parlor to find Lady Cordelia sitting in a chair across from the Bodens. "Hello, Anoria," Cordelia said, smiling. "Come here, please. We have a question we want to ask you."

Anoria was happy to see Cordelia. That month had been a wonderful treat. "I'm so happy to see you, Lady Cordelia. What question?" Master and Mistress Boden looked worried. "Have I done something wrong?"

Mistress Boden said, "Anoria, Lady Cordelia has asked for you to become her apprentice. She says you have the qualities a wizard needs to learn. And because it's a very large change in your future, we felt we should ask if you wanted it. You're quite welcome to stay with us, if you would prefer it."

Anoria was stunned. This was the last thing she had expected. "I could become a wizard like you?" she asked Cordelia. "Truly? Me?"

"Have you thought about it?" Master Boden asked. "You do understand that it will set you apart a bit?"

"I haven't thought about it, sir," Anoria answered. "I wouldn't really want people to be afraid of me, the way they are of Lady Cordelia. But she does a lot of good for everyone, if they only knew it. I'd like to do that kind of good for the world. So, yes, sir, ma'am, I'd like to try."

Cordelia smiled. "Run along and pack your things, then. You'll go home with me today." Cordelia paused a moment, then added, "And make sure you pack the things I bought you." She gave Gemma Boden a look. "I don't expect you to wear clothing you're about to burst out of at my home."

Anoria ran out of the room without waiting for the Bodens' response. She was happier than she had ever been.

Gemma knew she'd pushed about as far as she could without making this notorious wizard angry, but she was, in fact, rather miffed that it wasn't her own son being offered this apprenticeship. Not that she really wanted young Harold to be a wizard. But still . . . an orphan!

And she had the law on her side. No matter how disturbed Lady Cordelia might be, they still hadn't signed the apprenticeship agreement. Might as well be hung for a sheep as turned into a goat, she thought, and went on the attack.

* * *

"But what am I to do?" Gemma Boden asked, a sly grin seeping through her pout. "I can't hire Tess, since she found that man she likes and she'll be marrying soon. If Anoria leaves, who will help with the children?" Gemma's hands fluttered helplessly, an affectation that Cordelia found annoying. Still, though, Cordelia didn't want the Bodens to think up more objections. She decided to make a suggestion before Gemma found another reason to oppose the apprenticeship.

"Oh, is that the problem?" Cordelia asked. "Perhaps I can help there. Now, if I find you another child-minder, will you allow Anoria to become my apprentice?"

"I suppose so," Gemma agreed. "It will have to be someone as good with children as Anoria is. And perhaps a bit older. Tess made a big difference in young Harold's behavior."

Cordelia sighed internally. She'd had a talk with Tess about the Boden household. It seemed that Tess believed that a stronger hand from Mistress Boden and a bit more attention to the children from Master Boden were what the family really needed. "Very well," she said. "I shall find you another child-minder. Please ask Anoria to wait for me. I'll be back shortly."

Cordelia turned and directed a stern look at Gemma before she left the room. "And I expect that Anoria will be ready and the agreement will be signed when I get back."

Granted, the law might be on the Boden's side here. But Gemma was making Cordelia angry . . .

* * *

"I don't know, dear," Master Boden said after Cordelia left. "I can't say I actually approve of magic or wizards, but if Anoria has the talent for it it's probably best that she be sent to study with a powerful one. The Wizard Cordelia has been quite helpful, in a very quiet way."

Gemma thought for a moment. "It might be for the best, after all. If Anoria is a young wizard, I'm not at all sure I want her around the children, anyway."

"That is a point," Master Boden agreed. "Besides, you'll be pleased to know that a new school will be endowed, right here in Brookshire."

That concession had taken a good bit of bargaining.

CHAPTER 9

Location: Orphanage, Gent
Date: 19 Wovoro, 135 AF

Cordelia was annoyed with the Bodens. The man drove a very hard bargain. But the common wisdom said: Whoever wants the bargain pays for the bargain. Cordelia wanted Anoria as an apprentice, and there was no real advantage to the Bodens in releasing Anoria to Cordelia's care. That there was a clear advantage to Anoria didn't influence them much at all.

Anoria was caught in a vise, in some ways. In spite of the fact that the kingdom of Amonrai had fought a vicious war with the Servile States to eliminate serfdom, children remained the property of their parents or guardians. Naturally, in most instances, parents cared for their own children. But children without parents fell into the hands of whomever would take them in, whether a relative, an orphanage, or a family looking for a servant. And those hands might or might not be as caring as they should be.

Still, Anoria had the qualities a book wizard needed, even though she had no natural magic. She could concentrate, and she was determined. And endowing another school wouldn't be a problem. It would relieve some of the crowding at the Greenshire School, at any rate. Deaconess Willow, the schoolteacher, would be pleased to hear about it.

Cordelia arrived just outside of the orphanage in the city of Gent. It was the closest city to the villages, and she had a connection there. She had once turned the teacher of the Gent Home for Foundlings into a goat, after all. She went looking for Tilly Titum and found her in the schoolroom.

"Lady Cordelia, how nice to see you." Tilly smiled. "It's been a long time." Tilly had grown into a plain, but well-spoken, woman. She wore sturdy clothing, but it was of a better quality than had been available in Greenshire.

"Oh, you know me, Tilly," Cordelia said. "Busy, busy. But I've got a bit of a puzzle to solve, and you might be able to help."

"I'll be happy to," Tilly agreed. "I've often wanted to be able to return the favor you did me, even though it involved me eating hay and living in the open for a while."

Cordelia had arranged that Tilly could finish school, rather than go into service as her family had arranged. But that was after Tilly had been found in a tree on her property, spying on Cordelia. Twenty years ago, it was. In a fit of pique, Cordelia had turned the girl who was sneaking around her place in the woods into a goat and hadn't thought much about it. After the search parties started showing up, Cordelia used a spell to find the young nanny goat and popped herself and the goat to Greenshire, where she went around the town looking for the family who had lost a daughter, leading the goat. When she found the family, she handed the leash to the girl's mother, saying, "Here's your daughter. She shouldn't have bothered me," and popped back to her forest retreat.

The family went to the intercessor, who went to Count Whitehall, who put together a troop of soldiers and the best wizard he could find to confront Cordelia about her high-handed ways. It had been quite a tangle.

Cordelia was fresh from the Orclands and in no mood for polite society. That was why she'd taken what she thought was unused land in the first place. She'd known that it belonged to somebody, but hadn't really cared. All she wanted was to be left alone.

The old count had agreed to that for now, as long as she restored the girl child. Which she'd done, and a much-chastened Tilly had apologized and explained that she'd done it on a dare and because she'd wanted to find out what a wizard's house looked like. It made Cordelia feel guilty. The child wasn't an orc, after all. So, in recompense, she arranged for the girl's further education. Later, some time before the Servile War, the young count had worked out an agreement with Cordelia so that she would own and have rights over the land on which she'd been living. After the Servile War, there was another agreement with the king, but that was all years ago. This plain-faced, gentle woman was not the little girl she'd been back then.

Tilly laughed a tinkling laugh at the memory, and Cordelia found herself joining in. "As it turned out, you did me a favor. That story kept the children out of my woods for several years. And I still don't have as many boys trying to find me as there used to be. I'd say it worked out for both of us. Look at you, all grown up and in charge of your own school."

"And quite happy at it," Tilly confirmed. "Come, let's walk around and let me show you the school."

The foundling home had two buildings; dormitories were in one of them and classrooms in the other. Cordelia saw rosy-faced children out and about in the courtyard, all of whom seemed to think well of Tilly.

As they walked, Cordelia explained the type of person she needed, stressing that the Bodens seemed to be good people, if a bit misguided in their lack of discipline for their oldest son. "Someone like Tess, I think. You remember Tess, don't you?"

"Of course, I do," Tilly nodded. "We were in school together. No-nonsense Tess, I called her. Even at twelve, she didn't let anyone get away with anything. I've got just the girl, too. She's only been here for a month or so, but she likes children and she's very good with them, too. And she's the right age for the job, at sixteen. She'll be able to leave in two years if things don't work out for her. Imagine, putting a ten-year-old in charge of three children! What was your Mistress Boden thinking of? When Master Boden left here, I had the impression that he wanted Anoria as a child-minder during a wagon trip, not as a full-time nanny. Oh, look. This is my pride and joy."

Tilly gestured at a pile of building material. "We're getting ready to add on another wing," she explained. "That is, if the workmen ever get here to start the walls."

Cordelia walked over to the construction site and nodded. "The foundation looks well set. What's the holdup?"

Tilly sighed a bit. "The committee in charge of building got things a bit muddled. They scheduled the roofers before the wall builders. I've been trying to get it straightened out for days. Now, I'll just have to wait for the walls and reschedule the roof. At this rate, I might be able to have this finished by winter."

"Committees," Cordelia muttered. "How to make sure nothing gets done—assign a committee."

"Oh, yes," Tilly agreed. Then she stepped back in surprise. Cordelia made a gesture, and a wall stood in place. Three more gestures, and all of the walls stood, ready for the roofers. "There," Cordelia said. "That should save some time."

"Oh my," Tilly said. "That will save a fortune."

"Well, you're just lucky that Stone Wall spell is one of my natural spells." Cordelia sniffed. Many years ago, she had almost killed herself casting that spell again and again in a desperate attempt to counter the wizard who was working with an attacking army. By the time the siege was over, the spell had been internalized, and she would likely never forget it.

"And, tell your committee members that I said the money saved on the walls should be spent on books. If they argue, you can mention that I'm very good at that Goat spell." Cordelia's grin was full of mischief.

"Don't worry." Tilly's grin had just as much mischief in it. "I will. Now, let's go speak to Intercessor Ardith and get her permission. Then I'll find Anna, and I'll write a letter of recommendation for her. And explain to her about the way she'll travel."

* * *

Intercessor Ardith was staring in stunned amazement at the four walls of the new school. When Tilly and Cordelia tapped at her door, she turned from the window with a pale face. "What happened out there?"

"Intercessor Ardith, I'd like you to meet Lady Cordelia Cooper," Tilly said. "I was explaining about the building mixup, and she fixed it for us."

"Lady Cordelia, I'm pleased to meet you," Intercessor Ardith said. "Tilly has told me about you in the past. I've often wanted to thank you for the endowment of the school. And I'd like to ask you a question as well." The Wizard Cordelia Cooper didn't really intimidate Intercessor Ardith. She was secure in her faith in Barra and really wanted an answer to this question. "Why is it, Lady Cordelia, that you're willing to provide an endowment for the education of the children, but you don't provide for the feeding of them?"

Cordelia was quite taken aback and not at all sure she believed it. "You have trouble feeding them? Why? My understanding was that Baron Hargrove had adequately funded the orphanage. I set the funds for the school because I was concerned about seeing that the children actually got an education. I've run into too many people over the years who decided a good education was wasted on poor children." Cordelia suspected that she had just run into another. Priestess of Barra or not, this lady was looking at a long, healthy life as a sea turtle if she wasn't careful. "What are you feeding them anyway, caviar?"

"Mostly gruel with too much water and not enough oats," Intercessor Ardith explained. "We have hungry children going to the fanciest school in Gent. It's amazing, it really is. We have one of the best schools in the area. At the same time, I have to have the children work in the garden in an attempt to keep them fed properly. I'd just like someone to explain that."

The expression on Cordelia's face was darkening, and Tilly began to grow a bit nervous. Cordelia asked, "Just how much money are you receiving? When I set up that endowment, I was assured that the orphanage had enough funds to provide food. Where are those funds going?"

Intercessor Ardith went to her desk and opened her books for Cordelia's examination. "You can see here, Lady Cordelia. This is what I receive every quarter. We have a grant from the baron and the city pays one copper penny per day for each child who lives here. There are one hundred seventeen children in the Home. The baron's grant gives us just five hundred gold pieces a year, no matter how many children there are. When the baron's endowment was made, there were thirty-five children. With the additional funds provided by the city, it used to give us half a silver piece a day per child. But now there are one hundred and seventeen children. That works out to two coppers a day per child, or as close as makes no difference."

The intercessor was right, much as Cordelia hated to admit it. There were places in the world where two copper pence a day would be enough to feed and house a child, but this wasn't one of them. "I concede that the orphanage is not as fully funded as it needs to be. I, however, am not made of gold, nor do I lay golden eggs. I'll look into the matter and see what can be done. I'll be back in a short time," Cordelia said, and disappeared.

Tilly looked at Intercessor Ardith with worry in her eyes. "What do you suppose she's gone to do?"

Intercessor Ardith smiled. "I hope she's gone to fix things, I really do. I've long felt that something had to be a bit wrong with the way things were arranged. But I don't think she was aware of it. Merchant Jardin may be in for a bit of a surprise."

Location: Jardin and Sons Counting House, Gent
Date: 19 Wovoro, 135 AF

Very few people actually knew that Baroness Cordelia Cooper had anything to do with the orphan's home and school in Gent. She liked her privacy. One person who knew quite well that she had an interest in the school was Merchant Jardin.

Merchant Jardin was, in fact, backed up against the wall of his office. Having an irate wizard appear in your office will do that to you. Jardin was also in charge of the endowment the baron had made to the orphanage. "Yes, Lady Cordelia, it is only five hundred. When you asked if it was adequate, there were fewer children in the orphanage. If you will recall, I asked at the time for the authority to disburse funds to the orphanage should the need arise. You insisted it was strictly for the school. I've been doing what you told me, disbursing monies to the school. I invested the money, and when the surplus accumulated, I arranged to build another building. That's what I thought you wanted, a good school."

"Merchant Jardin." Cordelia stopped herself. She knew that if she authorized the disbursement of money for the orphanage proper, every copper half-penny would go there and the school would be back to no books and no buildings. "Show me the books, please. And, if you can, the books for the baron's fund as well as mine."

After a perusal of the books, Cordelia realized that Jardin had done a good job. His hands were tied somewhat by the restrictions set on the baron's investment. Worse, after the baron had made his endowment, the city had gradually dropped the amount it paid the orphanage per child. That amount had started at two pence per child. Then it dropped to one and a half, and finally to one. If she just set up an endowment for the orphanage, the city would probably stop its funding altogether.

"Very well," Cordelia said. "I'll set up another trust, but it won't be for a flat amount. Set it up to match the funding that the city provides. If the city won't provide for its orphans, I am not going to just take over for them. This way, it might even encourage them to fulfill their own responsibilities. I expect you to make the council understand that."

Merchant Jardin nodded. "I'll be happy to. I've tried, time and again, to convince the council that they were making a mistake by reducing the funding. Perhaps the knowledge that you've taken an interest will change some minds in the city."

"I'll have my factor, Bernard, send you the funds." Cordelia nodded. "And this time send me a message if the funds run short, although I don't think they will. You've done quite a good job, in fact."

When Cordelia disappeared, Merchant Jardin wiped the sweat off his face. Dealing with wizards was a chancy business.

Location: Orphanage, Gent
Date: 19 Wovoro, 135 AF

"I've checked into the matter, and the truth is, it's simply not practical for me to do much more than I have," Cordelia said when she popped back into Intercessor Ardith's office. She didn't mention that what she had done now included matching the quarterly payment by the city per child or a little bit of intimidation directed toward the city council. "The funds for the school only come to a hundred gold a year or so. Even if every pence of it were diverted to the orphanage proper, it would make little difference and would probably be followed by another drop in funding by the city. The children would still be hungry. And they'd be illiterate as well." She handed Intercessor Ardith a purse of additional funds. "This will help a little. But understand me; I won't have the school's funds diverted."

There were a hundred pieces of gold in the small bag. Intercessor Ardith's eyes had a peculiar mix of disappointment and respect in them. "Thank you, Lady Cordelia. At least it's something. And it will help quite a bit."

Location: Boden House, Brookshire
Date: 19 Wovoro, 135 AF

Tilly's and Intercessor Ardith's effusive letters of thanks and the addition of Anna to the Boden household did the trick. Anna took one look at the Boden children and fell in love with them. Gemma took one look at sturdy Anna and fell a bit in love herself. This girl wouldn't be leaving anytime soon, she felt. Sixteen-year-old Anna wouldn't have any trouble with young Harold. She could probably pick him up by the scruff of the neck if she wanted to.

Anoria was packed and ready, nearly delirious with joy at the prospect of a return to the forest.

Cordelia gathered her up and they went. Instantly.

CHAPTER 10

Location: Cordelia's Cabin, Greenwood, Whitehall County
Date: 7 Estormany, 135 AF

At first, Greenwood was a haven from the disturbances of day-to-day life in the village of Brookshire. There was no laundry to do and no children to care for. What chores there were, were things Anoria liked doing anyway: reading books, solving puzzles, working on her handwriting. Learning to draw the strange symbols used in magic was very interesting. Most of the mundane chores like sweeping, dusting, washing, and so on, were done by magic of one sort or another.

It didn't take long, though, before it became lonely for Anoria. Lady Cordelia was often busy with research into how magic worked, and there was no one else to talk to except Elegon, who was only interested in the garden. Besides, many of the books Anoria was set to study had words that she hadn't learned, and she hated to keep bothering Lady Cordelia. But mostly, she didn't want to show herself too ignorant to be a wizard's apprentice.

* * *

"So if I connect Wizard's Mark with . . ." Cordelia muttered.

"Lady Cordelia," Anoria whispered.

Cordelia looked up and snapped, "Yes, Anoria?" Cordelia immediately regretted snapping, as the girl jumped back.

Then Anoria caught herself and asked, "May I speak to you about something?" Anoria was dressed better as Cordelia's apprentice. Like Cordelia, unless she was in the village or a city, she preferred trousers and a tunic. The periwinkle blue color suited her quite well, Cordelia thought.

"Of course you may," Cordelia answered. "Is there a problem?"

"Well, it's not so much a problem," Anoria answered. "It's something that can be fixed, I'm sure. I'm just not sure how."

Anoria's face was creased with concern, and Cordelia began to grow a bit worried. What could be troubling the child? "What is it?"

"I don't understand this word," Anoria said, showing her the book she held. "In fact, I'm finding a lot of words I don't understand. And I've been thinking that I just don't have enough schooling yet. If I did, I wouldn't have this problem."

Cordelia considered Anoria for a moment. "You're thirteen, right?" She'd assumed that, but hadn't ever checked.

"No, ma'am," Anoria said, blushing a bit. "I'm eleven."

"Hmmm," Cordelia muttered. "I expect you're right. When I got apprenticed it turned out that I didn't have as much education as I needed, even for a natural wizard, which requires less knowledge than a book wizard. So I was sent back to school."

Cordelia didn't mention that her master had done everything he could to keep her ignorant and that it was Mrs. Brooks who arranged for her to go to school after Rojer's death at the hands of the Patty orcs.

"I was fifteen at the time. We'll have to consider this. You just don't have all the basics yet. Now, normally I could give you those basics, but somehow I don't really think that's the only problem. Is it?"

Anoria's face lost its blush and looked a bit pale.

"You're lonely, aren't you?" Cordelia asked.

"I wouldn't want you to think I'm ungrateful . . ." Anoria began. She stuttered to a stop and looked into Cordelia's eyes. "It is a little lonely, Lady Cordelia. I thought I would love it, really I did. And I do love the studying. But I miss Joanna."

Cordelia continued thinking and decided. "It's probably best if you spend the winters in Greenshire. You can go to the village school and finish up the basics. I suppose I could buy a house there. But I don't really want to." They were in Cordelia's work space, a niche in her magic workshop.

Anoria was still amazed by the workshop. It was a room forty feet long and thirty wide, with tables and shelves filled with the most amazing collection of this-and-that that anyone was ever likely to see. Potions and animal parts, elements and objects. A floating ball of ruby dust was next to a bucket of kracken heart. That bucket kind of gave Anoria the shivers, but the fully articulated skeleton that paced back and forth in the corner really gave her the willies. Anoria knew from her studies so far that human bones had their place in magic, even if it did scare her a bit. Most people from a village would be less accepting of animated skeletons, though.

So she quite understood that Cordelia wouldn't want to live in the village. Given a choice, she'd prefer to stay here too. But she didn't see that she had a choice. She needed more schooling as well as more company.

"Ah, perhaps I could stay with Joanna," Anoria ventured. "I could come back here on sixth and seventh day, maybe? And for the summers, when we don't have school. Or whenever you wished. I'm afraid it will be a while before I'm able to translocate the way you do."

"I would imagine so," Cordelia said. "That one takes a while. Very well. Let's go talk to Michael and Debra. You won't mind the traveling back and forth? And there may be times you'll have to stay for longer periods, too. I do travel a bit, now and then."

"Oh, no, I won't mind," Anoria said. "I like Joanna. And she likes me. I'll be able to help with Clarence, too. As much trouble as they are, I kind of miss the Bodens' children." As much as Anoria was pleased not to be involved with small children, something seemed to be missing from her life.

Cordelia couldn't imagine that. "Better get your fill of them now, then. Some day, when you go adventuring, you won't really have time for children."

"Adventuring?" Anoria was clearly astonished. "Why would I adventure? My dream is a home of my own. A place for me and any family I might have." After years of being stuck in this corner or that, sharing a bed with other orphans, Anoria had no desire for anything but her own home.

Location: Cooper Home, Greenshire
Date: 7 Estormany, 135 AF

Cordelia stepped up to Michael and Debra's door and knocked. Anoria had pointed out that perhaps part of Debra's problem was the sheer unexpectedness of Cordelia's arrivals. "That kind of thing can be very startling," Anoria said. "Kind of like having a mouse run over your foot."

"Ugh. I see your point, I guess," Cordelia agreed. "Michael's mother, Marie, never said it was a problem, so I didn't understand. I suppose we should start popping to a spot outside the village, too. Keep from scaring people."

"Well, sometimes, at least," Anoria agreed.

So, here they were, standing in the sun, knocking on the door like regular people. When she was honest with herself, Cordelia wasn't sure she liked this "regular people" business. Still, Anoria needed the schooling, and something would have to be worked out.

Debra answered the door and was clearly startled to see Cordelia standing outside. "Auntie, do please come in," she said, with a bit of trepidation. I didn't expect you."

Cordelia swept inside. There was no point in letting the regular people get too comfortable, after all. "I find myself in a bit of a quandary, Debra. Perhaps you might be able to help. I wondered if we might talk."

Debra was startled again, Cordelia could tell. When she thought about it carefully, Cordelia realized that she had never really come to know Debra. Perhaps the woman was intimidated by her. She supposed it was possible.

Michael, Debra, Joanna, and Clarence had apparently been having breakfast. Tess was clearing the table of the last of it. "Anoria," Joanna said, "It's good to see you. I've missed you."

"Why don't the two of you go catch up," Debra suggested. "It's been several weeks since you've seen each other. Chores can wait for a bit."

Anoria and Joanna giggled and walked away, arm in arm, chattering like magpies. It confirmed for Cordelia that the secluded life she led might not be what Anoria needed at this point in her life. A child needed friends as well as instruction and care. She shook her head and took a seat at the table. "I'm beginning to realize that I'm a little over my head in some ways," she admitted. "I've never had much to do with children, and I need some advice."

Tess stopped her eternal cleaning and sat down as well. "Problems?"

"Not problems, exactly," Cordelia said. "She's a child, and she needs more than I can give her. She's not used to being away from people the way I am. I could probably take a house in the village, but I'd be very uncomfortable doing that. I've simply lived alone too long. Anoria is happy with me, but she needs to complete her basic education. And, I realize now, I can't really provide everything a child needs. I wondered if you might have some suggestions."

Tess considered the matter for a few moments, as did Debra. Cordelia was relieved when it was Debra who made the suggestion.

"I suppose, with Tess leaving next week after the wedding, Anoria could come here for the school year, if you'd like. She's certainly no trouble. And without Tess around, well, I could use a little more help around the house."

"The wedding is next week?" Cordelia exclaimed. "I didn't realize it was so soon. I'll need to bring you your dowry, won't I?"

Tess grinned. "Well, I figured I'd better strike while the iron was hot, so to speak. Armand is forty, after all. Luckily for me, he married late and only has the one child, Gregory. After his first wife died, well, he just wasn't inclined to marry again. So, Gregory is fourteen and a well-behaved young man. He's insisting that he wants to become an intercessor of Barra, so he's very studious."

"Armand," Cordelia queried. "Armand . . . Is he that wool factor in Brookshire? The really nice-looking man who moved there for the quiet life?"

Tess nodded. "He is." Tess turned her nose up a bit and pretended to look down upon Cordelia. "I shall be a woman of wealth and distinction, Madame. I've no need for a dowry. My Armand wants me for myself alone."

Cordelia felt in a playful mood, so she turned her nose equally as high. "A woman of distinction? How so, Madame? I've seen you scurrying around, cleaning anything that doesn't move. How shall you adjust to a life of leisure?"

Debra began to giggle at the byplay between the two women. Related or not, they had many similarities. She turned her nose up just as high as the others and sniffed in imitation of Gemma Boden. "You shall have to allow Lady Cordelia to gift you with a Servant spell, Lady Tess. After all, a lady should not be seen scrubbing the floor."

Cordelia sniffed in reply. "I should be happy to. After all, we are related. And I should like to endow Lady Debra also, if she will allow it. Particularly as she has so kindly agreed to take on the extra burden of Lady Anoria and her care." Cordelia fell out of the pose she had assumed and looked at Debra with a serious expression. "Truly, Debra, I would. Anoria needs to study, not do chores. She likes children, but I'd rather she study than do housework. Helping care for Clarence is enough for her to do."

Debra sighed. "I suppose you planned this, didn't you, Cordelia?"

"Not at all, Debra," Cordelia corrected. "Not at all. I truly appreciate your suggestion, and I'd like to take you up on it. But I won't do it, not unless you let me do something in return. And you'll get used to the Servant spell a lot sooner than you think you will. Besides, Anoria will be able to make her own before you know it. You'd have to get used to one anyway."

"Very well," Debra agreed. "Although how I'm going to reassure my visitors is something I've got to figure out."

Tess resumed the pose of superiority she had let drop. "The same way I shall. By indicating that only a small-minded person would turn her nose up at magical help."

That thought hadn't occurred to Cordelia. Servant spells were something she had used for more years than she cared to count. "You don't have to use them all the time just because you have them, you know. You need not have the Servant spell serve tea."

Tess said, "We're joking about them, but you'll have to tell us both how to use them, Cordelia. We've never had a Servant spell. How long do they last? What do we have to do?"

"Well, it's called a Servant spell, but what it creates isn't a servant," Cordelia said. "It has no will or knowledge or understanding. It has neither hands nor feet. It's just a force that acts at your direction. And in doing that, it uses your skill and abilities. If you don't know the difference between a flower and a weed, your Servant spell is as likely to pull up the flower as the weed. So when I give you the item, we'll have to attune it to you."

"An item?" Debra queried, sounding nervous.

"Because a Servant spell that I cast would last about twenty hours, and you don't want me popping in here every twenty hours to recast it. It's not a major magic. I have a dozen Servant spells in my spell safe at home."

"Now you've got me curious," Tess said. "What is a spell safe? Why would a Servant spell you cast last only about twenty hours? And don't magical items take life force? I understood that some of them even require human sacrifice."

Cordelia paused and put down her tea cup. "That's going to take some explaining. In its simplest form, a spell safe or a magic item safe is a container you put magic items in while they mature. The longer you leave them in the spell safe, the more powerful they become . . . within the limits of the structure of the spell, of course. The Servant spell is one of the first spells a young wizard learns, and I laid up twenty of them before either of you were born, and I've made another hundred or so over the years." She shrugged. "It's something to do when you're, well, bored. Crafting the actual item takes a week or so, but the spell has to mature if you don't want to be renewing it every day or so, and that takes years. It's a lot like the little light coins they sell at the candle shop. They're not actually that hard to make, but after you've enchanted the coin, you have to put it in the spell safe for years before you can use it."

Debra still looked nervous. "B-b-b . . . I thought that it was a lot faster than that, Cordelia. I'd always heard about using life force . . ."

Cordelia's face was grim and hard. "Yes, that's the way they do it in the Servile States. And that's why not all of us were pleased when King

Johan made peace with the Southerns. The process is just the same up to the point of putting the item in the safe. But there are spells you can use to take life force from someone who is willing to give it and other spells to force it from them. And then that life force can be used to hurry the process of making a magical item. It's a quick and dirty way to get a magical item, and it works. If you're willing to kill someone to do it."

"I thought it didn't have to be fatal," Tess said.

"Oh, it doesn't. There were times in the war that we made magic swords for the soldiers and used their life force in the process. And they willingly did it. They asked us to do it. Because sacrificing a little bit of your life essence for a weapon to keep you alive isn't a bad bargain. Those are spells that a white wizard or a gray wizard uses to get an item in a hurry. But we're not all white wizards, and not all the intercessors are of the good gods."

"You mean holy magic can do that?"

"Oh, not Zagrod. Or the other members of the pantheon of light. At least not mostly. But the dark gods demand sacrifice. And they're not demanding flowers." Cordelia snorted. "You have to understand. To the gods it's the difference between being a vegetarian and someone who eats meat. Even Zagrod accepts our life force every time we pray. But it's tiny amounts given up freely. Like the difference between milking the cow and slaughtering it. To the dark gods, the fact that we can think and feel and understand just makes us tastier."

Debra and Tess both shuddered. Then Tess, ever practical, said, "Our tea has gotten cold," and went to replenish it.

CHAPTER 11

Location: Abel Home, Greenshire
Date: 3 Barra, 135 AF

"Double dog dare you," Wally Abel said.

The news that Anoria was going to live with the Coopers and return to school, now that she was a wizard's apprentice, had been met with nervous objections by both the students and their parents.

Laurence Firebird, intercessor's son or not, couldn't pass up a dare. Everyone knew that. And Wally was a little afraid of Anoria these days. He wasn't going to try it, not him.

"I bet she'll turn you into a pig," Wally said.

"Wally, you're just being stupid. All you have to do is think. It takes years, years, to learn how to do that," Laurence said. "There's no way she can know how to do that, even if she is a wizard's apprentice. She's just another girl."

"If you're so sure of that, you can't turn down the dare, then," Wally said. "You do it. If she doesn't turn you into a pig, well then, we'll all be all right. If she does, then the rest of us will know that we better not mess with her."

"I'm not afraid of a girl. I don't care if she is a wizard's apprentice," Laurence insisted. "But the last time I pulled a prank like that I had to say prayers for three hours a day for a week. If she turns me into a pig that's fine—it might even be fun. But I'm not going to be stuck praying all by myself, not again." Laurence thought for a minute. "I'll take the dare, but I want witnesses. You guys have to swear, if I get punished, you get punished too."

The other three boys weren't sure about that. It took some hemming and hawing, but they eventually reached an agreement. They would all take responsibility for the prank. With that in mind, the four boys went looking for a garden snake. Tommy Poll found one in his mother's recently harvested vegetable bed.

"Here you go, Laurence. The snake is ready."

"Okay. I'll pull the prank. Tomorrow. When we're leaving the classroom for lunch." Laurence took the snake home. It was just a harmless garden snake. He hoped Anoria wouldn't hurt a harmless garden snake. He liked snakes and hated to put this one to the inconvenience. Still, he wasn't going to let his friends think he was scared of a girl.

Location: Schoolhouse, Greenshire
Date: 9 Barra, 135 AF

It was the very first day that Anoria was back in school. She had moved in with the Coopers two days ago. The morning had been spent on what she had missed while she was staying with Lady Cordelia. She wasn't too far behind, partly because she'd been studying all sorts of things over the last half of the summer while apprenticing with Lady Cordelia. She was actually ahead in math.

"Just a couple of weeks and I'll be caught up with . . ." Anoria was saying to Joanna, when she felt the slither down her back. "Gaaahhh! What's that?"

Anoria wiggled her back, trying to figure out what was going on and heard the giggles from in back of her. Anoria began wiggling faster and felt whatever it was moving inside her blouse.

"Joanna, what is it? Is it a frog?"

"Hold still a minute," Joanna said, and pulled the neck of Anoria's shirt far enough out so she could see down the back. "Ah. Anoria. Don't panic, all right? It's just a garden snake."

The word "snake" got to Anoria right away. She danced and wiggled away, pulling her shirt out of her skirt and yelling. "Gahhh! A snake! Gahhh!"

The boys, all four of them, began laughing out loud. Finally, after what seemed like an hour to her, Anoria got her shirt loose and the snake fell to the ground. By this time, she was red-faced and angry. And she knew who must have done it. Balling up her fists, she marched angrily up to Laurence and punched him directly on the nose. It was a lucky punch. Blood spurted, boys yelled and laughed, girls screamed, and the teacher came running outside.

Deaconess Willow was not amused. Deaconess Willow had been teaching the school for several years. Laurence Firebird was more than any teacher should have to put up with, in her opinion. The upshot was that Laurence got to pray again. But this time he had company. All four boys were at their prayers directly after school. All the next week they prayed, the punishment imposed by Laurence's father. In school, the boys had to stand rather than sit for their classes.

As did Anoria. The punch hadn't been that lucky, after all.

Location: Schoolhouse, Greenshire
Date: 11 Barra, 135 AF

"Anoria Adrien, I'd like to speak to you for a moment," Deaconess Willow said. "The rest of you may go out and have your lunch now."

Anoria wondered if she was still in trouble for punching Laurence. She hadn't thought so, but you never knew.

When the rest of the children had gone outside, Deaconess Willow smiled. "Don't worry, Anoria. I'm not mad about your giving Laurence a bloody nose. I just wanted to check and make sure you were happy in your new situation. Apprenticing to a wizard must be very . . . unusual."

"I thought it would be," Anoria admitted. "But, really, it's a lot like school. I spend lots of time practicing runes with a pen and paper. Lady Cordelia is very insistent that my runes have to be perfect."

"Is that all?" Deaconess Willow asked. "You don't have to do anything different at all? Just study runes?"

"Mostly," Anoria said. "The one really different thing I do is called practice mode, but I can't do that when Lady Cordelia is away. I spent quite a bit of time in practice mode last summer."

Deaconess Willow still looked interested, so Anoria continued to explain. "Lady Cordelia says that practice mode shows me what my mind is doing. And I have to learn to make my mind do what I want it to."

Margaret Willow wanted to know details. She wasn't as suspicious of wizards as many members of the community were, but she wanted to make sure that Anoria wasn't being used as a source of power in some way.

"So how do you make your mind do what you want it to?" she asked. "You don't have to prick your fingers and draw blood or anything like that, do you?"

Anoria giggled. "No, ma'am. It might be easier though. When I'm in practice mode, I can see a lot of different colors and shapes in the air. I have to pick out the different colors and move them here and there. Sometimes I try to make them take another shape. Lady Cordelia says that when I form the shapes right and get them just the right color, I'll be ready to learn spells. They're mental exercises, she says."

"How do you move these colors and shapes?"

"Well, according to Lady Cordelia, they're like pieces of thought or pictures of what my mind is doing. And to make them move, I have to think about them moving the same way I think about moving my hands."

"Does that mean you can read minds?"

"Oh, no," Anoria assured her. "People don't all think the same way. When I am thinking about the number five, it makes a colored blob in my mind. Someone else would get a different blob when they were thinking about the number five. They would have to think about flowers or something to get the same blob I get when I think about five. Every wizard has to learn these exercises, though. Mostly it's just moving a blob here and moving another one there. I'd rather do the runes. All that blob moving is kind of boring. They don't always go where you tell them to, and most of the time when I try to move one, all the others go all over the place."

Deaconess Willow could see that Anoria was perfectly happy. Her own mind was comforted. It wasn't much different from learning the times tables, she supposed. That forced a child's mind to think in a certain way, just like that exercise did. She leaned back in her chair, much more at ease. "Very well. Do be sure and ask Lady Cordelia to let me know if there is anything I need to do, or know, about your training. I wouldn't want to interfere in any way. Go on out and have your lunch."

Location: Schoolhouse, Greenshire
Date: 18 Barra, 135 AF

A week or so later Deaconess Willow decided to have Anoria describe life with Lady Cordelia to the class. It was important that the children learn what Anoria could and could not do with magic. She was still curious about the topic, anyway. Besides, the children would explain to their parents, and it might prevent the fear of magic from getting out of hand.

"Anoria, I want you to spend the next week thinking about what it's like to be a wizard's apprentice and then give a talk about it. Say on next fourth day. Perhaps you could tell us a little bit about how magic works. I'm sure we would all be interested."

Anoria blushed a bit. Some of the children were much more reserved around her than they had been. Maybe talking about it would help. So she nodded and said, "Yes, ma'am."

Location: Schoolhouse, Greenshire
Date: 25 Barra, 135 AF

On fourth day, Anoria stood when called upon, walked to the front of the room, and faced the class.

"I don't really know all that much yet," she admitted. "I just started last summer. No one really understands how magic works, anymore than why lightning happens or rain falls. Wizards have learned that if you do certain things with your mind and body, you end up with a spell that works." Anoria paused and looked at her notes. She thought about all the talks she'd had with Lady Cordelia this summer. "Some people say that the first spells were gifts of the gods, especially Zagrod or Pago. Others say that the first magic came from the natural mages or dragons. Wherever it started, eventually someone figured out how to write down instructions for preparing a spell. The instructions are very important because magic is much too dangerous to just do. A little too much of this or a little too much of that, and a spell that is supposed to let you read magic will turn you into a rutabaga."

The class laughed at that, and Anoria began to feel a little more at ease.

"Sometimes the symbols used to record a spell tell you how to hold your hand or your arms, but mostly they tell you where to put the lights." Anoria paused, wondering how to explain the lights. "When you first become a wizard's apprentice, the wizard who is teaching you uses a spell that makes a bunch of lights. They are all mixed together, and they pulse and move all around your body, but mostly around your head. You have to practice moving them and shaping them. Most of what is written down in a spell book is instructions for where to move the lights and how to shape them for a specific spell. After your teacher uses the training spell and you have learned to move the lights around a little bit, the wizard teaches you to arrange the lights in a pattern and has you do that again and again until you can do it even if you can't see the lights. That pattern puts you in training mode, which is just like the training spell, except only you can see the lights.

"While you're still learning to get into training mode, you start to learn the symbols of the magic language." In spite of Lady Cordelia's preference for practicing writing the symbols in the special wizard's ink, Anoria went to the blackboard and drew a big, odd-shaped circle on it. She immediately saw that it wasn't right and realized that it was because if she had been writing it in wizard's ink there would have been parts of the circle that were darker and others that were lighter. Too, there was supposed to be a little squiggly bit in the upper left quadrant that she didn't think anyone could do with chalk on a blackboard. "Oh, drat!" Anoria complained, "You really have to use wizard's ink to get it right. Anyway, this symbol—but not exactly—is almost a picture of one of the shapes you have to concentrate on to make the magic . . . I guess . . . pot, for the Practice spells. Lady Cordelia says that the pot collects and holds the magic that is used in the Practice spells. And the Practice spells can be used to clean stuff or flavor food." Anoria didn't mention that the practice spells were all almost the same except for the last little bit. It was that last little bit that changed them from a flavor spell to a cleaning spell or a light spell and so on.

After Anoria had finished her explanation of what she understood about how magic worked, there were several questions from the class. They wanted to know how many spells she could do, and she had to admit that she barely knew any. She was still working on the Practice spells.

CHAPTER 12

Location: Greenshire
Date: 15 Justain, 136 AF

Through the fall and into the snowy winter, Anoria stayed with the Cooper family and only visited Lady Cordelia a couple of days a week, when Cordelia came and retrieved her. Joanna's house, as Anoria thought of it, was made of whitewashed stone with a slate roof. It had a covered walkway from the house to the barn and was two stories tall. The heat from the kitchen fires aided in heating the upper floor, something Anoria was very grateful for this winter. This winter was the hardest, snowiest, and coldest anyone could remember, even the Widow Mead. Widow Mead was the oldest person in the village and had been born here.

In spite of the explanation she had given early in the school year, some of the villagers as much as accused her of causing the bad winter. Anoria thought that would be silly, even if she could control the weather. She had to walk to school in the cold every day just like other people did.

"This walk to the village is sort of a problem," Joanna muttered. "Who would have thought the snow would be this deep so early?"

"True," Anoria muttered back. "The next time Lady Cordelia comes back I'm going to see if there's a spell to remove snow." Anoria's nose was as red as Joanna's. They were trying to stomp a path to the road, but it was a long lane from the house to the road. "I hope the village has cleared at least some of the snow off the road by now."

Normally, Greenshire had only a couple of months of heavy snow. This winter snow had started early, even before the Timu's Time celebration.

"I never saw it this deep before," Joanna agreed. "And I hope I never see it this deep again."

"I just want to be able to get to school tomorrow," Anoria said. "I hope everyone is keeping warm in this mess."

Most houses in the little farming village were stone with thatch roofs but were neatly whitewashed. Prosperity had spread over the last few years. The school was also whitewashed. It had one classroom and a small office in one end. Deaconess Willow stayed with one of the village families, rotating between them every year.

There was a village green, with two lovely old maple trees, surrounded by a loop in the road. On the outside of the loop were market stalls that were used on market day and empty the rest of the week.

"I'll bet the roof of our stall has caved in under the weight," Joanna said. "We'll have to fix it, too. Mother will need it, come time for market. And I've been working on the rose products, too. I got enough beeswax, sheep fat, and attar of roses to make a nice face cream. You'll have to try it."

"I'll be happy to," Anoria said after a sniff. The cold made her nose run. "We're both going to be chapped to our bones, between the cold and the wind. Look. I think I see the intercessor's roof. That's it, isn't it?"

The intercessor's house was at the northeast corner next to the temple. While this was a farming village and the focus of worship was on Barra, the goddess of the harvest, the other gods of the pantheon each had their own niche with a statue of that god. Zagrod, the god of magic and knowledge, was there, kind of off to one side, not in a place of particular honor. Noron, the god of war, had a niche, also. There were lots more niches, which was just as well. There were a lot of gods.

Each family owned, and was expected to maintain, a market stall, whether they used it or not. Once upon a time all the houses had been in the village, but now several of them were located as much as a mile outside the village on one of the four roads. The wizard road led off to Brookshire to the east and Herinshire to the west. At Brookshire, the wizard road turned north to the town of Copriceshire, where much of the village's crops were sold. There was a dirt road that ran north and south to the farms and fields.

"Yes, thank Barra," Joanna said. "If we've gotten this close, we should be able to make it into the village from here. Papa wants to know how much damage there is. And I want to stop by the temple, too. Papa always says that snow is good for the fields, but I think we've had enough for now, so an offering to Estormany is probably in order." Estormany, the goddess of weather, was fickle and quick to anger. Estormany was quite capable of keeping right on snowing till she was properly thanked for her gifts. "And I'd like to see if I can get Barra to smile on my efforts with the roses."

"Fine with me," Anoria said. "I'll light a candle to Zagrod while we're there." Anoria was always in search of knowledge. Zagrod was the god of wizardry and knowledge, so she had begun lighting candles in appreciation of his gifts.

"Joanna," Anoria said, when they finally reached the village, "is that Laurence walking the ridgepole of the temple? In the dead of winter? With ice on the roof?"

"You would think," Joanna said, "that the son of Barra's intercessor would be a little less . . . boyish. What does he think he's doing up there?" Laurence had red hair and freckles and was a well-known mischief-maker. He seemed determined to get in hot water every chance he got. Joanna had always liked him, trouble maker or not.

"I imagine someone dared him again," Anoria answered. "Remember last year? When he jumped off the cliff that overlooks the Garnet's pond. It's a wonder he didn't break his neck, it really is. That boy is trouble on two feet, Lady Cordelia would say. I'll bet, in two or three years, Lady Cordelia will catch him trying to find the house." Laurence was a trial to his parents, a vexation to his teachers. The girls had heard it said more than once.

"Probably," Joanna agreed. "He's just a mess. And if she does catch him, she ought to turn him into something really good. Like one of those nunkees you told me about."

"Monkeys, Joanna, monkeys. You're right. If ever a boy was a monkey, it's Laurence. He's nothing like Gregory, is he?" Gregory was Joanna's step-cousin, through Tess' marriage in Brookshire. A studious, quiet boy, Gregory had impressed both girls with his learning.

"Laurence dunked Aslinn Jaeger's braids in the inkwell." Joanna giggled. "She threw a fit! You should have seen it." Aslinn Jaeger's father, Adolf, was one of the more prosperous farmers in the village. Aslinn's long, blond braids were her pride and joy. Having the tips stained with ink made of oak galls and soot had not made her happy.

"There's no telling about him, there just isn't." Anoria grinned.

Laurence was often a joy to the other students. He was a clown. Sometimes Anoria could almost forgive him for putting the snake down her shirt. He was not always a very original clown, and it had to be said that his taste in humor wasn't very highbrow. In fact, it was quite the opposite. He was the boy who put frogs in teachers' desks and snakes in the outhouse. In spite of that, he was a fairly good student and often scored high in the weekly tests.

CHAPTER 13

Location: Cooper Home, Greenshire
Date: 5 Zagrod, 136 AF

Anoria returned from a late spring weekend at Lady Cordelia's with a fine evinwood box about four inches long by five inches wide and two inches tall. Joanna was extremely curious about it but didn't open it, just in case it might turn her purple or something.

"Just leave it alone." Anoria grinned. "You'll see tomorrow at school."

Location: Schoolhouse, Greenshire
Date: 6 Zagrod, 136 AF

All the children seemed to have spring fever today. Deaconess Willow was becoming quite annoyed. During the long, hard winter, the children tended to be relatively quiet and happy to be in the classroom. Now, though, with bright sunshine, several of the boys were fidgeting in their seats and disrupting the classes.

"Ow," Joanna Cooper shouted. Deaconess Willow looked up to see that Joanna had stood up and turned to face the boy who sat in back of her.

"What is the problem this time?" Deaconess Willow glared around the room. "Has Laurence poked you or something, Joanna?"

Laurence had already been in trouble twice this day. Once more and Deaconess Willow would send him to stand in the corner and make another report to his father. Not so surprisingly, considering that Laurence was a popular boy, Joanna shook her head. "No, ma'am. It was a bug that bit my arm."

Deaconess Willow accepted the rather lame excuse this time. She didn't really approve of Intercessor Firebird's chosen method of discipline, anyway. Forcing a child to pray for long periods of time seemed to guarantee that the child wouldn't turn to the gods in his adult life. Still, the children needed to settle down. Perhaps another test would work.

Just as she was about to tell the children to get ready for a history test, Anoria raised her hand. "Yes, Anoria?"

"I have an example of how magic works to show the class," Anoria said.

Deaconess Willow was grateful for the distraction. "Well, then, why don't you come up to the front and show us?"

"Yes, ma'am."

The girl got up, carrying an evinwood box engraved with what appeared to be magical runes. Deaconess Willow began to get just a bit nervous. Who knew what magic boxes contained?

Then Anoria began to speak, and Deaconess Willow began to get a little more nervous.

"It turns out that in magic, it's easier to animate something that used to be alive, and it's even easier to animate something that used to be animated. So wood is easier to animate than stone, and bones or skin are easier to animate than wood. That's why it's easier to animate a skeleton than it is to make a golem."

Uh oh, Deaconess Willow thought. Then realized that the box couldn't be big enough for a humanoid skeleton. But it might hold a pixie skeleton. Oh, dear. But it was too late to stop this now. And for the first time today, the children weren't fidgeting in their seats.

"Lady Cordelia animated this to give me practice in controlling skeletons," Anoria said, opening the box. And over the rim peeked the skull of a frog. It opened its mouth as though to ribbit, but no sound emerged.

All the boys laughed, and some of the girls screamed. Anoria put her hand out, and the frog skeleton hopped from the box into her hand. "This is Lord Ribbit," she said, grinning. "He doesn't even have the brains of a frog, just sort of what's left of the habits of a frog. Left on his own, he'll find a sunny spot and just sit there. And if a fly happens by, he'll open his mouth as though he were trying to grab it with his tongue. But, of course, he doesn't have a tongue anymore. But since he's animated and controlled by magic, I can make him do things."

With that, the frog skeleton sat up on his hind legs and his tail bone and waved his front legs in the air. The children laughed and started shouting various actions they wanted to see it perform. It presumably performed those actions that Anoria heard and had consented to, waving one front leg then another, ducking its head, that sort of thing, while Deaconess Willow and the children watched, fascinated.

"Lady Cordelia," Anoria continued, "explained to me that when something dies not much of it is left with the body. Just sort of the habits and the instincts. Of course, the poor frog never had that much more than habits and instincts to begin with. But awareness and understanding go back to the gods. So skeletons make useful tools for magic."

Deaconess Willow was glad that the time had come to send the children home. It had been a long, hard day, right up to the end.

CHAPTER 14

Location: Greenwood
Date: 2 Pago, 136 AF

"I'm so glad to be back here," Anoria said. School was out for the summer, and Anoria had turned twelve over the winter. Now she was looking forward to a summer of magic. "Away from boys and snakes and stuff like that."

Anoria didn't mention that some of the villagers were afraid of her. A little of their fear had rubbed off on her. In spite of the fact that she knew better, she was a little bit afraid that Lady Cordelia would do something drastic if she found out how they had acted, especially after she'd brought the frog bones to school. The children, at least the boys, had loved it, but among the adults there was a strong belief that a wizard who used bones was not a good wizard.

Cordelia stifled a smile. She'd had quite a briefing from Debra on the snake incident from shortly after Anoria went back to school. And the punched nose, for that matter. She knew about the reaction to the frog skeleton, too, and it didn't surprise her in the least. But skeletons and once-living objects were too useful a part of magic to be left out of a wizard's training, no matter what those prigs at the university in Kronisburg thought. Or what a bunch of ignorant villagers thought, for that matter.

"Well, this summer, we ought to get started on more of your training. But first, we'll take a quick trip to Kronisburg tomorrow. They have the best supplies there. And I'm running low on ink, anyway."

"Can't we just make ink? That's what we do for school," Anoria said. "It works."

"Not for spell books, it won't. The ink in a spell book needs to be especially sensitive to magic. The ink has to flow just the right way or you get blotches and can end up misreading the spell," Cordelia explained. "And you have to have special paper too. It has to be very smooth. Anyway, you've been practicing drawing runes all winter, so we need to get more of both."

Location: Kronisburg, Doichry
Date: 3 Pago, 136 AF

Kronisburg, in the nation of Doichry, was the most exciting, busiest place Anoria had ever dreamed of. It was a university town, and Cordelia seemed to know dozens and dozens of people. As they wandered through the cobbled streets surrounded by buildings—some of them five or even six stories tall—people would bow to Cordelia. Cordelia had dressed up for the trip, too. She was wearing a fancy gown with purple embroidery around the edges.

Their first stop was at a spice merchant's shop, much to Anoria's surprise.

Cordelia stepped into the shop and looked around as the shop owner bowed. "There," Cordelia said firmly, "that should do quite nicely." She pointed at a section of wall, one of the few that didn't have shelves full of spices against it. She opened her purse and pulled out a cloth. Anoria knew it was the doorway to one of Cordelia's spells. In fact, it was a spell that Cordelia had developed since Anoria had become her apprentice. It was a variation on the Spare Room spell but with a portable door. Cordelia's Portable Pantry, as she called it, held quite a lot. It was a woven doorway on a cloth but when it was hung, the door could be opened and led to a small room full of shelves. It wasn't a room in the real world, but like the spare room that Cordelia had created for Anoria and Joanna, it was connected to a spot in the real world so didn't totally disappear when the spell was turned off. It just sort of waited till the spell was activated again.

Cordelia waved her hand and a Servant spell hung the door against the wall. Cordelia made a little gesture, and the image of the door on the tapestry opened. Cordelia walked into the pantry and picked up a box. One whole wall of the pantry was filled with boxes of nutmeg.

Lady Cordelia brought the box out, set it on the counter, and opened the lid, letting the aroma of fresh nutmeg fill the shop. Then she smiled at the spice merchant—who had been watching with what looked to Anoria to be considerable consternation—and said, "I have fourteen more boxes just like this. Do you want them, or should I see if Krop and Sons is interested?"

When Cordelia was finished dickering with the merchant, he gave her a stack of gold coins. Anoria had never, until that moment, seen a gold coin in her life.

"You see," Cordelia explained when they got back to the street, "that's one of the ways I make money. I pop to a tiny island I know and I buy the spices for just a little bit of money. Then I bring it here, or to some other places, and sell it for a lot of money. The islanders are happy to sell it, and the merchants are happy to buy it."

"I wondered sometimes," Anoria admitted. "I knew you were rich, I just didn't know where it all came from."

"Lots of places," Cordelia said. "And I'll teach you all about them over the years. But right now, we need to go in here." Cordelia indicated a large, brightly lit shop.

The shop was amazing. There were wizard lights every few feet and magical items in a big counter made of glass. There were packets of every sort of magical ingredient: dried crystallized dragon's blood was next to the powdered bones of a hippogriff. There was even eye of newt. There was a case of enchanted scrolls, and a stack of flying carpets—not flying at the moment, of course.

Anoria had never had any money to speak of, but Cordelia's dickering with the merchant had her determined to learn more about it. After all, some day she was going to have to make a living too. Joanna had already made a start, what with her musk rose products. Anoria didn't want to get behind her friend or to be a burden on Lady Cordelia.

Because she was paying attention, Anoria was horrified at the cost of the paper and ink Cordelia bought. Cordelia handed the merchant the biggest part of the stack of coins she had gotten from the first merchant. Then, glancing around, she commented, "This place is even more crowded than the spice merchant's shop. Isn't there a bit of blank wall anywhere?"

"I have some blank walls in the back room," the shop owner said. "But why?"

"I need to hang my door to put this stuff away."

The shop owner blinked a bit but led the way to the backroom, and Cordelia repeated the business with the portable pantry.

The shop owner, a magic user himself, was even more impressed by the portable pantry than the spice merchant had been. Actually, it seemed to Anoria that the magic shop owner was more knowing of the spell itself. The spice merchant was impressed with the portable pantry, but he would have felt the same about a Light spell or Servant spell he hadn't seen before. The magic user, as would be any knowledgeable magic user, was impressed by the structure of the spell.

* * *

"Wow," was all Anoria could say, as she and Cordelia left the shop.

"Wow, what?" Cordelia asked.

"I didn't realize paper and ink were so expensive."

"Quality costs a bit." Cordelia shrugged. "It's mostly the ink, not the paper, you understand. The ink that is used in a spell book needs to be of specific colors and retain its vibrancy without fading. If you visualize a symbol that is supposed to be red but has faded to pink, you could blow yourself up. Only a few people make wizard's ink, and they're very secretive about their process. From what I understand, they use magic moss in making it. I'm not sure that's true, but that's what they say. So it's expensive, and it's a fact of life for a wizard. But then, we're very well paid for what we do."

"Do you think we could figure out how to make our own?" Anoria asked.

"I doubt it. There is something special about the colors of wizard's ink, and it never fades. Don't worry about it right now. You've got to try the food here. It's much, much different from what you have back in Greenshire."

Location: Greenwood

Date: 7 Pago, 136 AF

Over the next few days, Anoria was haunted by the amount of very expensive ink she had used over the winter. She hadn't known how expensive it was at the time. Still, now that she knew how much it cost, she felt guilty with every mark she made. She hated to use up any more of the ink in practice.

"Lady Cordelia?"

"Yes," Cordelia answered.

"Couldn't I practice runes on a slate? I just hate to use up so much of this expensive ink."

"No, dear, that isn't the way it works, I'm afraid. You have to use the correct paper, the correct ink, and the correct pen. You write differently on a slate and develop the wrong habits. Then, when you're recording a spell for real, you end up pressing too hard or not hard enough. When you read it in a hurry, you make mistakes in crafting the spell, and that can be deadly."

Anoria nodded at that. Cornelia had explained that spell-crafting focused on accuracy and speed, in that order. She had also said that for an adventuring wizard both were essential. The books that you read from as you crafted the spells had to be totally accurate and completely clear and legible.

"Why this sudden concern over money, anyway?" Cordelia asked.

"It seems that training me is costing you an awful lot of money. And I know that wizards are generally paid a great deal to take on apprentices. But the Bodens didn't pay you anything to take me on, and, well, you've done so much for me already. I don't want to cost you so much," Anoria said. The cost of the paper and ink had been preying on her mind for days. Yet Cordelia continued to insist that she practice the rune drawing every day.

"Anoria, if you were a seamstress' apprentice, the seamstress would be providing fabric for you to practice on, correct?"

Anoria nodded. Fabric was expensive too. But fabric scraps could still be used, not thrown away or burnt, like the paper.

"And if you were a baker's apprentice, you'd have to learn to bake, so the baker would furnish you with flour, yeast, and eggs, right?"

Anoria nodded again.

"So, you see, this is merely a part of training costs. As to the Bodens not paying me, well, I chose you as an apprentice because of your mind and talents. And I'd rather spend the ink than waste the mind. Yes, wizard training is very expensive, largely because of the cost of the special ink. But, in the end you will be a fully trained wizard, and that is what I want."

"You're sure?" Anoria asked. "Because it seems just terrible to me. From what I've seen, just one simple, very simple, spell must cost more than a hundred gold pieces, and Mr. Miller sold a good milking cow for less than three gold pieces. The Servant spell, for example. You just gave away two amulets of Servant spell last year. How can you afford to do that? And how would I ever craft enough Servant spells to pay the cost of the ink? How will I ever pay for the cost of my training? A tailor's apprentice works for his master for seven years, learning. And in all that time, he's making money, at least some, for his master. How will I ever make you money instead of costing you money?"

That was a good question. Cordelia had used several magical items and a unique spell to pay for her studies at the university. That was a much quicker payoff than average. "Anoria, the cost isn't what is important here. What's important is that I pass on my knowledge. That's why I took you on as an apprentice, not to make a profit off you. Anyone who is willing to solve puzzles like you are is fully capable of becoming a wizard. It's my job to see you learn to be the best wizard you can be." That was both true and not true. Cordelia did care about preserving her magical knowledge, but she had come to care for the little, blonde waif with the serious expression.

It took a while to convince Anoria that Cordelia simply wasn't worried about the cost of her training. Cordelia decided not to mention that she was considering sending Anoria to the university in a few years, but she had to go into some detail about the way she made money, as well, before Anoria understood. While she was explaining it, Cordelia began to realize that, for wizardry as a whole, the expense of training was a "very bad thing." The cost limited the number of apprentices one could train, and the cost of training at the wizard's college at the University of Kronisburg limited that sort of education to the very wealthy. And that was the main reason that the cost of having wizardry done was so very, very high. It was something Cordelia had always known, but hadn't thought about that much, not in many years.

Cordelia began to consider the future. What would Anoria do to make a living? It took years for any wizard to learn the Translocation spell, so Anoria couldn't take advantage of things like the cheap spices the way Cordelia did. In fact, most of the spells that made Cordelia rich were very high-level spells.

It took the intensity of adventuring to gain levels quickly. As Cordelia had come to know Anoria and to love her, she had also come to realize that Anoria would never make a good combat wizard. Anoria really liked people. She could get angry with them, just like anyone. But even at her most angry, she didn't want them hurt.

Adventuring, fighting wars, and killing people, even bad people, would hurt something deep inside Anoria. As bad as that was, what scared Cordelia was that the very kindness in Anoria's nature might well make her hesitate at the wrong moment and be killed. Would Anoria, who didn't have the temperament to adventure, ever gain the power to be able to train another apprentice? Cordelia doubted it.

CHAPTER 15

Location: Cooper Home, Greenshire
Date: 17 Barra, 136 AF

Another summer with Cordelia had passed, and Anoria was back in school in Greenshire. She had learned the Practice spells over the summer, and she was in the process of learning to use their weak magic.

"He's a menace," Anoria fumed as Joanna wiped at the spreading stain on Anoria's blouse.

Joanna hid a smile. "Who?"

"You know very well that I'm talking about Laurence Firebird," Anoria said. "The snake last year was bad enough, but this is just too much. Not only did he get ink in my hair, but he got it all over my shirt."

"You did trip him, Anoria," Joanna pointed out. "You really can't claim that it's all his fault, not when you tripped him." Joanna was rather fond of Laurence in a way. He often made her laugh.

"I wasn't trying to trip him, was I?" Anoria said, defensively. "It's not my fault that he was trying to sneak up behind me. I just tried to stand up. He's the one who was in the way."

Laurence Firebird had become the bane of Anoria's existence. Deaconess Willow had had each of the older children go over what they had learned over the summer. The smith's apprentice had described that the metal needed to be glowing different colors for different things. When it was Anoria's turn, Deaconess Willow had even had Anoria demonstrate a Practice spell for the class. Laurence had interpreted that to mean that Anoria was still "just a girl" and had picked on her, playing a number of pranks. Then he'd decided to try the old braid-in-the-inkwell trick. Anoria had moved suddenly, and Laurence had dumped the inkwell down the back of her shirt instead. It was a new shirt too. Pale blue, her favorite color. Now it was ruined with an ink stain.

"I'm going to get even," Anoria muttered. "Somehow."

Joanna had been trying not to giggle. Doing her best to keep a straight face, she asked, "How?"

"I'd give him warts if I could," Anoria muttered, finally beginning to see the humor. "I just can't yet."

"Does he know that?"

Anoria felt as though a light had dawned. She had given her talk, but she might be able to convince Laurence that she hadn't demonstrated everything. "No, I don't suppose he does. I can do a couple of little things now. I could make it seem like his lunch was overspiced. That one is easy."

"So that's what you do," Joanna suggested. "Overspice his lunch tomorrow. Then whisper that if he doesn't leave you alone, you're going to give him a great big wart on his nose. That ought to do it, don't you think?"

"Maybe," Anoria said. "Maybe. Meanwhile, I think I can get this stain out with the Cleaning spell. I'll try it when we get home." The Cleaning spell was one of the practice spells and as such it was crafted in almost the same way as the other practice spells, like the flavor spell. Anoria couldn't contain spells yet. She had to craft a spell and cast it as soon as it was crafted, or keep concentrating on it until she cast it.

* * *

Anoria was appalled. "Oh my," she said. "I didn't know it would do that."

Instead of removing the ink stain, her Clean spell—one of the practice spells—had spread it even further over the new shirt. It was lighter in color, but the blackish ink didn't do anything for the light blue shirt. "Oh my."

"It was ruined to begin with," Debra comforted. "Really it was. There's just not a lot a person can do with that nasty ink. Oak galls and soot just don't want to come out."

"But it was new," Anoria wailed. "And now I'll have to wear a stained shirt all year."

"Maybe if you tried it again," Joanna suggested. "If you could keep spreading the stain, you might be able to make it even all over the shirt and have a darker blue."

"I'll try it," Anoria muttered. "In a couple of days."

"Why a couple of days?"

"I can only do one Practice spell at a time," Anoria explained. "I'm still not very good at it, so it takes a long time to get ready. And I've already got a use for tomorrow's spell." The glint in Anoria's eyes was a little scary. "I'm going to fix Laurence Firebird."

Debra decided that this was one of the things that a parent was just better off not knowing and left the kitchen rapidly. Besides, Laurence Firebird was a menace. Really.

Location: Schoolhouse, Greenshire
Date: 18 Barra, 136 AF

Anoria planned it carefully. She waited until Laurence and his friends were sitting in their favorite place next to the school wall, in the sun. Then she cast the Flavor spell. Laurence had just taken a big bite of his ham and cheese on bread. After a couple of chews, he spit it out, gagging. "Gah! Phooey!" he yelled. "What's wrong with this? It's awful. Gah!"

Anoria smiled and waited until the bell rang, watching Laurence dance around and gag. As they were walking into the building, she slipped up behind him. "I did it, Laurence. And I'll do it again. What's more, if you say one word, try one more thing, I'm going to put a great, big, gigantic, hairy wart right on the tip of your nose. Leave me alone, or else."

Laurence's face paled a bit.

"I mean it," Anoria warned. "I'll do it. Try me."

The words "try me" were a mistake. Anoria knew it as soon as they slipped out. Laurence was not easily intimidated and was incapable of backing down from a dare. Anoria had just dared him.

His eyes glittered a bit. "I'll fix you," Laurence promised. "Just you wait. I'll fix you."

Location: Schoolhouse, Greenshire
Date: 24 Barra, 136 AF

Anoria was nervous all the next week. Laurence had promised to get even. He would, she knew. It was just a matter of waiting for it. Several of the other children were egging him on as well. They wouldn't do anything themselves, but they were perfectly willing to think up pranks for Laurence to pull. "Let's head home, Joanna," she said. "He's gone, I think. And we've got things to do. We can't stay here all night."

"About time," Joanna said. "He's been gone at least a half hour, and we need to get home." Joanna was almost jiggling with impatience.

The girls slipped out of the school's front door and began the walk home. They walked faster than normal because they knew Debra would worry if they were late. As they hurried, they forgot to be on the lookout for Laurence.

* * *

"Here they come," Laurence whispered. "Wally, hand me that bucket."

"She's going to be really mad," Wally warned. "Just leave me out of it. I got you the pig stuff, but I'm not going to throw it, not at a wizard. You'll have to do your own dirty work."

"Shh. Just another few seconds."

As Anoria and Joanna walked past the large shrub, Laurence stepped out behind them and dashed the pig manure that filled the bucket all over Anoria.

Anoria turned slowly around, her eyes flashing fire. Laurence laughed like a maniac.

Joanna shouted, "You rat! I didn't have anything to do with it." Joanna's clothes were liberally spattered with the same smelly mixture that covered Anoria.

"I will get you for this, Laurence Firebird," Anoria promised. "I will get you for this."

CHAPTER 16

Location: Schoolhouse, Greenshire
Date: 18 Banth, 137 AF

The war had continued throughout the year with only occasional tense truces. Laurence had treated it as a competition with rules. He had not blamed Anoria for the things that happened by chance, like when he got kicked by a cow in the Mason's field. He could have done so, but he was a fair boy. As the son of the intercessor of Barra, Laurence could probably have caused her a lot more trouble with the villagers. Instead, he had insisted that she hadn't caused it because she couldn't. She wasn't that powerful a wizard.

In return, Anoria had not told on him when he pulled his stunts. This "war with rules" had continued past both their thirteenth birthdays and had just about worn Deaconess Willow to a thread.

"So you see, Lady Cordelia, they declared war on one another," Deaconess Willow explained. "Normally these little battles last a week or so and then go away. But not this time, I'm afraid."

"I had some concerns," Cordelia said. "Debra told me that Anoria was constantly in trouble this year, always coming home with something all over her. I just didn't know if she was having trouble because of the wizard training or not."

"Not entirely," Margaret Willow said. "In a way, the war might even have helped. Several of the other children are afraid of her, reflecting the attitudes of their parents. They urge Laurence on, but don't get involved themselves." Deaconess Willow shook her head. "Laurence is a scamp and a troublemaker, but he's honorable in his way. He actually defends her. He insists that she couldn't do the things some of the children accuse her of, because if she could, she'd have done them to him.

"I do have some concerns of my own. Just how much can Anoria do with her magic? It wouldn't be a good thing if she were able to blast Laurence into dust, for instance. And since several other children were affected by her, ah, misdirecting the magic, I feel I really need to know what to expect. Those Practice spells were quite bad enough to deal with. Frankly, another year like the one just past will have me going crazy."

Cordelia stifled a laugh. Deaconess Willow looked worn out, and it wouldn't be at all nice to laugh at her. But Deaconess Willow began to grin a bit, herself. Both women began laughing.

"I must say," Deaconess Willow said with a bit of a hiccup, "that it was an interesting year. They did, at least, limit their antics to the schoolyard, after the ink incident. Laurence even thanked Anoria once. He said he could now eat anything, whether it was dried worms or three-day-old fish guts. They finally declared a truce about a month ago."

Cordelia wiped a few tears of laughter from her eyes. "You needn't worry, Deaconess Willow. It will be a few years before Anoria can do any real damage to anyone. Not that I think she would. I'll have a talk with her this summer, though. At least she got plenty of use out of the Practice spells."

Location: Greenwood
Date: 18 Estormany, 137 AF

It had been a busy summer. Anoria had gone beyond the Practice spells and learned other sub-spells and spell components. She was practicing making magical items. Cordelia wanted Anoria to have a solid base of knowledge. Cordelia was keeping her busy studying magical theory. They had made half a dozen short trips throughout the summer, but they were working trips, not holidays. This close to Anoria's return to school, Cordelia wanted her to have a real break from work.

"How goes the study?" Cordelia asked. She and Anoria were having lunch in the garden. Anoria had set her books aside for the moment and fallen on lunch as though she was starving.

"Not bad," Anoria mumbled through a bite of bread. She paused a moment and swallowed before continuing. "Not bad. The Practice spells only take a few minutes to prepare now. Of course, I had a lot of chances to use them this year."

"You and Laurence aren't going to have another war, are you? Because Deaconess Willow is a very good school mistress, and I wouldn't like having to find another."

Anoria shook her head. "No. We gave it up as a bad job. It's just as well, too. I was having trouble finding something else to make his food taste bad. We agreed. No more war."

"Good." Cordelia sat for a moment, enjoying the late summer day. "Now, we haven't done anything but study all summer. Time for a treat, I think. Is there any place you'd like to go or do?"

"Anything is fine with me," Anoria answered. "But Joanna is after me to ask you about more fragrant flowers she can grow. Her rose scents are going well, but she'd like another one. So far she's got roses, lavender, and rosemary in her garden. Can we go and see if she can come?"

"I don't see why not. And the University of Honth has a marvelous botanical garden. I expect she'd enjoy a trip there."

Location: University of Honth
Date: 20 Estormany, 137 AF

"Oh my," Joanna said. "What is that?"

"It's called a greenhouse," Lers Hammond explained. "In the winter, when it's cold, the glass lets in light but keeps the wind out. So we can grow unusual blooms, even in the dead of winter."

"Does it ever get cold?"

"It does at night," Lers said. "But the university allows wizards to attend, after all. Those students, to help pay their expenses, come and use heating spells in the winter. The university pays them, and it helps pay for their ink, you understand."

"Oh my."

Lers Hammond smiled down at the girl. She had no wizard talent at all, but he'd rarely met a young girl with such a knowledge of, and interest in, plants. She could only be about fourteen, judging from her looks.

"Lady Cordelia says that you've been making perfumes," Lers said. "And that you've become quite good at it."

Joanna nodded. "I enjoy them a lot. And it doesn't hurt that I've managed to acquire a dowry by making and selling scents, either. But I'd like to branch out a bit. Perhaps grow some unusual herbs, make other perfumes, that sort of thing. Do you have anything different that would grow in Greenshire? The town is a bit north of here."

"Quite a bit north, I'm told," Lers grinned. "Lady Cordelia mentioned that. There are a few things you might be able to grow up there in the wilds of the north. But you'll have to dig them up and keep them inside over the winter. Otherwise the cold will kill them."

Joanna smiled up at the scholar. "Just give me directions. I'll follow them."

"Well," Lers muttered. "I do have an excess of lily of the valley pips. Perhaps they might grow there. Go ahead and plant them when you get home, since they're resistant to cold. As well, I have some culinary herbs that come from the far south. There's one called bazil. It has quite an unusual flavor. And a very spicy scent. Let's go see. You won't be able to plant the seeds yet, of course. It's nearly fall, and these plants can't take a freeze. Planting them will have to wait for spring."

Location: Greenshire
Date: 2 Barra, 137 AF

On the first day of school, Anoria wondered if Laurence really intended to avoid another war. As it turned out, he didn't want another war, but a contest was in the offing.

Laurence, as the son of Intercessor Firebird, was forced to undertake studies over the summer, and Anoria, as apprentice to Cordelia, had also spent the summer with books and study. A side effect was that very early in the school year, the two of them were vying to be the head of the class.

Deaconess Willow was happy that neither of them were covered in muck or starving from spoiled-tasting food, but she began to wonder if she could keep up with their thirst for knowledge. They had turned their war into a friendly competition, and each had advantages. Anoria'd had trips to the other parts of the world and so could give lectures on the geography and culture of other places. Though Laurence didn't enjoy it, he had a solid knowledge of the Amonrai pantheon and the legends of the various gods. Both had a solid base in mathematics. They had caught up with and even passed students a year older than they.

Deaconess Willow put their knowledge to good use. Both Anoria and Laurence lectured the young scholars on magic, geography, and mathematics, which gave Deaconess Willow more time to help her struggling scholars. The whole class, from the youngest to the oldest, did especially well that year, because Laurence was a natural leader, and his interest in study infected the whole school.

* * *

Joanna longed for spring. Snow-covered fields and roads, while pretty enough, didn't satisfy her need for growing things. It wouldn't even have to be a flowering plant, if only she could grow something during the winters.

So she snuck books on plants to school and often read them while she was supposed to be reading, oh, a history lesson or a geography lesson. This particular book might help her, since it was all about plants that grew in the far away, frozen south. She had borrowed it from Aunt Cordelia on a weekend trip back to Greenwood with Anoria.

"Ahem."

Oh, rats, Joanna thought. "Yes, ma'am?"

Caught, Joanna knew. Deaconess Willow, with her sneaky, silent walk, was standing right at her shoulder, with a full view of the book Joanna was hiding in her geography text.

"Are you studying the continent of Centraium, Joanna?" Deaconess Willow asked.

"Um. I'd finished that section, ma'am."

"Did you?" Deaconess Willow asked a couple of questions about Centraium, which Joanna—luckily for her—knew the answer to.

Joanna wasn't sure if the deaconess was pleased that she knew the material or was upset by it.

"Very good, Joanna. Now, why don't you go up to the front of the class and tell us all about plants of the southern wastes?"

Joanna complied, knowing that argument would only make this more difficult. She rose and walked up front, carrying the book so she would have pictures to show the other students.

"Off the south coast of the Orclands are a series of islands where it snows and rains most of the year," she started. "The summers are very short and happen in the middle of our winter. There's a kind of plant there that grows in frozen ground. In the summertime—their summertime—it builds up a big ball like a giant potato. But when the snows come, it eats its own potato to live through the winter." This was about all that Joanna had so far learned about the frozen Janis plant. So she took the easy way out, turned her book's pages toward the other students, and began to show them various pictures.

It was a near thing, and Joanna didn't quite escape unscathed. Mistress Willow assigned her to lecture on the continent of Centraium the next week.

CHAPTER 17

Location: Cooper Home, Greenshire
Date: 9 Banth, 137 AF

"You're sure it's not too early?" Anoria asked. "It does get a lot cooler at night, you know."

"Professor Hammond said that if I put a blanket or something over the seedlings at night that they ought to make it," Joanna explained. "So that's what I'm going to do. He said that the blanket will protect them from the frost, which is what kills the seedlings."

Anoria and Joanna had dug the plot they were working on in the middle of Cashi last fall. Now that it was Banth the days were warm, but the nights could still frost. They had built up foot high sides to the north, east and west of the small plot. "Lers said to protect them from wind," Joanna said. "It never occurred to me to do that. The southern exposure will keep them warm in the day, and the walls will keep the wind off. It can't hurt to try."

Anoria shrugged. "Fine with me. He certainly knows more about gardening than I do. What's next?"

"We've already planted the bazil. Next we'll try that tomatum thing. Professor Hammond says it's good to eat. He even gave me a recipe for something called . . . ah . . . splageti, I think. You remember, we had it for lunch that day. It was good. If I get enough tomatums, I'll try it. It uses the bazil, as well as garlic."

"Whatever you say."

Location: Cooper Home, Greenshire
Date: 14 Pago, 137 AF

"It looks like worms," Michael insisted. "I'm not going to eat worms." Michael's face was stubborn, but Debra noticed that he had a twinkle in his eyes. She, in turn, hid her grin and let him tease their daughter.

"It's made of eggs, wheat, and salt, Papa," Joanna said with a touch of exasperation. "It's not worms, but just another way to use wheat. We ate splageti down in Honth last summer. If you'll just try a taste, I'll bet you'll like it."

"Why can't we just have bread from the wheat?" Michael wanted to know.

"We can. We are, Michael," Debra said. "And yes, it doesn't look like turnips, I know that. But it smells good, and the girls have worked very hard on it. Just take a bite, will you?"

Michael muttered some more. The plate of white, wormy-looking things had a red sauce of some sort, but it did smell good. "It still looks like worms."

Location: Greenwood
Date: 15 Pago, 137 AF

"And then he said 'it still looks like worms.' " Anoria giggled. She was back at Greenwood after a weekend with the Coopers, while Cordelia spent the weekend adding a few hundred more yards to the wizard road. "But once he tasted it, he ate every bit and went back for seconds."

"I've often felt that Greenshire would benefit from a little more culture." Lady Cordelia put on a severe face. "Locking oneself into habits is not a good thing, after all. And, truth be told, I've never been all that fond of turnips." Cordelia was a bit tired from pushing herself to finish that dratted road. Some days she wished she'd never agreed to tie so much of Whitehall County together with wizard road, but it was useful. Anoria was always going on about how much better Cordelia's roads were than the dirt roads.

"Turnips are easy to grow," Anoria pointed out. "And they taste a bit better after frost, for that matter. And they keep just as well as the cabbages do. The tomatums will all die when the first frost hits, and they're no good for winter storage. Professor Hammond says they get all mushy and rotted. But Joanna is planning to save the seeds so she can grow them again next year. What she really wants is a greenhouse, like at the university in Honth. She says she could grow the tomatums and all sorts of flowers all year round."

"Well, she could always use a Breadkeeper to keep the tomatums fresh," Cordelia said. "But making glass by magic is a fairly high-level spell. There are people who make it without magic, but it's very expensive even so."

"As expensive as a Breadkeeper?" Anoria asked. "You know almost no one can afford a Breadkeeper."

"What about drying the tomatums," Cordelia suggested. "The elves slice their meat thin and dry it in the sun. So do the orcs. So I wonder what would happen with the tomatums."

"Every time you wonder something, we wind up with a pile of work, you know."

Cordelia grinned. "Nothing comes easy. I just wondered what would happen if Joanna sliced up the tomatums and dried them in the sun. Then, when she wanted to make the splageti sauce, she'd just have to add water. The same thing goes for the bazil, as well. Dry some of it this summer, just like the beans. See what happens."

"Can't hurt to try," Anoria agreed. "It turned out that after we had the splageti and Michael told people about it, they all wanted a taste. Joanna took a huge pot of splageti as her dish for the midsummer festival. Almost everybody liked it. Well, once they got over the worm thing, anyway.

"Aren't there any simpler spells for making glass?" Anoria went on. "Maybe a spell to turn stone into glass? Or to make stone clear?"

"Not that I'm aware of," Cordelia said. "The spells to make stone, or to shape stone, are fairly complicated, difficult spells. And making anything transparent on a permanent basis is fairly high-level magic. But I'll check the library, and we can look into the possibilities next summer."

CHAPTER 18

Location: Cooper Home, Greenshire
Date: 3 Barra, 137 AF

Anoria straightened her new dress and began to comb her hair. "First day of school again, Joanna. I'm glad to get back."

Joanna saw the mess Anoria was making of her attempted hairdo and took the brush and pins away. She began combing it herself and soon had Anoria's hair neatly arranged. "There," Joanna smiled. "You're just hopeless at hair, you know."

"Yes, I know," Anoria sighed. "And my hair is so dull-colored, too. I'd give anything to have yours instead. That black hair of yours is just beautiful."

And it was. Joanna's hair had always been beautiful, thick, curly, and raven dark. In fact, Joanna was beautiful, as far as Anoria was concerned. They had both grown a few inches in the last year, but Joanna was beginning to curve, while Anoria was still, as she said, built like a stick. "How is it that we're the same age? Both of us are fourteen years old, and you look like a lady while I still look like a little girl."

"Different girls grow at different speeds, Mother says," Joanna answered. "And there's nothing wrong with your hair color, either. The sun has lightened it very nicely. Now, here, try some of this." Joanna held out a container of scented cream. "This is new. I decided to try adding some other herbs, so this one has some rosemary extract. Aunt Cordelia quite likes it."

Anoria took a dab of the cream on her finger and sniffed. "Oh. I like this scent too. It's sort of fresh smelling. Where does it go?"

"On your hands, silly. Maybe that cream will help take out those ink stains. And use more than that. How was your summer, by the way? You got here so late last night that we didn't get to talk at all."

"Oh, wonderful," Anoria said. "We went to a lot of places and met a lot of people. It will take me all winter to tell you about all we did. And we'd better get going. Clarence's legs are shorter than ours, so it will take longer to get to school."

The girls clattered down the stairs and into the kitchen for breakfast. Anoria looked out the door and saw a beautiful early fall morning. The air had that crisp, crackly feeling that you only get on the very best days. She was glad to be back home.

Location: Schoolhouse, Greenshire
Date: 3 Barra, 137 AF

Everyone at school had grown a lot over the summer. Even scrawny Laurence Firebird had put on inches and pounds. "He's starting to look like a young man," Joanna said, eyeing Laurence. "Instead of looking like a ragamuffin or thief."

Greetings were passed around, and the young people filed into the classroom, preparing for another session of schooling. Some were more prepared than others. Joanna, because of her studies for her herbal and floral products was well ahead of many other girls, who had spent the summer helping on farms or in shops. Anoria also spent a lot of time at her books, as well as practicing runes for her future spell books. Laurence, whose father was the local intercessor, had always done well in his classes, mischief or not.

Over the last three years, the fear of Anoria and her wizard's apprentice status had faded. Now, most of the children treated her the same way they treated each other. Joanna had gained a lot of status with her scented products, as well. She was well on her way to a healthy dowry of her own, in addition to being near to owning a thriving business.

* * *

"Joanna," Anoria said after classes were done for the day, "Let's stop by the temple. I want to light a candle to Zagrod and thank him for his help."

Anoria heard a snort from behind her and turned to see Laurence standing there. "Hello, Laurence."

"You're going to thank a god for what?" Laurence asked. "Why bother? You're the one who does the work, aren't you? What good does a prayer do?"

"And here you are, the son of the intercessor," Joanna said, shifting the weight of her latest herbal to her hip. "Anyone would think you didn't respect the gods."

"I'm not sure I do." Laurence shrugged. "My father does, of course, but I've never seen any evidence to prove anything. And with him always trying to push me into the gods' service, well, you know how it is. I wish he'd just let me alone about it."

Larendo Firebird was an intercessor and a fairly decent one. But he wasn't one of the lucky few whose prayers were rewarded with spells. Whether a god provided spells when an intercessor prayed was up to the god. Sometimes they did, but more often they didn't. It was the rare intercessor who could do magic, and such intercessors often rose quickly in the temple and were almost never assigned to small villages. Laurence Firebird's father was convinced that in some way he had failed as an intercessor because the god of harvests didn't choose to gift him with spells of healing or spells to help the harvest.

It gave Intercessor Firebird a quiet bitterness and his son a distrust of the gods. That difference in response had driven a wedge between the father and son. A slow, quiet war had gone on between them since Laurence was about seven and decided that if the gods didn't like his daddy, then he didn't like them. Intercessor Firebird was intent that his son should follow in his footsteps and become an intercessor of the god of harvests. Laurence was intent that he would never in his life pray and mean it. For such a prayer, it seemed to him, must inevitably result in further degradation of his father, whom he loved dearly, either by his son also being deemed unworthy of magic, or—worse—by prayers being answered for the son when they weren't for the father.

Intercessor Firebird was, in a way, right to be concerned that he had failed. He was a highly intelligent man but did not have the sort of mind that could handle close contact with the will of a god. He was too stiff in his opinions, too unwilling to see the other side, but that stiffness reflected a core of uncertainty, which meant that a god's voice would crush his mind. Because of that uncertainty, Intercessor Larendo Firebird was unable to admit he was wrong.

Laurence's big trouble, at fourteen and suffering the brunt of his father's displeasure, was that he was beginning to see the gods' point, although he didn't know that. He had started to wonder what the addition of proof of divine favor would have done to his father's stiffly held beliefs. He wanted out and away from home. He didn't want to be caught in the struggle between his father and the gods.

"What will you do, if you don't want to become an intercessor like your father?" Anoria asked as they neared the temple. "Almost everyone winds up doing what their parents want, I think."

"Not me," Laurence said. "He's going to push me too hard one day, and I'll pack up and leave. I'll go soldier, if I have to."

Soldiers weren't well thought of, Anoria knew that. Which made a lot of sense, considering that a soldier's job was killing people. But that wasn't all of it. There had been a war when Anoria was just a baby. It was called the War of the Servile Provinces, and the kingdom of Amonrai had lost. The provinces within the nation of Amonrai which insisted on keeping serfs and slaves had split off into a nation that called itself Southern Amonrai. That nation hadn't lasted very long before it had split into other nations, because the only thing holding them together was their conflict with the free provinces. Now there were a dozen nations to the south of Amonrai that were fighting among themselves.

There were also raids from the Servile Provinces across the borders into Amonrai and the occasional raid by the wild elves that lived in the west. That was what kept the army busy these days.

CHAPTER 19

Location: Cooper Home, Greenshire
Date: 15 Zagrod, 138 AF

"No, I'm not really sure I want to go," Anoria admitted. "Yes, I like the dancing part, but I'm not really looking for a husband, at least not yet."

"Well, none of us are," Joanna said. "We're still too young. The idea behind the dances is to let people from different villages meet. And we're lucky we're sort of in the middle of so many villages and have that big square. That way we get a lot of visitors." Joanna twirled around a bit and asked, "How do I look?"

"Really beautiful, as always," Anoria said. "Let's go then. I'll be going back to the forest in a day or two, when Cordelia gets back. I guess we'd better enjoy the evening. I'll be back at the wizard studies, trying for the next higher spells before you know it."

"Do you still love it?"

Anoria's face lit up, making her much prettier than she thought she was. "Oh, yes. I do. And Cordelia and I do so many wonderful things together. And she learns new spells too. Did you know it took her nearly a year to figure out how to fix the roads? But it only took her two months to figure out the spare room. And, last year, we found out that you can use Wizard's Mark to make a highly complicated spell usable for a less skilled wizard."

"I doubt you'll ever get it low enough for me." Joanna grinned. "But if you get a chance, work on a spell to, oh, keep milk fresh like a Breadkeeper does. Something anyone could use."

"Oh. You mean like a spell to recharge a Breadkeeper? That's not a very complicated spell."

"It is for me!" Joanna said.

"Well, for me, too," Anoria said. "But that's because I'm still an apprentice. I have prepared it several times and then released it, but Lady Cordelia says I'm not ready for casting real spells yet."

The girls went downstairs and were met by Michael and Debra, who were anxious to leave for the village dance.

"Let's go, how about it?" Michael said. "You know the dances are the only time I get to see Tess anymore. I miss having her around."

* * *

The village square was decorated with late-spring blooms and vines. The atmosphere was festive, and a wandering minstrel was playing dance music. They'd no more gotten to the square than Joanna was surrounded by half a dozen young men, all begging for a dance. Laurence Firebird asked Anoria, and none of the young people took a break until the minstrel begged for a little time to rest his fingers.

Laurence walked Anoria over to a refreshment booth and bought them both a cup of cider. They sat down on a convenient bench to rest a moment. "So, you'll be away again all summer," Laurence said.

"Yes. Summer is when I get most of my training," Anoria explained. "At least for the next year or so. After that, I'll be finished with school and probably won't get back here more than two or three times a year. I've got to work hard and finish."

Laurence looked a bit downcast for a moment. "I've enjoyed talking to you this year," he said. "You're a lot . . . I don't know . . . deeper . . . than most of the girls around here. You think about things outside of Greenshire and Brookshire."

Anoria and Laurence had spent quite a bit of time talking about this, that, and the other over the winter. Laurence was interested in everything, as long as it didn't involve any kind of religious study and often snuck away from the temple quarters. He'd even begun to help Joanna with her herbal compounding, just as a way to avoid his father. He had also found that he truly loved working with plants and animals, something he had rarely experienced except at harvest time.

"I love it here, though," Anoria said. "I'd really never leave if I didn't have to. I spent so much time without a home, and now, with Lady Cordelia and Joanna, I have two."

"You wouldn't want to go live in the wide world some day?"

"No, not me." Anoria smiled. "I want to stay right here, or in the forest. It's just home."

Laurence nodded, but didn't look convinced. He looked around and changed the subject. "Look, there's Joanna's step-cousin, Gregory. Let's go talk to him."

Gregory, as usual, was quiet and reserved. He was a couple of years older than Joanna, Anoria, and Laurence and was entering the seminary of Barra in the fall.

"I imagine you've got your life all worked out for the next twenty years," Laurence told Gregory in a sneering voice.

"Oh, hush, Laurence," Joanna said. "What are your plans, Gregory?"

"Well, Laurence is sort of right," Gregory admitted. "I'll be going to the seminary this fall, and, assuming I get through it all right, I'll probably end up as a village intercessor, just like your father, Laurence." Gregory shrugged. "I've always felt a calling to the service of the gods."

"You can have 'em," Laurence said. "I don't know what I want to do, but I know that isn't it. I just wish I could get my father off my back about it."

"Can't help you there. I'm not even in the seminary yet. He's not going to listen to me. So I guess Anoria and I have our lives pretty much settled. She's going to be a wizard, and I'm going to be an intercessor. What about you, Joanna?"

"Not keep house, that's for sure," Joanna said. "I like distilling my perfumes, but I sure don't like spending hours rubbing wet clothes against a washboard every week. And I don't like churning butter or sweeping floors or carting water from the well, either."

"That's the same way I feel about chores," Laurence said.

"But somebody's got to do them," Gregory pointed out. "And this isn't the Servile States, where they keep slaves to do that sort of thing."

"I know," Joanna said. "I'll have Anoria make me spells to do all the stuff I don't like."

"Hey, wait a minute," Anoria said. "Cordelia hasn't let me cast a real spell yet. I just form them and then release them, for practice. It'll be years before I can start developing spells. And just the ink to write them down costs a fortune."

"Why's that?" Gregory asked.

"It's special colored ink, and it's really dangerous if your spell book fades. If you get the wrong color, it can make a spell go wrong."

"Oh, I didn't know that. Intercessors don't have spell books. Even those who can do magic. They get their spells from the gods, fully formed. Not that I'm ever likely to be able to do that. But Intercessor Tomsom explained how it worked, back when I lived in Gent."

Tommy Poll had stopped to listen, and said, "I guess I'll be a farmer like my papa. I kind of like it, making things grow."

"I'd like that better than being an intercessor," Laurence said.

"Enough about that, Laurence. I've been hearing about it since you were ten. We understand, really. You don't want to be an intercessor!" Tommy said, laughing.

"He had another fight with his father, I bet," said Anoria.

"That would explain it," Tommy agreed. "You want to dance, Anoria?"

CHAPTER 20

Location: Spice Islands
Date: 14 Pago, 138 AF

That summer was the first time that Anoria went to one of the spice islands where Cordelia traded. And it was there that she found the beginnings of a way to make her own living some day. She and Cordelia were walking along the dusty road when it happened. "What is that smell?" Anoria asked, sniffing the breeze.

Cordelia sniffed a bit and smiled. "It's called sindal. It's a very fragrant shrub that grows here. I've always loved that scent too. The problem is that the shrub is very thorny, as well as rather spindly. It won't grow anywhere else either."

"Is the scent in the flowers?"

"No, it doesn't flower, I don't think. We have some time, so we'll go look at one. Knowledge is never wasted."

After a short walk, following their noses all the way, Anoria and Cordelia found a patch of the sindal shrubs. The scent was marvelous, but, to put it very kindly, the shrub was nothing much to speak of. The largest of its branches was about as big around as Anoria's smallest finger. The thorns were sharp and wicked, as Anoria soon found out. "Drat!"

"I did warn you." Cordelia grinned.

"I know. I just wanted to collect a bit for Joanna. I'm sure she could find a way to make a lovely perfume with it. But those thorns!"

"I'm afraid it's not much use, Anoria. But a perfume would be a lovely thing to have."

Anoria thought for a moment then asked, "Do you suppose one of the Servant spells could gather it and remove the thorns? It wouldn't hurt one, would it?"

"I shouldn't think so. The Servant spells don't really make servants, you know. They have no will of their own. Really, they're just programmed bits of magic. You've been practicing that spell lately, haven't you? Do you think you can use it?"

Anoria had prepared that spell and several others in the mornings and released them in the evenings any number of times, with Lady Cordelia observing to make sure she was doing it right. Lady Cordelia was teaching her to keep spells ready for casting. She had never been allowed to cast any of them before, though. These weren't like the Practice spells, which were just bits of magic carried around and used by concentration. These were real spells.

"I believe so."

"Try it then."

Anoria concentrated a moment and invoked the spell. Her first Servant spell came into existence. There was a slight tug at her mind, a connection between her and the structure of magic. Now she really understood that the servant wasn't really a servant but a tool. A thing, not a person or an animal. Anoria gave it its instructions, and it began gathering branches of the thorny shrub until there was an armload in front of Anoria. "Lay it on the ground to dry," she instructed. "Collect all you can, and then remove the thorns, and . . ." She stopped. "Um . . . Lady Cordelia?"

"Yes?"

"There's no wall."

"And?"

Anoria felt like Lady Cordelia was waiting for her to do something. She just wasn't sure quite what. So she thought for another moment. "Could we use a Servant spell to hold up the tapestry for the portable pantry?"

"That would work," Lady Cordelia agreed.

The Servant spell was put to holding up the tapestry, Lady Cordelia invoked the Portable Pantry, and Anoria went in and fetched a box.

She told the Servant, "Go back to collecting the sindal, then place the stems in here."

"I'm proud of you, my dear," Cordelia said. "Very pleased and proud. You've learned well. But you really don't have to speak out loud to the Servant spell."

Anoria flushed with pride and embarrassment. This was the best spell she had used yet, even though it would probably only last about half an hour. "I sort of have an idea for what to do with the sindal, but it's going to take some study."

"I expect we can manage that, and I'm curious about what you're planning." Cordelia smiled. "That fragrance is quite pleasing, isn't it? We'll just wait here for a bit while your servant does its work."

They watched as the invisible servant did its work, breaking the branches, striping the thorns, and putting the thorns in the box. Then they had it hold up the tapestry again, so that Anoria could put the box in the pantry. When all of that was finished, they went back to the village and its market and continued their shopping trip.

Location: Greenwood
Date: 19 Pago, 138 AF

Anoria's face broke into a big grin when they popped back to Cordelia's forest home. "I always enjoy the things and people we see when we travel, Lady Cordelia. But I'm always glad to get home."

"It has become a real home, hasn't it?" Cordelia said. "I wasn't sure, you know, when I came back here. Wasn't sure I could stay, didn't know if the villages around here would accept me. Being a wizard tends to set you apart from people. You get used to it, but magic, well, it makes a permanent change."

Anoria nodded. "I know. When I first met you, I was terrified. But that isn't right, you know. There's no real reason to be terrified of a wizard. Once people get used to us, well, they become more accepting. Like the kids at school. The first year they were even afraid of me, then Laurence put the snake down my back, and they saw I was just a regular girl."

"Well, that depends on the wizard, Anoria," Cordelia said. "Magic is often used in warfare, and we've already been over the fact that magic can be powered by stealing life force, by sacrificing animals, or even people. There are whole classes of wizards that any sane person hates and fears. And there are circumstances where even the kindest of wizards can be dangerous, like anyone who has power." Then Cordelia looked into Anoria's disappointed eyes. "But that doesn't mean that our neighbors have to be afraid of us. And you are a regular girl. Just one who happens to know a little magic."

They had continued walking through the garden as they talked. Anoria loved the garden, Cordelia knew. She often brought her books outside and studied there. "I'm not sure I'd want to be that 'regular,' Anoria. The people can keep a little distance, as far as I'm concerned."

"I'm sure they will, Lady Cordelia." Anoria grinned. "There's that pig story, after all. But Greenshire is home to me, and I want to stay here. So I don't want people to be afraid of me."

"Oh, stop calling me lady! I'm practically your . . . aunt." Cordelia felt her heart warm as she watched the bright smile that bloomed on Anoria's face, then they started walking again.

Cordelia had never removed the upper access door to her underground home. Anoria still needed it, so she had become accustomed to using it as well. Cordelia considered Anoria's statement as they entered the house and began to wonder, again, just how Anoria would ever be able to afford to train another wizard, some day. Economics couldn't be avoided, after all. It took money for training. It took money to research spells and to record them. Sometimes it even took money to use them, if they had an expensive or hard-to-come-by component, like a scale from a living dragon.

"We're going to have to consider what direction your training will take, Anoria," she finally said, after they were settled into their home. "It seems to me that we need to develop a different sort of training. You've said you don't want to adventure, so we'll have to concentrate on developing spells you can use to make a living and have enough put by to take an apprentice yourself. Training others is the only way to keep the skills alive."

"I've been thinking about that," Anoria said. "It will be years before I can translocate, anyway. What if I concentrated on spells to make things? Like the sindal wood. I wonder if I could produce a spell that would form the wood into beads. And another to drill a hole in the bead. And another to string the beads into jewelry. If I could do that, I'd have a product to sell. And that would bring in money."

"Hmmmm," Cordelia muttered. "A fair bit of money, considering that the scent is unique. You know . . ." Cordelia looked at Anoria's earnest face. "You just might have an idea there. But I thought you had Joanna in mind for the sindal wood."

"I do." Anoria grinned. "I'll bet the thorns and the shavings from bead making could be ground into a powder. Then Joanna could extract the oils, just like she does for the rose petals. And she would have another perfume to sell. And because I furnished the wood, well, I ought to get a part of the profits, don't you think?"

"Hmmmmm."

Location: Greenwood
Date: 28 Pago, 138 AF

Anoria, after nearly four years of practice, was quite good at drawing and writing the runes for spells. She knew what they meant and was a dab hand at copying. She simply needed more practice preparing and casting spells and more time for her concentration ability to grow into learning the really difficult spells. Developing the spells to make the jewelry would be good practice. So, although Cordelia knew a very complicated spell that would produce the same effect, she and Anoria set to work devising alternate spells Anoria could use to make her product.

It took several weeks, but Anoria developed the spell design on her own. Sort of on her own, at any rate. There was no way Cordelia was going to let Anoria do something as dangerous as researching a new spell without looking over her work to make sure that the new spell would be safe to prepare and use.

Cordelia looked over the spell design and pointed to a particular rune. "What do you mean by this?"

"That's the Wizard's Mark spell," Anoria explained, "Cast on a piece of wood with a nail in it. I used the Wizard's Mark to connect to the . . ."

Cordelia nodded, and went through the rest of the spell, noting the symbol and the structure, and that the spell used the position of Wizard's Mark to control how the sindal wood would be held and spun. "You know, this might work," Cordelia commented. "Bring me that plank over there." Taking the plank, Cordelia cast a quick spell and forced a nail through it. Then she cast Wizard's Mark on the plank in the indicated position. "Very well. Now go stand over there, Anoria. I don't want you too close when I cast a new spell. Even one as simple as this."

Then she cast the spell and watched with amusement as the stick of sindal wood spun above the nail. The spell carved the beads. But it was much simplified by the special plank that helped control the magic. "A very good idea, young lady. You're coming along quite well. I am somewhat amazed at the variety of uses to which a Wizard's Mark can be put. Now, I want you to practice forming that spell in your mind three times a day for a week before you actually try to cast it. And I want to be there when you prepare it the day you use it the first time."

"Do you think it'll be ready by the time I go back to school," Anoria asked.

"It should be if you're diligent," Cordelia said. "But let's set it aside for the moment. Let's not work for a bit. I'd like to visit someone, and I'd like you to meet her."

Anoria's face lit up. "You have the most interesting friends, Cordelia. Who is it going to be this time? Another spice gatherer?"

"Not at all. These are orcs, not friends. You'll see soon enough."

Location: Orclands
Date: 29 Pago, 138 AF

The Orclands were an island continent in the southern hemisphere. That continent was primarily occupied by orcs, and the gods they worshiped were the sort that insisted on human sacrifice. So the orcs had been sacrificing each other and anyone else they could get their hands on throughout their history. They had also, in imitation of their gods, enslaved, murdered, raped, generally brutalized, and occasionally ate one another with gay abandon. The general attitude was: get the other guy before he got you.

Two hundred years ago the Kingdom Isles had invaded the Orclands to put an end to human sacrifice and cannibalism. Also to pick up some more territory. The Kingdom Isles now controlled about a quarter of the Orclands, and they treated the orcs about as badly as the orcs treated each other. Well, they didn't do human sacrifice, and they didn't eat the orcs. But forced labor and other abuses—those things the Kingdom Isles' representatives here in the Orclands did practice. Still, there were a good number of orcs that took the Kingdom colors, and there were orc tribes on the borders of Kingdom territory that were at least semi-civilized by human standards and terribly effete by orc standards. It was in one of these bordering tribes that Anoria found herself.

"They're not so bad," Cordelia told her, as they looked around the "courtyard." It was an open space of white sand surrounded by white cliffs that each seemed to have one or more cave entrances in them.

Anoria had never met an orc, but she had seen drawings. The pictures didn't do them justice. They had short bodies and long arms, wide shoulders, and their jaws stuck out enough to be almost a snout. Their skin was a pasty white, but covered in a greenish down. The down extended into hair on their shoulders and heads, and they wore very little clothing. What clothing they had was made from animal skins that hadn't been tanned all that well, from the smell. They carried wooden swords with bits of sharp stone embedded in the wood. And they had Anoria and Cordelia surrounded just moments after they had popped into the "courtyard."

Cordelia said something in a language full of grunts and glottal stops, and one of the orcs said, "We speak human tongue!" in Kingdom. "What you want?"

"I'm told you make glass here," Cordelia said. "Is that true?"

"We have glass. Good glass. Very expensive." Then he named a price that didn't strike Anoria as all that expensive. Not exactly cheap, but not very much at all compared to what glass jars or panes cost in Amonrai.

"Well, let's see what you have," Cordelia said. "Then if I like it, we can get down to haggling."

They were led into the caves, which were rather better lit than Anoria was expecting. The orcs had used their own glass to fashion crude skylights. Cordelia and Anoria were shown glass beads, glass jars, small glass sheets about six inches wide by eight inches tall, and even mirrors about the same size as the glass sheets. It was a showroom.

"I'm impressed," Cordelia told the orc with the best leather vest, which looked to Anoria to be some sort of reptile skin. "How do you make glass?"

It was the wrong thing to say because the orcs raised their weapons. Aunt Cordelia managed to get the orcs mostly calmed down, and they were taken to see the emperor of the northern orcs. Anoria would later learn that the emperor of the northern orcs actually ruled fewer orcs than there were people living in Whitehall county. And, slowly, they got some of the history of orcish glassmaking.

There was, as it happened, a fire elemental that lived in one of their deeper caves. They fed the fire elemental this and that, foods it was particularly fond of, and it burned pretty hot. The caves acted as an insulator, and there was a pool of molten glass that the elemental maintained in fairly liquid state.

As the fire elemental swam, it left the glass a little more liquid in its wake. And an orc with a stone cup on a long pole would reach in and scoop up some of the liquid. They had experimented with adding different things to the cave of fire, to the point that by now they had mostly clear glass. They had also worked out several ways of using the stuff. For one thing, even outside the pool the cave of fire was really hot.

There were other sources of glass around the world. Aside from powerful spells to make glass, the orc's elemental wasn't the only elemental to wander, or be drawn into, the material plane. But the orcs had, by chance more than anything, good sand for glassmaking. And their fire elemental was quite a large one. They also had an iron box full of what looked to Anoria like molten silver. They poured the molten glass onto the molten silver, and the glass would spread out flat on the molten silver before it cooled enough to get hard. Anoria was surprised that they let her and Aunt Cordelia see the wide, flat buckets full of molten silver, but later realized that the orcs were keeping parts of their process secret. However, seeing what she did of the orc's process for making glass made her wonder about the secret process for making wizard's ink as well. She began to think about whether or not she and Cordelia could do the same thing with the people who made wizard's ink.

The orcs mostly sold their glass to the Kingdom agent for this area, and there was a considerable increase in price over and above the cost of shipping before it got to the intended user. But it was still much less expensive than magically created glass, because there were very few wizards who had the skill to cast such spells and even fewer of them who happened to know the particular spells involved. Cordelia, though she had the skill, didn't know those spells and was more interested in finding a way for Anoria to make glass.

"Very well," Cordelia told the orc's emperor, who wore armor even in the excessive heat. "I'll buy one hundred panes of your flat glass and a dozen of those jars."

And then they got down to haggling over price. Cordelia managed to talk them down by about a quarter, and even Anoria could tell that the orcs were convinced that they'd gotten the best of the deal. Later, Cordelia told Anoria that it probably was better than the price they got from the Orcland trading factor and that she herself was going to make a considerable profit, since she effectively had no transport costs. The orcs were deeply impressed when Cordelia set up her portable pantry to store the glass.

They parted with mutual protestations of undying friendship. Cordelia placed her hand on Anoria's shoulder and said, "I've got to get out of this heat for a while." Then they popped out.

CHAPTER 21

Location: Wild Wood, Western Amonrai
Date: 29 Pago, 138 AF

Anoria was surprised yet again when they popped into deep forest. "Oh, it's so much cooler here, Cordelia. Thank you."

"I'm not happy when it's too hot." Cordelia grinned. "Of course, I'm not happy when it's too cold, either."

Anoria laughed. "I'd just begun to wonder about the wizard's ink again. Do you suppose we could go and visit the ink makers? And maybe figure out how they do it?"

"I'm afraid not," Cordelia said. "I don't even know who makes it. And I do know that learning the secrets of making wizard's ink has been tried before, with generally fatal consequences to the wizard who tried it."

"Oh." Anoria was only disappointed for a moment, because she began to look around her. The trees were not at all familiar. They were a bit like pines, but not. Their needles were different and grew all along the bottom of the branches, and their trunks were very thick. They produced a funny kind of hard fruit. Anoria picked one of them up. "What do you call this, I wonder? It looks like a pine cone, sort of."

Cordelia didn't answer, but the tree Anoria was standing under did. In a whispery voice, it said, "It is a cone."

Anoria jumped.

The tree giggled a bit. It was quite a young tree, Anoria later discovered.

"Did you speak?" she asked.

Giggling, the tree answered, "Yes, of course. Did you think I couldn't?"

As Anoria and the young tree engaged in the conversation of young things, Cordelia found herself smiling. Young things were something she was becoming very fond of, lately. She asked an older tree, one she knew from an earlier trip, "Is Vindriss home?"

In the more ponderous tones used by older aware trees, it answered, "She is. We've told her of your arrival. She's on her way. It takes a little more time to tree walk than it does to translocate, she said. So it will be a few moments."

"Thank you," Cordelia said. It paid to be polite to the aware trees. "We will wait. May I sit?"

"Please do, Lady Cordelia," Vindriss said, as she walked out of another tree, dressed in her usual gray robes. What brings you to my bower? Not that you aren't welcome. I haven't seen you in years."

"Just a visit, Vindriss," Cordelia said, hugging her old friend.

"Not an adventure, then," Vindriss smiled. "I had hoped you weren't going to ask me to help slay a dragon or something. The older I get, the less I like to leave these woods. Let me find us some refreshments and we'll talk. Who is the child having such an interesting conversation with the baby?"

"My apprentice, Anoria," Cordelia answered. "I'm introducing her to magical creatures. And these trees are certainly magical. I thought of you and this forest right away. You don't mind an unannounced visit, I hope."

"Not at all," Vindriss answered.

Anoria had finally noticed her presence and stood up to be introduced.

"Anoria," Cordelia said, "this is my friend, Vindriss, a druid. Vindriss, my apprentice, Anoria."

Location: Greenwood
Date: 4 Wovoro, 138 AF

It was quite a nice visit, Anoria thought. She now knew more about druids and their beliefs as well as more about dryads and elementals. For a vacation, the week had been full of learning. They had also made another trip to Honth, where Cordelia sold the orcish glass at a considerable profit.

Anoria was glad to be home again, just the same. Visiting was fine, but there was just no place like home. She added another bundle to her luggage as she prepared for the trip to Joanna's home, ready for another year at school. In addition to the sindal shavings, she had a bundle of the long, needle-like leaves the aware trees had gifted her with. Their scent was sharper and stronger than rosemary, but not quite the same as regular pine needles. Joanna might be able to use them for another perfume.

Location: Cooper House, Greenshire
Date: 3 Barra, 138 AF

"Joanna, Joanna, I'm so glad to see you," Anoria said, sniffing the scent of Joanna's stillroom. Joanna was becoming quite a good scent maker, and the crowded shelves of the room reflected that. The combination of scents was nearly overpowering in its intensity. "It was such an interesting summer, but I'm so happy to be back."

Joanna turned from her mortar and pestle and smiled happily. She walked over to hug her friend. "It's wonderful you're back," she said. "And what is that amazing scent?"

"Ah, we have a lot to talk about," Anoria said. "But tell me everything. What's been going on around here?"

"Oh, just the usual," Joanna pulled a face. "Nothing ever changes here. It's the same old village. Now, let's get something to drink and talk about that smell. Is it really coming from that necklace?"

Location: Greenwood
Date: 3 Barra, 138 AF

While Joanna and Anoria were enjoying their reunion, Cordelia was thinking about glassmaking. She spent a few hours going over her notes on the spell to make a pane of glass. It was a fairly complex spell that used a small quartz crystal, and Cordelia was having real difficulty in making it fit with what she'd seen among the orcs. After all, the only magic involved in the orc-made glass was the fire elemental.

After worrying over it for most of the morning, Cordelia popped out to the most recent stretch of road she'd made, and cast "shape land," a fairly powerful spell that did not actually make the road, but rather shaped the ground. In doing so, Shape Land encouraged the plants out of the roadway. In this case, two small trees were moved from what would be the center of the road off to the side of it. Once that was done, she cast a spell that turned earth into stone. Then she repeated the process two more times, producing just under one hundred fifty feet of wizard road.

Then, having done her duty to the count, she went home to think about how to make glass.

Location: Cooper House, Greenshire
Date: 3 Barra, 138 AF

Anoria and Joanna became partners over that winter. They worked together to make perfumes and jewelry and had quite a good profit by the time spring arrived. Anoria's ability to concentrate grew, and she was becoming more powerful, just as she had hoped.

She renewed her acquaintance with the children of the village and began to look for more things she could develop spells for. And Laurence Firebird was becoming a special friend, as well.

Laurence had grown another inch or so over the summer. Tall and gangly, he looked like he might some day grow into his height. A lock of his red hair was perpetually hanging in his eyes, and he often blew at it to get it out of the way. Still, Anoria found herself growing quite fond of him.

"I'm just sick of the praying," Laurence moped. "Father insists that I pray at least an hour a day, and not a single time have I felt anything but, well, irritation at Father. Why can't he understand that you can't force this kind of thing? You either have a calling, or you don't."

"I don't have an answer, Laurence," Anoria told him. "And, since I never knew my father, I suppose I can't really understand what you're going through."

CHAPTER 22

Location: Cooper House, Greenshire
Date: 26 Noron, 139 AF

"Another year, another village dance," Joanna said. "And this year we both look like ladies, so you've got no complaints."

Anoria nodded happily. She was finally beginning to fill out a bit and looked more womanly. She was still thin and willowy, but at least not so sticklike, in her opinion. "I'll never look like you, though, not even in a new dress."

"And why should you? You're fine, just the way you are. Let's go. My feet feel like dancing." Joanna was telling the truth. Her feet, in the new black slippers, were tapping rapidly.

The village square was again decorated and festive-looking. And because Greenshire prospered, more and more people came to buy the products at the market stalls. It was busy and crowded with young people from all over the area. The dancing went on for hours, with youngsters slipping away from the elders to snatch a quick kiss in the darkened byways.

Laurence and Anoria thought they had slipped away, but Larendo Firebird was keeping a special eye on his son tonight. Laurence was simply not putting enough effort into his religious studies this year, and Larendo thought he knew why. When he saw them slip away, he followed. Laurence was not going to be allowed to do as he wished, not at only sixteen years old.

Location: Town Square, Greenshire
Date: 26 Noron, 139 AF

"And just what do you think you're doing?" Intercessor Firebird's voice thundered out of the darkness.

Anoria and Laurence jumped guiltily, just as he thought they might.

"You, wizard girl! I'll thank you to stay away from my son," Intercessor Firebird snapped. "And you, Laurence, what do you mean, sneaking away like that? Thought you'd have a little fun with the girl, eh? Fine way to jeopardize your career as an intercessor that is."

Intercessor Firebird looked like an avenging angel, swooping down upon the miscreants.

Anoria and Laurence had been talking about Laurence's problems with his father. Laurence was nearly at the end of his rope. He suddenly reached that end. His face flushed bright red. "I'm not going to be an intercessor, Father. I have no calling. So what if some intercessors can heal? Most can't. The gods don't care about the people. How could they?"

Larendo flew into quite a rage. He shouted and stomped his feet. A crowd began to gather. "You, you ungrateful whelp . . ."

"What should I be grateful for? All you ever do is insist that I work harder and pray more. That's a laugh. Pray! What good does it do? What good has it done you? I'll never serve the gods. They don't deserve it!"

Larendo lashed out at Anoria. "I suppose you're responsible for this, aren't you? With all your unnatural learning and spells. What are you trying to do, steal my son away?"

Anoria was stunned at the accusation. She had been trying to understand Laurence's feelings, not draw him away from his father. Intercessor Firebird was managing that quite well on his own.

Even some of the watching villagers objected to that. Anoria and her devotion to Zagrod were well known. She usually lit a candle to Zagrod at least once a week. Lately she had taken to making especially scented candles to light for her devotions.

Larendo didn't care for the muttering around him. He grabbed his recalcitrant son by the ear and dragged him away, continuing his recitation of Laurence's faults.

Laurence's face grew even redder as he shouted back at his father.

Joanna came running up to comfort the weeping Anoria. Larendo had been harsh in his condemnation of her, but even worse in his condemnation of his son. It had been a difficult scene to watch. It must have been an even more difficult one to have been a part of. Anoria's eyes were red and her nose stuffed up.

"Come on, Anoria," Joanna whispered. "Let's get out of here. We'll go home."

Location: Cooper Home, Greenshire
Date: 7 Zagrod, 139 AF

"So you see," Debra explained, "Larendo Firebird blames Anoria for his son's leaving during that night. And Anoria has been miserable ever since. I think she may have had some feelings for Laurence, even though she's a bit young for it." Debra looked worried but composed.

"And the villagers, what are they saying?" Cordelia asked. "If they're blaming Anoria for this, things could be difficult for her."

Debra waved a hand in negation of that thought. "No, well, not everyone, but quite a few of them have sympathy for her." Debra rose to go and check the pot on the stove, lifting the lid and sniffing. When she put the lid back down, she continued, "Oh, a couple of the grumpy types are claiming that the intercessor was right, but the people of Greenshire know Anoria. And they know that Intercessor Firebird was pushing Laurence to be an intercessor. That's the biggest reason the poor boy ran away. This will blow over sooner or later, at least in the village. I'm more worried about Anoria. She's drooping around here like a weeping willow, to tell the truth."

"Puppy love?"

Debra nodded. "Which doesn't make it any less painful, as I remember from my own youth. So, she's droopy and weepy, Joanna is droopy and weepy because she is, and generally, I'm tired of droopy, weepy girls." Debra's face was a study. Cordelia could see both impatience and sympathy playing in her expression.

"I have some old memories," Cordelia muttered. "I'm not so ancient that I don't remember what it felt like. So what are you suggesting, Debra?"

"I'm suggesting that they could both use a change of scenery, Cordelia. And I'm suggesting that I could use a break, as well. We've done well enough this year to hire some help in the house, so I'll take over the perfume making and train someone to help with that. You take both girls and get them over the weepy stage, please. It won't hurt to get them away from Greenshire until all the fuss settles down."

Debra's sigh was a bit irritated, as she wiped her hands on her embroidered apron. "I know it hurts. I even sympathize with the girl. But that doesn't make having the nonstop waterworks around all day any easier to bear."

Cordelia grinned into her tea cup. "Oh, I imagine I can keep them busy."

CHAPTER 23

Location: Spice Islands
Date: 14 Estormany, 139 AF

It was a busy summer. Cordelia kept both girls hopping. They collected spices from the islands as well as sindal wood and aware tree needles. Joanna looked at every unusual plant everywhere they went, searching for more perfume materials. Anoria practiced her magic and gained strength, as well as studying the spells Cordelia was working on to make glass.

Joanna was sniffing an unusual bright pink bloom when Anoria brought herself to ask Cordelia a question about her progress. She'd started as an apprentice, of course, then progressed to a caster and, very soon after, a crafter. Because Cordelia had started her practicing the crafting of magical items even before she'd become a caster, she'd progressed more quickly than was usual, especially for a non-adventuring mage.

"One more year, I think," Cordelia replied to her question. "If you keep learning at this rate, about one more year should see you to wanderer rank rather than crafter. After that, well, I suppose you could set up on your own."

The stunned and hurt look on Anoria's face made Cordelia realize that Anoria thought that Cordelia was trying to get rid of her. "Not that I want you to," she hastened to add. "It's just that you could if you wished. There's always more to learn. We never stop doing that, even if we don't actually wander."

"I want to learn," Anoria assured her. "I never want to stop. And I never want to leave you."

Cordelia's heart was warmed by that statement. "Then we shall go along as we have been. Except that I think you've learned all you can from the village school, so unless you just want to, I see no reason to spend the winter in Greenshire."

"I've finished with it too," Joanna said, joining them under the spreading tree. "I want to work on my perfumes and unguents and concentrate on building the business up. What I'd most like to do is earn enough money to build a glass house, like the one we saw in Honth. Then I could extend my plantings a bit, and maybe grow this flower."

"We're working on glass, Joanna, but it's a very complicated spell. Much above my level," Anoria said. "And having glass made by hand is just plain expensive. Enough glass for a house? How would you ever afford that?"

"Well, partner," Joanna said with a smile, "if you don't make any progress, I'll just have to raise enough money to buy the glass myself. Things are going so well with the perfumes and scented jewelry that I really believe we can do that, even if it will take years."

Location: Greenwood
Date: 27 Cashi, 139 AF

Anoria was sitting in the library, with her feet propped up on the desk.

Cordelia shook her head in mock despair. "Honestly, Lady Anoria, if the townspeople could only see you now. Hair bundled up with a jeweled stick holding it out of your face. Trousers. My heavens, what a sight you are."

Anoria grinned widely, hazel eyes sparkling. "One of the best things about not living in Greenshire is not having to follow the rather outmoded ideas of proper dress. How is a person meant to get any work done when dealing with cumbersome long skirts?"

Cordelia, herself dressed in trousers and a tunic, put on a severe face. "Ladies do not sit with their feet above the waist, Madame. And, as you should well know, trousers are for doing dirty farm work."

Anoria put on her own version of a severe face and grumped, "Lady Cordelia, you have surely ruined the girl. She has no concept of her proper place in the world. What shall we do with her?"

Cordelia laughed a ringing laugh and collapsed into a chair. "I've no idea. We shall have to consider an appropriate punishment, I suppose." Reverting to her normal manner, she asked, "What are you researching? Still working on the Tray spell?"

The Tray spell was one of three spells that Cordelia and Anoria had worked on together as a way of simplifying glassmaking to a level of magic that Anoria could handle. They had already developed the two Separation spells they needed and a Melt spell, but that just left them with globs of glass. Getting the glass into a flat pane was proving difficult.

"Well, I do have a responsibility to the partnership," Anoria said. "And I might have found a way, although I'm not sure I can use it. It's pretty complicated, and I don't know if I can manage either spell."

"What do you have?" Cordelia asked. Anoria often found simple, less complicated ways to accomplish the most amazing things.

"Take a look here," Anoria said, showing Cordelia some of the notes they had made at the glass foundry in the Orclands. "They use some melted metal, or something like a melted metal, to pour the glass on when it's very hot. What if we use some kind of a shield spell?"

Cordelia sat in the chair she'd added to the library and put her own feet on the desk, then studied the notes Anoria pointed out. "Hmmmm. Wizard's Mark won't help us here I don't think. Perhaps an enchanted framework . . ."

The two fell into study for a while. Then they began their experiments.

Location: Cooper House, Greenshire
Date: 27 Banth, 140 AF

Michael read the letter aloud that night at supper. "It's from Tess. 'Dear Michael and family,' it says."

"Yes, dear, we know that part," Debra said. "Get to the meat of it, please."

Joanna and the hired girls giggled a bit at this byplay. Debra always acted a bit impatient with her husband, but everyone knew that as far as she was concerned, the sun rose and set in his very words.

Michael stuck his tongue out at Debra, causing a few more giggles. " 'Gregory is in his last year at the seminary and will be coming home this summer for a break. Because he's going to be an intercessor of Barra, god of harvest, it's been suggested that he spend his break on a farm and work. I just wanted to check with you and make sure it's all right. He'll be home in about two weeks, so please let me know as soon as you can. Love, Tess. ' "

"Won't it be wonderful to have an intercessor in the family?" Debra smiled. "Of course, he's more than welcome. I'm sure you can keep him busy."

Michael nodded. "It's a farm. One minute you're rushing to get something done, the next it's raining and you can't do anything. But we'll manage, I expect. I can always use help with the haying. And then there's that greenhouse of Joanna's. I can use some help following Cordelia's directions."

CHAPTER 24

Location: Greenwood
Date: 7 Noron, 140 AF

"You're sure you don't want to come along?" Cordelia asked again. "You'd be quite welcome. And I'll be gone for at least four months. The prince has quite a lot of building he wants done."

"I'm very sure," Anoria said. "It's a nice enough castle and all that, I know. But I got my fill of the courtly life when we went there last year. I'd rather not have to change my dress fourteen times a day, thank you very much. And I'm grown, Cordelia. I'm sixteen, you know. You don't have to worry about me. I'll stay at the farm and work on the greenhouse, instead."

"I almost wish I could too," Cordelia grumped. "You're right about all that changing. Why the princess feels you must have a different outfit for every hour of the day is totally beyond me. Still, I agreed to do this. And it does pay very well."

Location: Cooper House, Greenshire
Date: 19 Noron, 140 AF

"All right," Anoria said, looking at the rather strange addition to the farmhouse. "It's on the south side; that's good. And you've installed a dark stone floor, which is also good. Now we just need the glass."

Joanna clearly didn't understand why the addition had had to be built in this specific manner. "It's kind of strange looking, Anoria. All those crossing beams make it look like a giant tic-tac-toe game. And why did it have to be exactly two-by-two foot divisions?"

"Because of this." Anoria opened the small portable pantry that Cordelia had made for her and brought out a flat, square piece of metal a bit over two feet by two feet. It had a rim around the top edge and four legs that could be extended to different lengths. She set it up very carefully, explaining, "It has to be set perfectly horizontal and I can only do one window pane at a time." Anoria went back into the pantry and brought out a small pot and a scoop. "And this." Anoria headed for the stream, which ran through the farm not too far from the house and was very convenient.

Anoria began talking as she walked. "I couldn't use the spells I wanted to use. I'm not skilled enough yet. So I had to do it another way, and it takes three spells."

"But you can make glass?" Joanna asked. "Because having that strange framework attached to the house has Mother wondering what the neighbors are going to say."

"Yes, I can. It's just going to take a while to get it all done," Anoria said. "Like I told you, this way takes three spells for each pane of glass. The first one separates the sand by weight. The second separates it by color. The third one is tied to this little table and melts the sand into glass." Anoria and Joanna walked back from the creek with a scoop full of sandy, wet soil. Anoria dumped it, without ceremony, in the pot. She set the scoop down and invoked "Separate One."

This was a spell that removed all the sand that weighed too much or too little. It left about a third of the sand in the pot, and the rest was pushed out of the top. Then she invoked "Separate Two." It pushed the sand that wasn't clear out of the pot. Anoria muttered something not entirely ladylike, and Joanna giggled. Anoria was becoming more and more like Cordelia every day.

Anoria began trudging back to the creek and Joanna followed. "It's going to take two scoops per window pane. There isn't really enough of the transparent stuff in the creek sand." The girls headed back for Anoria's odd little pot. A few minutes later she had cast the two simple spells again and was ready for the final spell.

She poured the sand onto the table and invoked "Melt." The sand on the table glowed red and began to melt. The new-made glass was floating on a plane of magical energy. The glass then cooled as the energy was sent back to the plane of fire from whence it came.

"We made a right mess the first time we did this," Anoria said. "The metal melted and mixed with the glass, and we got a ruined table and a pane of bubbly glass. We had to start over."

"Why?"

"Don't know," Anoria admitted. "No idea. But Cordelia put a sort of magic separator between the metal and the sand, since we did get a pane of glass. Sort of. Now it works fine."

It left a flat, smooth square of glass. Anoria carefully removed the glass from the form and set it aside. Then, sighing, she got out her spell book. "The sand at Greenwood has more of the transparent stuff in it. If we could use that sand, I'd only have to cast the separate spells once for each pane. I can't separate more than one scoop at a time, either. So, using the sand from the creek here means I'm going to have to do it twice for every pane. Now I'll have to spend an hour preparing the spells before I can make another pane for the green house."

"Well, you ought to at least put your separating pot down by the creek and save steps. But, what about the other colored sand?" Joanna asked. "Why do you have to separate it out?"

"It doesn't make clear glass if you don't separate it out," Anoria explained. "At least that's what we think. It was hard to tell from the references we had, to tell the truth. We think it would make glass that was whatever color the sand is. Some of it is red, some black and stuff like that. That won't work for the greenhouse. All the colors might muddle together and wouldn't let in enough light for plants."

Anoria, and even Cordelia, for that matter, didn't really know how the combination of spells worked to make glass, nor did they realize quite how different their glass was from that produced in Ethwap, one of the glass-making cities. The spells had been a result of researching the way non-magical craftsmen made glass in far off Ethwap. Then Cordelia contacted a being of the plane of fire who owed her a favor. She had asked it several questions. The answers had provided the basis for the table that was used in melting the glass. The table bordered on being a magical item in its own right. Much of the control of the magic was vested in the table rather than in the spell.

Joanna thought for a few moments, twirling a lock of hair around her fingers. "It would let in more light than scraped hide does, wouldn't it?"

Anoria looked a little annoyed at the interruption, but her face cleared after a moment's thought. "Probably. I don't really know, though. We've only tried making clear glass. We could try it, but the panes might be opaque and not let any light through or they might be colored glass and let some light through."

"Think about it, Anoria. Glass is very expensive. That's why so many people have scraped hide on their windows. So, even not perfectly clear glass would probably sell to someone who wanted a window in their cottage, right? If they had an opening the same shape as your table, that is."

Anoria nodded. "I could do it in a different shape, too, like a rectangle, if I had a table that shape. But I don't have one. I just can't do anything much bigger than this is, no matter what shape."

"And the colored sand . . . couldn't you do something with the colored sand? Bottles or something like that?"

Anoria's forehead creased in concentration, her spell preparation forgotten for the moment. "I don't know. I'll have to see what kind of spell would shape a bottle. And I'll have to figure out a way to adjust the spell to separate the sand by all the different colors, too."

Joanna rose and patted Anoria's shoulder. "You prepare your spells. I'll get a bucket and fill it with sand, so you don't have to walk back and forth to the creek. Then I'm going to Greenshire and measure windows. I'll bet we can sell glass windows to every village around here."

Joanna started walking away and then called back over her shoulder, "This is even better than a spell to keep milk fresh. This will make money. We can always make cheese with milk. Come to think of it, that makes money too."

Location: Cooper House, Greenshire
Date: 5 Zagrod, 140 AF

Gregory was returning from Brookshire to Greenshire when he saw the glitter of glass in the framework. Two panes had been installed so far. Why so few, he wondered. It surely couldn't take that long to install a glass pane. He continued up the lane, admiring the glitter.

As he drew near the house he saw Joanna and her friend Anoria bending over an oddly shaped table. Just as he entered the yard, the table suddenly glowed red. He began to hurry, afraid that there had been an accident. "What . . ." he began to say, but Joanna waved him off.

"Don't touch it yet. It's still hot."

The glow began to fade, and in less time than he thought was possible, the table had cooled. "What is that?"

"That," Joanna said, "is the next pane of glass. Though at this rate it's going to take a while to make them all.

"Three a day, probably," Anoria muttered. "At least for the first couple of days, until we get a bit better organized. It looks like it's going to take two of each of the easy spells for every time I do the hard one. If I leave the placing until later and concentrate on just making glass, I should be able to get five panes a day."

"You're a wizard, then?" Gregory asked. "I knew you were an apprentice, but I always assumed . . ."

"What?" Anoria asked sharply. "That I was apprenticed as a nanny or something? There's nothing wrong with wizardry, you know, no matter what some people think. It is not unnatural, and it is not evil."

Gregory raised his hands, pretending to cower away from her. "Yes, ma'am. No, ma'am. Whatever you say, ma'am." He grinned. "I never suggested there was, ma'am. Please don't turn me into a frog, ma'am."

Anoria couldn't help but giggle a bit at the fearful face Gregory made.

"Actually, Anoria," he said, "I was about to say that I had assumed it would take longer. I know you're a few years younger than I am. I didn't think you could cast spells yet."

"I started young," Anoria said, pleased that someone had noticed her progress. "I've been using spells for several years. Cordelia says I could probably set up on my own in a year or so, but I'll never leave her. She's been too good to me."

CHAPTER 25

Location: Cooper House, Greenshire
Date: 20 Pago, 140 AF

"I managed six panes today," Anoria said, eight weeks later. "The greenhouse is done, thank heaven."

"What's next?" Michael asked, as he poured himself a cup of cider. He offered the pitcher around, and Anoria refreshed her cup as well.

"I still think you ought to try the glass another way," Joanna said. "Just try it without that second Separate spell and see what you get. I've been looking around at the village. If a person built a frame, sort of like the greenhouse frames, couldn't you cut the glass to fit the frames? That way, say, if a person needs a three-foot by four-foot window, you could cut glass into pieces, fit it into the frames and fit the frames to the windows. You wouldn't need a differently sized table then."

"Wouldn't the glass break if you tried to cut it?" Anoria asked. "I'm willing to try it. I just don't have any idea how to cut it."

"There must be a way," Gregory said. "My father bought Tess a mirror. It's certainly not as big as the glass panes you make, so there must be a way to cut the glass."

"Mirror. Mirror," Joanna muttered. "That's another thing we should investigate. Mirrors are incredibly expensive."

"Joanna," Debra sighed, "do you ever think about anything but making money? There is more to life, you know."

"Sure," Joanna answered. "I think about spending money too. And you've complained about that often enough, since Cordelia taught us about shopping."

Michael snorted into his cider, and everyone around the table began to laugh. It was true. Joanna liked spending the fruits of her labor just as much as she enjoyed earning those fruits to begin with.

Debra rolled her eyes a bit. "Well, it sounds to me like Anoria is going to need some help. Gregory can look into how to cut glass. Michael can look into how to build the frames Joanna spoke of. And Anoria can see what happens when she tries a different spell."

"And what shall you do, Madame?" Michael asked, putting on a fruity voice.

"I," Debra said, "shall have another cup of cider, please."

Location: Cooper House, Greenshire
Date: 25 Pago, 140 AF

"All right," Anoria muttered. "We'll see what happens." Anoria threw a scoop of separated sand on the table. There was enough sand to make a pane, so she invoked the Melt spell. When it was finished, there was a pane of glass there, but it most certainly was not clear. When she held it to the light she could see glints of different colors in the glass. Over all, though, it would let in more light than scraped hide, even if it was rather greenish in color.

Anoria set the pane aside and decided to try the new version of the second Separate spell. It had taken her a week to figure it out. But if she adjusted two runes on the pot and adjusted two of the forms in preparing the spell, it should push the different sands out of the pot in different directions, rather than randomly. So the pot should separate the different colors of sand into separate piles. She shrugged. "No way to know except to try it." Anoria was more than a little nervous about that. She was almost sure that Lady Cordelia would disapprove, but she didn't want to disappoint Joanna.

The results were disheartening. She had a tiny pile of bluish sand, a larger pile of clear sand, and small piles of other colors. But the very largest of the smaller piles was a reddish brown. Muttering some more, Anoria swept the differently colored piles into containers and carefully labeled them. She had prepared three of the first Separate spell as well as three of the new version of the second Separate spell. She used all six spells before she had enough of the reddish-brown sand to try a pane of that color.

"Anoria, come in for lunch," Debra called. "The dratted sand isn't going anywhere, you know."

Anoria was glad of the break. She was running a bit low on energy, anyway. "Coming," she said, happily leaving the experiment behind for the moment.

Location: Cooper House, Greenshire
Date: 28 Pago, 140 AF

"Drat," Anoria said, just as Gregory walked around the corner of the greenhouse. Joanna was inside, happily arranging benches and tables to suit her plans.

"What's the matter, Anoria?" he asked.

"This is just strange," Anoria said. "Strange. I've made all sorts of glass, but look at this. That's not glass."

"No," Gregory agreed, "it isn't. It looks like iron, but I've never seen iron so thin. How did that happen?"

"No idea. I tried to make glass from the reddish-brown sand, and this is what I got. I wonder why."

Gregory looked at the thin sheet of iron and thought for a moment. "Reddish-brown? Do you have any left? Can I see it?"

"There are a few grains left," Anoria said, handing him the wooden container. "Why iron? This is just strange."

Gregory licked the tip of his finger and picked up a couple of grains of the sand. He sniffed it, and then placed it on his tongue. His face creased in thought. Spitting the grains out, he said, "Rust."

"Rust?"

"Iron rusts, Anoria, unless it's kept oiled. Maybe this is rust that somehow gets into the sand."

"Strange."

"The natural world has many surprises," Gregory agreed. "What else have you done today?"

Location: Cooper House, Greenshire
Date: 29 Pago, 140 AF

"Well, Joanna," Anoria pointed out, "I told you I'd try it and I did. So we have four panes of the greenish glass. Now what are we going to do with them?"

"Father," Joanna asked, "can you fit frames to the windows? Something like the frames for the greenhouse but made for the windows?"

"I can," Michael said. "But what good is it going to do? The windows are three feet by three and one-half feet. The panes Anoria can make are too big on the one hand and too small on the other."

"That's where I come in, sir," Gregory piped up. "I did some research and had a tool made. I can cut the glass. Anoria let me practice on one that came out too dark. If you divided the window frames into fourths, we would need the panes to be about seventeen inches by twenty-one inches. We would have wood around all four sides and a wooden cross-piece in the middle."

"Show me," Michael said. "Prove you can cut it, and then we'll see. I'm not buying a bunch of wood from the sawmill until I know you can cut that glass."

"Right after dinner, sir," Gregory said. "I'll bet you'll be surprised. When I went to see Tess and Father this past fifth day, I also spoke to the smith in Brookshire. He was able, just barely, to duplicate a glass-cutting tool."

"Just show me," Michael said. "Scraped hide has done well enough for centuries. Why do we need glass windows, anyway?"

* * *

After dinner Gregory demonstrated his cutting tool.

"How can that cut the glass?" Michael wanted to know. "That wheel won't cut through that."

"I read a book, sir," Gregory said. "And you're right. It doesn't cut the glass. It 'scores' the glass." He used a straight piece of wood to keep his line going in the right direction and ran the tool over the glass. The scritching noise made Anoria shiver a bit. Then Gregory used the tiny knob on the other end of the tool to tap the scored line. He placed the pane of glass at the edge of the table and forced the free edge down. The glass snapped cleanly into two pieces.

"You see how that works?" Gregory asked. "A single score across the pane, a few taps, and a little pressure. Now I'll do it again for the length of the pane." Gregory demonstrated the cutting technique again. "It took a few tries to get this right," he said. "But I kept at it."

Gregory cut the four panes to the correct shape and laid them side by side on the table. "You see? If we frame this glass this way," Gregory laid out a + sign with some wood pieces, "then we put more wood like so." Gregory surrounded the odd shape with straight pieces of wood. "All we need now is a way to attach the glass to the frame. I think we can do that with very thin wood, attached on the inside of the frame. And it's not a lot of wood, either, so it won't be that much expense."

Michael stared at the contraption for a moment, then grinned. "Ayup. We can do that."

CHAPTER 26

Location: Richlieu House, Greenshire
Date: 9 Wovoro, 140 AF

Charlene Richlieu, wife of the local wheelwright, finished washing the dishes and reached for the wooden container of Joanna Cooper's hand cream that she kept close to the sink. "Drat," she said. "Gayla, did you use the last of the hand cream?" Charlene cast an irritated look at her sixteen-year-old daughter, who looked guiltily down at the floor. "I've told you and told you to stay out of it," Charlene said. "It's hideously expensive, and it's the one thing I buy for myself. Now I'll have to walk out to the Cooper's and get some more. I don't want to wait for the market day."

"I'm sorry, Mother," Gayla said. "It just smells so good. And I do love the way it makes my hands feel."

"Then you can just find a way to make your own money to buy it," Charlene said. "And you can think about that while you finish cleaning the kitchen. Then you can start heating the water for washing the clothes. I'm going to the Cooper's."

Charlene stormed through the house. "Drat the girl," she muttered. "She knows that cream is mine. I'll have to start hiding it."

On her way back out, Charlene grabbed her wooden container and made sure Gayla was doing her chores. She left the house and began walking the half-mile trip to the Cooper home.

It was a lovely summer day, and Charlene began to enjoy the walk. It never hurt to have a break in the routine of keeping house. As she turned up the Cooper's lane, she noticed a kind of glitter in the light. She winced at the brightness of it and began to hurry. "What on earth is that?" she asked the air. "I hope nothing is wrong at the Cooper's."

Charlene made the last turn into the Cooper yard only to be faced with one of the oddest sights she had ever seen. There was a framework of sorts that stretched most of the way across the Cooper house. It looked like some sort of grid of wood. Inside each of the squares a pane of actual glass glittered in the sunshine. Charlene stopped and stared. How could the Coopers have afforded that much glass? True, the family was doing right well these days, but this was just outside of enough. There was a middle-sized fortune in glass alone.

"Hello, Charlene," Debra said. "I thought I saw someone coming up the lane. Would you like a cup of tea?"

Charlene was still staring at the greenhouse. Her eyes followed the wooden supports up the side of the house, and then she noticed that Michael was hanging a window upstairs. "How . . . how . . ." she began, and then stuttered to a stop.

Debra knew that Charlene wanted to ask how they could afford so much glass, but decided not to offer her any information. Charlene was a well-known meddler and gossip in the village. She would find out soon enough. No need to make it easy for her.

"It's a very pleasant place to sit," Debra said, hiding a small smile. "Right now, it's a bit too warm in there, so come on in. I'll make us a cup of tea. Did you need some more hand cream?"

Charlene shook off her stunned look and nodded. "I certainly do, Debra. I think Gayla is using it all over her body, considering the way it disappears. And, yes, I'd love a cup of tea."

As they walked through the greenhouse, Charlene noticed that it was very warm. "It's almost too warm in here, Debra. Almost hot."

"Time to open a vent then," Debra said. "It can get too hot on sunny days, we've found. Just a moment." Debra climbed a ladder to reach the top pane and placed a block of wood to hold it open. Charlene could feel the heated air begin to rush through the vent. It seemed to work almost like a chimney.

"Good heavens," she muttered.

Debra hid a smile. She knew the tale of the greenhouse would be all over the village by evening. "We didn't realize how hot it could get. Michael had to hinge one of the panes to let the heat out. It works quite well. Come on inside."

In the kitchen, Debra bustled about making tea and waited for Charlene's questions. They would come; they always did. It was just a matter of waiting.

"I haven't seen trader's wagons in town, Debra. Where did all that glass come from? It must have come from a long way off," Charlene said.

Debra had to hand it to Charlene this time. It was a masterful way of approaching the subject of "how much did it cost." "It came from the creek right outside, Charlene. Joanna wanted a special room for growing plants. It's called a greenhouse. She and Anoria saw one, once, on a trip to Honth. Anoria researched how to do it, and the two of them made the glass. All it takes is sand and heat. We have sand; Anoria uses magic for the heat."

Charlene shifted a bit uncomfortably. Wizardry used to make Debra uncomfortable as well, but she had grown accustomed to it now. "And they've made enough that you can use it for windows, too? How interesting," Charlene said. "It must make for a much brighter room than scraped hide does."

"It certainly does," Debra agreed. "They're even considering selling it, if anyone happens to want any. It does take a bit of time and work to produce, though. And, as well, summer is busy on a farm. We've all got other work to do."

Debra hid a smile in her tea cup. Charlene Richlieu couldn't bear that anyone should have something she didn't have first. She liked to set trends in the village and had been the first to recommend Joanna's creams and scents. Debra thought that Joanna might just owe Charlene and her busybody ways a discount on the windows. She made a note to mention it to her.

Location: Coooper House, Greenshire
Date: 11 Wovoro, 140 AF

Gregory pressed the glass cutter against the glass with a hard pressure. They had practiced with the cheaper, colored glass, some of which were easier to cut, some harder. This was the first of the truly clear glass he had worked with for cutting. They hadn't wanted to experiment with the clear glass, because it was more valuable. Now that he knew what he was doing, he expected the screech of glass being scored by the cutter. But it didn't come. Nor was there the scratched line in the surface of the glass. He might as well have been using a feather duster.

He tried again pushing harder. Nothing. He looked closer . . . maybe the faintest trace of a line but he couldn't be sure. Meanwhile the glass wasn't doing any good for his cutter.

"What's wrong?" Joanna asked.

"I don't know." Gregory said. Then he stopped himself. He didn't know what the problem was, but he could make a pretty good guess. "You cut glass by scoring it, by scraping against it with something hard," he told Joanna, thinking out loud much to her evident disgust. "Harder than the glass or almost as hard as the glass. Once you have a score mark, you can use that weak point to break the glass in a line. But I'm not getting the score mark, and the only reason for that is because the tool"—he held up the cutting tool—"isn't hard enough or the pressure on it isn't strong enough. This is the same tool I used on all the other glass, and I'm pressing as hard or harder than I ever have. On all the other glass, we got score marks. That just leaves one possibility. This glass is harder than any of the other glass that we have tried it on. As hard as I pressed on that last try I would have thought I would have gotten at least some scoring. I think there is something different about this glass. Different from the glass the orcs make; different from the glass you get from anywhere else. It's harder."

He thought for another moment. "I want to try an experiment."

"What experiment?" Joanna asked.

"I want to drop the glass pane and see if it breaks."

"You break it, you buy it." Joanna pointed her finger at him.

Gregory sighed and picked up the glass pane and indicated to Joanna that she should step back. Then he tossed the pane, and it landed on some rocks, and then bounced.

"Everything I've read about glass talks about how easy it is to break. This is different."

After some more discussion, Gregory and Joanna went looking for Anoria. Maybe she would know what was different about this glass.

"I know they put something in the melted glass at Ethwap," Anoria muttered, as the glass cutter scraped over the glass without making the scratching sound that so bothered her, but also without leaving a score mark. "We always thought it was just so the sand would melt faster. I saw one of the orcs, a really old one, sprinkling something across their pool of liquid glass that their fire elemental swam in. Wherever the elemental would swim, the glass went whiter and more liquid. The orcs would always scoop out the melted glass right behind the elemental. But I have no idea what he was sprinkling. That was the big secret they wouldn't share.

"Well, now it's time to experiment. I wish I could get to Greenwood with its library and alchemical supplies, though."

"What did the powder the orc was sprinkling look like?" Joanna asked.

"It was just a white powder," Anoria said. "Not always the same white powder, but it was almost always white, or at least close to white."

"Well, that makes sense," Gregory said. "If you're making clear glass, you want to start with white."

"So we'll try putting white stuff in with the sand," Joanna said. "What about salt?"

They experimented for days. Some additions had no effect at all, some additions turned colors, and some additions made glass that was too fragile for a window and shattered when they tried to cut it. Finally, they got a mix that seemed to work.

Location: Cooper Home, Greenshire
Date: 29 Wovoro, 140 AF

"How much?" Adolf Jaeger asked with an outraged face.

"Two silvers a pane," Joanna repeated, determined not to back down. Adolf, in her opinion, was a bigoted, bullying busybody. He would never get a discount from her. "The lower quality glass is two silvers a pane, and the clear is three."

"But my windows aren't the right size. I need a different size."

"The only way to do that is to cut the glass to size, Farmer Jaeger," Joanna explained again. "Rob Benedict, the carpenter, can build whatever frame you need. We simply don't have time. We can cut the glass to fit, but we still have to make it with the same spell, and it takes the same amount of time, no matter what we do."

"But she just stands there and wiggles her fingers at it," Jaeger objected. "That hardly seems to be worth two silvers."

"Anoria has been studying for five years to learn it," Joanna said stiffly. "and spends hours crafting the spells that she uses. If you want to use five years, then you can make them yourself. Anoria will even teach it to you, assuming you're willing to dedicate the time. Meanwhile, if you want our glass, it's two silvers for the lower quality and three for the best. We'll cut it to your specifications, and you deliver it to Rob Benedict. What he charges you for the frames is between you and him."

Joanna'd had this same argument several times so far. No one wanted to consider the amount of time and study that had gone into learning the spell or the amount of time it took to craft the spell before it was used. Glass, anywhere, was at least two silvers a pane, likc it or not. The villagers could pay it, or do without. After all, they were saving all the transport costs.

"What about the pieces that are left over?"

"We usually let a bunch of them accumulate and then remelt them," Joanna explained. "It saves time."

"I'll want the scrap you cut off," Jaeger said. "I'll get my money's worth, and you'll not keep what I've paid for."

"That's just fine," Joanna agreed. "I've no idea what you'll use them for, but you're right. The cutoff pieces belong to you. Just try not to cut yourself. It's really easy to do that."

Jaeger huffed a bit, but handed over half the agreed-on price. "Here are the measurements," he said. "When will the glass be ready?"

"In three days," Joanna answered. "It will take that long to make it."

"Three days!" Farmer Jaeger's face began to redden again.

"If you'd rather wait three months for it to get here from Ethwap, that will be just fine with me," Joanna said. "Do you want it or not? If not, you can have your money back."

Jaeger deflated a bit. All the women of the town were after glass windows, at least on the side of the house that was visible to the road. "I'll take it," he muttered. "Three days, right?"

Joanna nodded, and Jaeger left. He was still a bit huffy about it, but Mistress Jaeger had been making his life miserable for two weeks now, as Joanna had heard from gossip. "Serves you right, you old crow," she muttered.

"Boo."

Joanna jumped at the sound from behind her and turned to see Anoria grinning at her.

"Joanna," Anoria asked, "why three days? You know perfectly well that it could be ready tomorrow."

"Because he made me angry." Joanna sniffed. "And what's more, it doesn't hurt to make them wait. They'll just want it that much more. Besides, if you're ahead of the demand, maybe we'll have time to try the colored glass. I really want to know about that."

CHAPTER 27

Location: Cooper Home, Greenshire
Date: 15 Estormany, 140 AF

Debra smiled to herself as she watched Joanna, Anoria, and Gregory try their best to get organized. Anoria was using spells as quickly as she could craft them, something Debra was still surprised to find she was comfortable watching. The greenhouse was proving to be a wonderful addition to their home too. Debra was sitting in a chair next to a small table, surrounded by warmth and sunshine. It would be marvelous on a sunny winter day, she thought.

Still, the young people had her smiling. "Clarence, please don't bump the table again," Joanna said with a certain amount of annoyance. "It will get all this stuff mixed up again. If you want to help, go fill the buckets."

Clarence, at a rather rambunctious eight years old, happily complied. He was always happy to dig sand out of the creek. He grabbed two buckets and a scoop to fill them and ran toward the creek bank. Debra knew he'd come back with full buckets and dirty clothes again.

"All right," Anoria muttered. Where's the container for the white stuff?" Debra could see about thirty small piles of differently colored sand on the table. Anoria and Joanna had appropriated nearly every container in the house in an attempt to keep all the colors and weights separated. By far the largest contained transparent sand. It was what had made such wonderfully clear glass. It looked white to Debra, but Anoria insisted it was transparent. Second was the reddish-brown color that produced a thin sheet of iron. It was almost half as big as the white sand. The white sand that Anoria was talking about was a bit different from the transparent. It was chalky and looked more like whitewash.

"White stuff," Joanna said, checking labels. "Here, white stuff. What's next?"

Anoria carefully placed the white powder in the container before saying, "Ahhhh, brown stuff, the really dark brown stuff."

Joanna handed her the appropriate container and looked over Anoria's shoulder. "The bluish green next?"

"Yah."

In all, separating all the weights and colors of powder took a good while. The youngsters had been working on collecting all the different colors for a couple of weeks now. Many of the containers contained very tiny amounts of powders; several others contained quite a bit. One even contained a little bit of what Debra thought was gold.

"All right, then," Anoria said. "I don't see the point in making more of the iron, so let's just set that aside for now. What color shall we try first?"

"I like this blue," Gregory said. "Let's try the blue first."

The Melt spell made Debra a little nervous, but Clarence was at the creek, and the girls and Gregory moved back. Debra watched nervously as Anoria cast "Melt."

When the table cooled, Anoria held up a deep blue sheet of something to the sky. "Drat," she said. "It doesn't let any light through at all."

They all examined the flat rock for a while. Debra rather liked it. True, it wasn't glass, but it was pretty. "I'd like to have that," she said. "It's just the thing to set the stew pot on top of. It will keep it from burning the table."

"Oh," Anoria said. "I hadn't thought of that. You're welcome to it. I don't know if it would cut down like the windows, so it's just as well for you to have it." The three experimenters fell into conversation for a while.

Finally, Gregory, after a bit of thought, said, "Anoria, do you have any more of the Melt spell prepared?"

"Two," Anoria answered. "I knew we were going to melt today, instead of all that separating. Why?"

"Well," Gregory answered, "how about making another couple of sheets of the iron, then? We'll think about this other. Maybe one of us will have an idea. Meanwhile, though, I'd be willing to bet that the blacksmith will have a use for that iron. He'll probably be willing to buy it. And I want to stop by the temple, as well."

Anoria shrugged off her irritation at the blue rock. "Fine with me," she said. "At least it isn't separating all those little colors of dirt."

Location: Blacksmith Shop, Greenshire
Date: 15 Estormany, 140 AF

The sign over the door of the shop showed a horseshoe and an anvil. William Hagen was the local blacksmith and farrier as well as the owner of a substantial farm he had inherited. His wife, Marlene, ran the farm and directed the farmhands. William's vocation was the working of metal, any metal. He just loved it.

"Ah, young Gregory," William boomed. "How much longer will you be with us? I understand you've your last year of seminary to complete."

Gregory smiled. William was such a cheerful person that it was hard to take offense at his personal questions. "About another six months of school," Gregory said. "Then I'll be off to a village somewhere. No idea where, of course. Wherever there's a vacancy. I'd certainly like it to be near here, though. I've loved the Brookshire and Greenshire area ever since Father and I moved here from Gent."

"Ah," William smiled. " 'Tis a very good village, this. I'm quite fond of it myself. And what's that you're carrying, young Gregory? Looks like iron of some sort."

Gregory laid the five sheets of Anoria's iron in front of William. Falling into the local dialect, he said, "Aye, 'tis. Young Anoria, in her experimenting with the glass, she discovered this. I'd thought that it might be somewhat useful to you."

William examined the thin iron sheets. " 'Twill, indeed. Hinges. Very good hinges it will make, and 'tis already flat and even. Very little work to do, aside from cutting and drilling the holes. Where did this come from, boy? I've never seen such."

"Mistress Anoria, when she made the glass, discovered that some of the sand was iron. She was trying to make a pane of glass but got this instead. I'd thought you might find a use, so I had her make more. If you can use it, well, I'd expect she could make a bit more as well."

"Can," William agreed. "And I'll not be quibbling, either." William's cheerful face was beaming. " 'Twill save more time than you can imagine, this. Already flat and smooth. Very little working to do. What's she asking for it?"

"Six copper a sheet," Gregory answered. A sniff behind him drew his attention, and he turned to see Larendo Firebird.

"Pandering for the wizard?" Larendo asked in a superior voice. "I shouldn't think a person who hoped to become an intercessor of Barra would do such a thing. I certainly wouldn't, and I wouldn't have an association with a notorious wizard, either." Larendo extended a stirrup that needed repair to William and was surprised when William didn't extend his hand.

"I'll be thanking you not to be calling Mistress Anoria 'notorious,' " William said. "It's very helpful, she is, and Lady Cordelia as well. They've both done quite a lot for this village, what with the schools and the glass and all. I'll not be wanting your business, Intercessor, not if you're going to be spreading such, such . . ." William's vocabulary failed him at that point.

"Wizardry is not normal," Larendo began, and Gregory cut him off.

"That is not your decision, Intercessor Larendo," Gregory said, and fell back into his more educated vocabulary. "While many in the temple are suspicious of wizards—and I will concede, not without cause—there is no actual stricture in the temple to prevent an intercessor from associating with a wizard."

Gregory ended his speech with the words, "Or, for that matter, becoming one." He glared, triumphantly, at Larendo. The various temples might have a problem with wizards, but the gods certainly didn't. There was more than one intercessor who was also a wizard, and some of them received spells from the gods they followed. Granted, most of them were intercessors of Zagrod, the god of knowledge, but not all. More importantly, in the last few months Gregory had started receiving spells from Barra. Only the most minor, so far, but Gregory hadn't even officially taken his final vows yet. Whatever Intercessor Firebird thought about magic, clearly Barra didn't object.

Larendo Firebird gaped at William Hagen, who was nodding vigorously. William was, in all truth, a very powerful man in Greenshire, and it behooved Larendo to pay attention to his preferences. Deciding rapidly that this was not the place to air his personal feelings, Larendo nodded. "True. That does not prevent a certain distrust, however."

"Might be." William sniffed, in imitation of Larendo's own sniff. "Might be. But 'tis a fair bit better to judge on actions and not on hearsay."

CHAPTER 28

Location: Cooper Home, Greenshire
Date: 23 Estormany, 140 AF

Clarence, it had to be admitted, was a bit bored with the stream and the sand. He was almost looking forward to school. Life on the farm could be a little too . . . rural. Most of the other boys his age were actively working on the farms, running errands and so forth. But with Anoria, Joanna, the hired girls, and Gregory around, as well as the hired man Michael had taken on, Clarence was at loose ends.

He sat in the greenhouse and ground a charred stick against the tile floor and muttered to himself. "I'm bored, I'm bored, I'm bored." He had quite a little pile of ground charcoal when Debra found him sulking.

"Clarence, what kind of mess are you making now?" Debra asked. "Grinding a stick against the floor someone has to clean! How very kind of you." Debra's face was quite cross. "I suspect we shall have to find you a chore, since you can't seem to occupy yourself without making messes."

Clarence grabbed a broom and began to sweep. "I'll take care of it," he muttered.

"I'll take care of it, what?" Debra asked.

"I'll take care of it, ma'am," Clarence corrected. Mother could be a little short-tempered when she wanted to be. It wasn't a really good idea to upset her.

"Fine," Debra said. "And when you've finished that, Anoria has a proposition for you. It involves being paid for work, I might add. Please finish and come to the kitchen." Debra's eyes grew a bit more kind as she said, "There are some fresh cookies."

"I'll be right in, Mama," Clarence said, breaking into a big smile. Cookies weren't everyday fare, after all.

Debra left the greenhouse to return to the kitchen. Clarence, in a hurry, gathered the charcoal dust. Rather than take the three seconds needed to dump it outside, he dumped it in one of Anoria's many containers. He shook it up a bit, just in case anyone noticed the black powder on top of the rusty red powder.

This operation, of course, took longer than dumping the charcoal outside, but Clarence didn't notice that.

Location: Cooper Home, Greenshire
Date: 23 Estormany, 140 AF

"Gregory is a very learned person, isn't he?" Joanna asked, after the girls had given up the experiments for the day. They were in the room they shared when Anoria was visiting, each studying a different book.

"Hmmmm?"

"I said Gregory has two tails and a pitchfork," Joanna said.

"Um hmmm."

"Anoria, will you please stop that?" Joanna asked. "Hello? Hello? Joanna would like Anoria to answer her. May I have your attention, please?"

Anoria looked up from the book she was studying and grinned. "I heard you. I just wanted to see what you'd do if I agreed he had two tails. And, Mistress Joanna, I'm trying to figure out why the dratted glass comes out looking like a rock or as a piece of iron. Glass that won't let light through it isn't much use, is it?"

"Actually, I think it would be good for perfume bottles," Joanna said. "If you can figure out how to do bottles, that is. A lot of herbs retain their healing properties better if they're kept in the dark. And, as far as it being too dark . . . maybe if you put some of the transparent sand with the colored sand? It couldn't hurt to try it that way."

"Hmmmm . . ."

Location: Cooper Home, Greenshire
Date: 24 Estormany, 140 AF

"All right," Anoria said. "We'll give this a try. I have three Melt spells ready." Anoria used yet another container to measure out nearly enough of the transparent sand and then mixed in a small scoop of the blue powder. After it was well mixed, she poured it onto the little table. Standing back, she invoked the Melt spell. Gregory and Joanna watched, wondering what would happen. When the heat had returned to the plane of fire, Anoria picked up the result and held it to the sun.

"Oh, look," Joanna said. "It worked, it worked!"

And it had. Anoria was holding up a two-by-two-foot pane of sky blue glass. It sparkled in the sun.

Anoria set it carefully aside and grinned. "What next? Let's see what happens next. There's enough transparent sand to try two more; then I'll have to do more separating. What do we have the most of?"

"This brown stuff, I think," Joanna said and began to mix and measure. "I wonder if it will make brown glass. Brown glass would be good for keeping herbs away from the light."

"We'll see soon," Anoria smiled. "When Cordelia gets back from her visit, I'll check the spell books and see if we can find a way to shape it."

Anoria used "melt" again, but the result was not in the least brown. She held up a beautiful, translucent pane of golden-yellow glass to the sun.

"Wow," Gregory said. "It's almost the color of ripe wheat. Beautiful, just beautiful."

The girls were both very excited by now. "What next?" Joanna jittered. "What next?"

"Let's try the bluish green," Gregory suggested. "That would be pretty."

The result was more than pretty. The bright red glass sparkled in the sun like a ruby.

"Why, I wonder," Anoria mused as she wrote down the results and measures, "does the bluish-green powder make red glass? And I wonder what does make green glass."

"We'll find out, sooner or later," Joanna said, laughing. "Red glass. Can you imagine?"

Location: Cooper Home, Greenshire
Date: 25 Estormany, 140 AF

"Mistress Anoria." William Hagen smiled. "It's good to see you." He was standing at the door of the little glassmaking shop Michael had built for Anoria. It was a small building with good windows and a table and shelves for all the various containers of colored sand.

"Thank you, Master Hagen," Anoria smiled back. "It's always good to see you too. What can I do for you?"

Anoria was sorting sand again. It was a boring chore but had to be done to get properly colored bits of sand. She swept a pile of the bluish-green stuff into a container and straightened. "Forgive me," she said to Master Hagen. "We've found that a good breeze can undo a day's work if we're not careful. So I've learned to sort all this stuff right away."

"Not a problem, not at all," William smiled. "What you've done with the iron, can you do it some more? It's made some good hinges, and now that people are wanting so many windows, they're buying hinges to hang them with. Then they can open the window to let the air in. So I've sold every hinge I made, and I need some more. Same price as before, six copper a sheet."

"I can do three sheets right now, I think," Anoria said, reaching for the container of reddish brown sand. "Did you want to wait, or would you rather not watch?"

William settled onto a stool Anoria kept to sit on and grinned even more widely. "It's metalworking, of a sort. I'm always interested in that, no matter how it's done. Wizard or not, good metal is good metal. I'll watch if you've no objection."

Anoria grinned a bit herself. Quite a number of people were fascinated to watch the glass melt. Gayla Richlieu had spread the word about it, and Anoria was getting used to having the occasional audience. She measured out the sand she needed and used "melt." William even leaned forward a bit to watch more closely. When the sheet had cooled, Anoria took it out of the table and handed it to him.

William looked at it closely. "It's not the same as before," he said. "Darker." William flexed the sheet a bit. "Not so easily bent, either. How have you changed it?"

Anoria stared at the container in wonder. "I don't know. We've always put that color in this container. Give me a moment and I'll separate it and see what has happened."

"Aye," William said. "This is steel, not iron. And I'll buy it. Seven copper a sheet. But I want to know how you did it."

"So do I," Anoria muttered, scooping the offending powder onto her melting table. "So do I."

Anoria and William bent over to watch. She used the first Separate spell and the sand shifted. Reddish brown sand lay in one pile and a few tiny black flecks lay in another.

"What in the world," Anoria said, "is that? It wasn't there before. I know it."

William dampened his forefinger with his tongue and picked up some of the tiny black flecks. He examined them intensely and even walked to the door to get more light. "Charcoal."

"Charcoal?" Anoria asked, forehead creased. "Charcoal. I wonder how that got in there. I'll separate the rest of it and melt your iron sheet for you."

"Nah," William grinned. "Leave it. In fact, mix that back in, if you would. It makes sense, in a way. When I make steel, I put it in with charcoal and heat it. What you had before was wrought iron. What you have here is steel, but some steel is better than others. I'd have to test this to see how it works. I'll buy it, though, and probably all that you can make. If it's good steel, it will save me a lot of work."

Location: Cooper Home, Greenshire
Date: 25 Estormany, 140 AF

The fortuitous addition of the charcoal was explained that evening at supper. Debra looked sternly at Clarence when Anoria told what had happened. "Clarence, I expect you can explain it, can't you?"

Clarence shifted uncomfortably under his mother's glare. "Yes," he said, face reddening. "I'd made a mess with a burnt stick. I swept it up, but I threw it in the container. I didn't mean to do anything wrong."

"You just got yourself another job," Debra said. "Now you get to grind burnt sticks into powder for Anoria. For a week. Perhaps you'll learn not to be so lazy. She may not need it now, but I'm sure William Hagen will want more of that steel."

"I hope not too much," Joanna muttered. "We get seven coppers a sheet for the steel, but two silvers for the glass."

Michael made a grunting sound and prepared to make one of his rare speeches. "Money isn't everything, daughter. William Hagen is a good neighbor and a good man. Doesn't hurt to be on good terms with him. Or anyone else, for that matter."

"Besides," Anoria said, "I learn something new with every melt I do. Doing glass all the time would be boring, and I wouldn't learn as much."

CHAPTER 29

Location: Cooper Home, Greenshire
Date: 27 Estormany, 140 AF

Gregory had a couple of weeks left of his break and wanted to try something. All the colored glass was beautiful, but it was useless for windows. He borrowed a piece of paper from Anoria and sat down to draw a picture.

"Look at this," he said. "I think I can make a picture with the glass if I can just figure out how to hold all the different pieces together." Gregory had drawn a simple picture of the god of harvests watching over a wheat field. "I found out that I can cut wavy lines as well as straight ones, and I've been practicing on the scraps."

Not everyone in the village wanted the leftover glass, unlike Farmer Jaeger. There was a growing pile of scrap glass in the greenhouse. It was even becoming a bit of a danger. Like all village folk, Gregory hated to waste anything. "There is one thing I'd like to try, Anoria," he said. "We've got that golden yellow glass, but it doesn't look quite enough like wheat to me. If we sprinkled shards of that dark brown piece in a pattern on the yellow glass, do you think you could remelt it and see what happens? I'd like to have an impression of wheat waving in the breeze."

The whole family was becoming interested in this project. Even Clarence piped up, "I'll break that dark brown piece for you, Gregory."

Debra cast Clarence a reproving glance. "You'll need to find a safe way to do that, judging from that cut on Gregory's hand."

"Glass cutting is a bit of a tricky business," Gregory admitted. "That healing salve of Joanna's helps a lot, I've noticed. But I really want to try this, I do. I'll be going to Brookshire tomorrow, to see Father and Tess. I'll try to think of a way to hold the pieces together while I walk. Would you go ahead and try the remelt, Anoria?"

Anoria nodded and took a sip of her after-supper tea. "First thing in the morning," she said. "I'm tired of melting iron and separating sand anyway."

Location: Cooper Home, Greenshire
Date: 27 Estormany, 140 AF

"Clarence, be careful," Anoria said. Clarence was being a bit too enthusiastic about breaking the sheet of brown glass. "I don't want to step on some tiny splinter and cut my feet."

Clarence calmed down his breaking a bit. Then Gregory very carefully collected some of the smaller shards, both for his fingers' sake and for the art's sake. He started placing the shards on the melting table, arranged in a pattern that would make a picture. The dark brown glass was placed on the yellow pane in the hopes that when the melt happened, the two colors would bond together.

"All right," Anoria said. "Stand back, both of you." Then she cast "Melt."

When the table cooled, Gregory rushed over. The dark brown glass was still sitting on the yellow pane and apparently totally unaffected by the spell. "What happened?"

"The spell has to have just the right amount of material," Anoria said. If there's not enough material, the spell won't work at all. If there's too much, the excess is ignored. The spell doesn't affect it. We started with a full pane of glass and didn't need any more, so the brown glass was ignored."

"So, does that mean I get to break the yellow glass," Clarence wanted to know.

Anoria and Gregory looked at each other and grinned. "Yes, I guess it does," Anoria said. "But be careful!"

Two small cuts on Clarence's fingers later, Anoria thought they had the right amount of glass. Any excess would be ignored, after all. "Stand back," she said, and invoked the spell again.

The table heated and cooled, and on the surface a uniform pane of glass appeared, with a few shards of leftover. Gregory picked up the pane and held it to the sun. "Oh, drat."

The glass was now a uniform yellow, but a shade darker than it had been. "That's not going to work," Gregory muttered. "Not the way I wanted."

"There must be something about the spell that mixes everything up evenly. And it's not something I can change by myself. Lady Cordelia would kill me if I tried changing a spell without her," Anoria said, feeling increasingly guilty about the changes she'd made to the sorting spell. It hadn't seemed dangerous at the time, but she was beginning to think that something could have gone wrong in a very bad way. Honestly, she wasn't sure what could have gone wrong. The spell already separated the particles of sand by color. All she'd done was adjust where it put them.

"She might kill you if the spell didn't!" Gregory said, unknowingly making Anoria feel even guiltier. "Even I know that changing spells is dangerous. We'll have to come up with some other way."

CHAPTER 30

Location: Cooper Home, Greenshire
Date: 4 Barra, 140 AF

"Anoria, what have you been doing?" Cordelia asked. "You came here to make the glass for the greenhouse, but you look exhausted. You've had four months. You shouldn't be that tired."

Anoria did look tired, but triumphant at the same time, and more than a little nervous. "Look, Cordelia. Look at this spell. I worked it out myself."

Cordelia looked at the spell Anoria had written down and was amazed. "You tried this? It works? It works just like this?"

"It does." Anoria nodded. "And I'll bet I'm the only person who's ever done that too. You know, if you look around at most glass, it's kind of greenish-colored, no matter how expensive it is."

Cordelia didn't know whether to hug the girl or strangle her. What she had done was amazingly clever, and it was truly a very minor modification of the spell. At the same time, even very minor modifications could have significant and unpredictable consequences. A different very minor modification of that spell could have kept separating particles until it used up all the magic in the area, leaving Anoria, the pot, the ground, and anybody else within a couple of hundred feet separated into their component parts. Anoria knew better! But it worked. And Cordelia didn't really feel comfortable with the idea of punishing Anoria for getting it right.

"I was quite pleased with the fact the glass we made was clearer and finer than the glass they make in Ethwap. But, Anoria, you know better than to experiment with a spell without supervision." Then Cordelia pointed at a rune in the spell description. "What would happened if you had adjusted this rune to be a bit bluer?"

Anoria looked and admitted, "I don't know."

"It would have made the spell break out of the separating pot and divide up your elements, each into their own individual color. And when I got back, all there would have been was various piles of dust where Anoria used to be. And quite possibly where Joanna used to be. And Debra. And little Clarence. You're not ready to do spell experiments yet. This one worked, and it was very clever. But at the same time, it was a very, very dangerous thing to do. What made you do it? You had to know I would object."

"Well, I was explaining to Joanna about separating out the different colors of sand, and she suggested that we try making different colors of glass with it, and so I did, and we did . . ." Anoria's voice trailed off as she realized that her explanation in no way justified the risks she had taken. "But it worked!"

"Slow down," Cordelia said. "And let me think."

After a few moments of quiet and another look at the spell, Cordelia's brow creased. "All you did was adjust a component to the spell, a very simple one. You've caused it to separate the different colors of sand. Instead of just isolating the clear sand, it now isolates all of the different colors into separate piles, is that right?"

"Yes." Anoria nodded. "And then we collect all the different colors into separate containers by hand. Once they're separated, it's easy to tell which color is which." She hesitated and then went on in a rush, "I did the same thing to the Separate by Weight spell."

"And then you can make panes of colored glass?"

Anoria nodded hopefully. "Sort of. At first, I thought it was kind of silly. But Joanna said there might be a use for it. We tried making glass out of the different colored sand, and it didn't work all that well. It did do some interesting stuff, though. It turned out that the red in brown dust is some strange kind of iron. When we put it on the table and cast the spell, we didn't get glass."

"Girl," Cordelia said with a certain amount of asperity, "don't keep me waiting like that. What did you get that time?"

"It was strange, really it was. The reddish-brown dust, well, it turned into a thin sheet of iron. Isn't that strange? After that we tried mixing some of the different colored sands in with the white sand and got some interesting colors, but it's still strange. The reddish-brown sand made the glass green or brown, and the more there was, the darker it got till you couldn't see through it. We got a really lovely blue, though."

"What is anyone going to do with colored glass?" Cordelia asked, interested in spite of her better judgment. "Wouldn't it be kind of gloomy in a window?"

"Well, it was Joanna who suggested it," Anoria said. "We were talking about the colored glass, and she said that we ought to add some clear back to it, to make it translucent. Then, Gregory jumped in. You know, Tess' stepson? He saw a bunch of broken glass and sort of liked the color combinations. So he figured that if you take the colored panes, and you could cut it into shape. Then you can put all the shapes together into a picture."

"How do you hold it together?"

"That was the clever part." Anoria beamed. "Gregory said that you could use soft lead, if you made thick wire with a groove on each side. He calls it 'caming lead' because he said it came to him in a dream. He got someone in Brookshire to make what he wanted, and then he made a picture for the temple. It hangs in the window, and the colors are just beautiful when the sun shines through it."

Cordelia was very pleased on the one hand, but still concerned that Anoria might push herself too fast and get hurt. Anoria was finding ways to make a living without going on dangerous adventures. The girl was overtired right now, and adventuring wasn't any more dangerous than modifying spells. She'd worked too hard.

But glass was very, very expensive. And colored glass, well, that was something difficult to do. The glassmakers often made colored glass but had very little control over how the color came out. Perhaps it was because the separating spell separated the sands better.

Cordelia thought that, for now at least, she would let the matter of adjusting spells go. After all, Anoria hadn't come to any harm. "Let's go take a look at this picture window," Cordelia suggested. "It sounds beautiful."

"Gregory says that every temple in the country will want a picture like it," Anoria said.

Cordelia suddenly had a feeling that she was going to hear an awful lot of "Gregory says" for a while.

Location: Temple of Barra, Greenshire
Date: 4 Barra, 140 AF

The window in the temple was mostly green, yellow, and blue. It showed the god of harvest looking over the harvesting of wheat. Cordelia imagined that temples dedicated primarily to other gods would show other scenes. The local intercessor was somewhat cold to them. Apparently the fact of the new window had not made him comfortable with having a wizard in the area. It was still a lovely window, though.

On their way out of the temple, they were approached by the village smith. He wanted to order more sheets of iron and steel from Anoria. Cordelia was amazed at all that Anoria had produced over the summer. All the discussion that followed made her wonder what other uses the table and its associated spell could be put to.

CHAPTER 31

Location: Greenwood
Date: 12 Barra, 140 AF

"It's good to be home." Anoria smiled at Cordelia over her cup of cocoa. "I like summers in the village, and I made a good bit of money this year, but it's nice to have a break. I want to do some studying and see if I can develop a few more spells this winter."

"You may have created a monster, you know," Cordelia said. "Glassmaking will bring in a fair amount of money, but it will also take up a lot of time. And the steelmaking, well, it's not so much of the money, but steel is a very useful thing to have."

Anoria nodded. "I used up all of the supplies before I left. William Hagen has all he's going to get until winter is over, and I can dig more sand out of the stream. And I made stacks and stacks of glass panes for Joanna to sell. As well as a stack of colored glass for Gregory to take to seminary with him. Did you know that he's getting spells from Barra?"

"Hmmm," Cordelia said. "No, I didn't. Is he going to go adventuring, do you think? You know that many intercessors do go adventuring as part of their service to the gods, though it's less common for Barra's intercessors than for Noron's."

"I don't think he will," Anoria mumbled through a bite of pastry. She stopped trying to talk and took a sip of cocoa. "He said he was going to ask for Greenshire as his temple. He's got no more urge to wander than I have, really."

"Speaking of which," Cordelia said, "We've a bit of traveling to do this winter. Spices, paper, ink, that sort of thing. And study. There's a good bit more to learn, for both of us. A wizard who doesn't study, well, that's a wizard who's not doing her job."

"And, this year, I can do a bit of buying myself," Anoria was pleased to announce. "I've made a bit of money and there's this, as well." She handed Cordelia a small, covered, wooden box. "There's not a lot, but I couldn't see letting it go to waste."

Cordelia opened the box and saw a small pile of gold dust. True, it wasn't much. "Where did this come from?"

"The sand. When I sorted out the sand there were usually a few flecks of gold. Not much, sometimes not any. But that accumulated, and I kept it. It was another useful side effect of the Separate spell."

"And I suppose you'll be wanting to separate dirt wherever we go this winter, won't you?" Cordelia grinned. "Ah, well. Everyone needs a hobby, don't they?"

Location: Seminary, Gent
Date: 20 Cashi, 140 AF

"You've got to see this," Professor Andiris told Professor Mallory. "It's pretty amazing, I think."

Professor Andiris knocked on the student's door and waited for an answer.

"Come in," came the muffled reply, over the sound of tapping.

The two professors entered to see an unusual sight. Normally a seminary student would be immersed in his books at this hour, but Gregory was standing at a table, tapping what looked like horseshoe nails into a piece of wood the size of his table. "I told you I wanted Mallory to see this, Gregory," Professor Andiris said, "so I've brought him along."

The seminary was located in an old castle on a hill. The rooms for the senior students were located on the west side of the seminary, so at this hour of the evening the sun was shining in the unshuttered window. The scene on the table was incomplete, but there was a finished one in the window.

Both men looked at the window, and Mallory exclaimed, "My word. The image is lovely, but the effect on the room is glorious."

"It is nice, isn't it?" Gregory smiled. Then he indicated the scene on the table. "This time I'm doing a window to represent Barra at the beginning of spring."

Professor Andiris marveled at the representation. "You've caught that springtime feeling, my boy. I can almost smell the fresh-turned earth."

Professor Mallory was senior to Andiris in the temple and happened to be in charge of parish assignments. He knew about Gregory and his spells. "An interesting hobby. Quite unique," he said. "Going to be difficult to keep it up, though, when you go off on your quests."

"Ah," Gregory said, a bit uncomfortably. "I'd like to talk to you about that, sir. It's just that I've got no wish to wander, never have. I'd most like to have the parish of Greenshire. I feel called upon to be a village intercessor, not a High Intercessor."

"Greenshire does have an intercessor, doesn't it?" Mallory asked.

"Larendo Firebird," Gregory answered. "He's a very intelligent man. I spoke to him several times this year. A bit rigid, perhaps, for a village intercessor. I think he'd be happier in administration, quite frankly."

"You're sure?" Mallory asked. "The gods have a way of getting us to go where they want us to. And they often do it whether it's what we want or not. The quests Barra will send you on will hone your skills and bring you more rank, you understand."

"Quite sure, sir," Gregory said. "A village intercessor, that's what I want. Always have. And it seems to be what Barra wants for me."

Mallory stared a bit longer at the window Gregory was making. "You know, Gregory, I have a bright, western exposure in my office. Do you suppose you could produce a window for me? Even, perhaps, a small representation of Zagrod to hang in the window? I think the sun shining through purple glass would be a lovely sight."

"I'll see what I can do," Gregory agreed. "A book in black and white, surrounded by purple?"

"Exactly."

Location: University of Drakan, Dragon Lands
Date: 14 Coganie, 140 AF

"Eeep," Anoria said. "I never dreamed it would cost that much. Five thousand gold. I'll never have that much."

"Well, it's just an estimate," Cordelia said. "It could take more. But we could probably produce something that will use the sorting spells you already have for about five hundred gold. But something that worked all the time, without a spell every time? No, that would take a lot more research and would be a powerful magical item. Which means a lot more gold and time."

Anoria slumped back into the chair. "Drat. Drat. Drat," she muttered. "Somehow, some way, we really need to develop a way to make writing spells cheaper. I wonder if you could use Wizard's Mark to write spells into the spell book."

"Wizard's Mark is a bit more limited than that," Cordelia explained. "We've used it for a lot of things, but it just isn't big enough or strong enough to write spells all day."

"An improved Wizard's Mark, maybe," Anoria suggested. "Something that would write all day?"

Cordelia started to say no, but stopped herself. "I'll look into it," she said. "We might be able to do something like that. I'll think about it. Meanwhile, let's go traveling. I'm tired of snow."

Anoria giggled. "I doubt you'll ever be able to just stop your wandering ways, Lady Cordelia. You're off to visit or travel every time you get rested up."

Location: Cooper House, Greenshire

Date: 17 Coganie, 140 AF

"I understand," Joanna told Rob Benedict, the local carpenter. "I rather miss the added income myself. But we've used up all the big panes of glass. All I've got left is the trimmings from those. Which," Joanna's eyes gleamed a bit, "I'll be happy to sell you. I suppose you could build many-paned windows with them. Or, come to think of it, you might want to build doors with windows in them."

"That might do," Rob mused. "When the visitors from the other villages around here saw all the windows, I had quite a rush on them. Now they're clamoring for more. And here you are, out of glass." Rob took a sip of the hot cider Debra had prepared. It had been a cold walk, she knew.

"Anoria will be back in the spring," Debra said. "They'll just have to wait, just as William Hagen will have to wait for more steel. We can't help that Anoria isn't here, after all. The girl has her training to do. She's not exactly the property of the folk, and I wish people would understand that. She's her own person and not at the beck and call of just anyone who wants something anytime."

"Aye," Rob murmured into his mug. "It's just she's familiar to us all and very helpful when she can be. I think we all miss her when she goes away. Even old Widow Mead, back on market day, said something about missing Anoria's smiling face around the village. And did you hear the latest news?" Rob extended his cup for a refill and took one of Debra's ginger cookies as well.

"What news?" Joanna asked. "I didn't feel like digging a path through all that snow on market day, so I stayed home and made some more salves and perfumes."

"The intercessor, Larendo Firebird," Rob said. "He's gone and gotten himself a new job with the temple. Moving to Gent this spring, he is. We'll be getting a new intercessor of Barra."

Debra's smile brightened a bit. Relations with Larendo hadn't gotten any better for her family even though he had stopped speaking against Anoria, at least in public. "Do we know his name yet?"

"Expect we'll hear that about the time he or she shows up." Rob drained his cup. "Very well, then. I'll buy the scrap glass. Perhaps there's something that can be made of it. And the wife, she wants another flagon of the rose perfume. The plain kind, not the sindal combination. I like her to smell like a flower, not that heavy smell from the sindal."

Joanna was happy to comply with that request. "I've a new scent for men, as well," she mentioned. "Take a whiff of this and tell me what you think." She opened a large jug and waved it under Rob's nose. He took a sniff.

"A bit like rosemary," he said. "Sharper, though. Has a woodsy smell to it."

"Just right for a man, I thought," Joanna said. "I'm calling it 'after shave.' Father uses it after he shaves in the morning. He says it makes his face feel good. Here, take a sample and try it in the morning. Let me know what you think." She poured a sample into a very small jug. "And, I'll want that little jug back, please, sir," she added. "They're hard to find, those small ones. We may have windows, but bottles are a whole different thing. I've asked Anoria to see what she can do about that."

Rob sniffed. "Nice enough, but I don't think so. I'm a carpenter, so I always smell like wood."

"Ah, well, then," Joanna said. "I'll see if someone else wants it. It's got to smell better than pig manure."

"But pig manure is what the women around here are used to!" Rob said with a laugh.

CHAPTER 32

Location: Greenwood
Date: 14 Justain, 141 AF

"What are you looking into now?" Cordelia asked.

Anoria, as usual when they were home, was engrossed in a book. "Joanna wants a better way to make bottles," Anoria muttered. "So I'm trying to find a way to shape the glass into a bottle shape. And knowing Joanna, I expect she'll want bowls and cups and who knows what else."

Cordelia felt her preoccupation with developing a way to make recording spells less expensive fade a bit. "Now that's an interesting application," she said. "How would we do that?"

"No idea," Anoria admitted. "I was thinking about the glass table and started looking at how you made it. But it's a little too complicated for me, so far. I was about to ask you about it."

"Hmmm," Cordelia muttered. "Hand me that book, please."

Location: Greenwood
Date: 11 Banth, 141 AF

"Well, we can do it," Cordelia decided. "And it will be worth it too. At least in the long run. We only have to make the table once, after all."

"But we have to make a different table for each thing we want to make," Anoria pointed out. "That's a lot of money. An awful lot of money."

Cordelia shook her head at Anoria. Anoria noticed that there was a strand or two of silver in Cordelia's hair now, and wondered just how old Cordelia really was. Cordelia was a little vague about her age. She didn't look as old as she probably was, Anoria was pretty sure.

"Honestly, Anoria," Cordelia said. "I've never met two girls who were so concerned with money. Joanna with making it and you with saving it. Spending is what it's for, you know. I've been explaining that to you for years. True, it will cost some money for each table. It will take time to develop each one, as well. That's part of the challenge of it. It's a puzzle to solve, just like the puzzles you used to solve in your books. If I'm not concerned with how much it costs, why are you worried about it? I've explained a dozen times that I want you well set up."

Anoria still felt that she should pay for her training. It was just what people did. "I just still feel like the training costs too much. I've always felt guilty about that."

Cordelia smiled. "I know that, dear. But if I'd had a daughter, I'd have hoped to train her. I didn't, not until you came along."

Tears began forming in Anoria's eyes. "You think of me as a daughter?"

Cordelia rose from her favorite chair and came to hug Anoria. "Well, of course, I do, you ninny," she said. "Why would I have put up with you all these years if I didn't?"

Location: Cooper House, Greenshire
Date: 20 Noron, 141 AF

When Anoria and Cordelia arrived at the farm in early spring, it was to a house filled with happiness. Tess and her husband, Armand, were visiting and thrilled to bits. When Cordelia asked what was going on, there was a rush of explanations, with so many people answering that she couldn't make sense of it.

She raised a hand to stop the babble. "One at a time, please. Debra, what is going on?"

It was Tess who answered, eyes shining. "Gregory is going to be the intercessor in Greenshire. He should be arriving any day now. We're so proud of him."

Debra was beaming as well. "Imagine. An intercessor in the family. It's wonderful, it truly is."

Joanna had drawn Anoria aside to ask about the research and report on the demand for glass. "It's just amazing, Anoria," she said. "Demand for it grows and grows. Did you find a way to make bottles? And how about bowls?"

Anoria sighed a bit. It looked like it was going to be a very busy summer. "Not yet, Joanna," she said. "It takes a lot of time to make the tables, and we figured out that we'll need a different one for every single size of anything. We have to modify the spells for each one. I only have my glass sheet table, so far. We did make a better sorting pot, though. I just have to pour the sand in it, use the spell, and the sand will sort out of holes in the rim. It's a lot more efficient than all that brushing different colors around. It sorts a lot more of the sand for each spell too."

"Good," Joanna said. "Really good. Gregory's letter says he's out of colored glass, and there is a big demand for his windows. We'll all be busy this summer."

Location: Blacksmith Shop, Greenshire
Date: 22 Noron, 141 AF

"But you don't seem to understand," Widow Mead said. "My eyes just aren't what they used to be, I'm afraid. Winters are always hard on a person, but being locked up in the dark with just a few candles or lamps, well, it's awful. So I went to visit Marlene. And those windows! It's so wonderful. Bright sunshine coming in. The room was warmer. I've just got to have some windows for the cottage. The clear ones."

William Hagen looked at his mother-in-law with a bit of irritation. Would the woman never let up? He knew all that. He was there when it happened. Marlene was his wife, after all. "Mother Mead, I've ordered them. Anoria says it will be about a week before the glass is ready. Just give the girl time. It seems like every single person in every village around here is scraping up enough money for windows."

Widow Mead drew herself up to her tallest height. Which, it had to be said, wasn't really all that high. "I'm going to go talk to her myself. I'm old. I won't have as many years to enjoy them as some people. Every day makes a difference to me."

As she left the blacksmith shop, William just shook his head. The old woman was made from rawhide and bone, in his opinion. He had no doubt that she would outlast him and the rest of the village as well.

Location: Cooper House, Greenshire
Date: 22 Noron, 141 AF

"I'll try," Anoria said with a sigh. "I'll try." Anoria looked at the large slate on which she tracked the glass orders. There were just too many people who wanted—no, needed—the windows. Having light in the winter saved on both candles and lamp oil. The added warmth from the sun shining in helped people stay warm. More could be done in the long winter months when better light was available.

It seemed that everyone had realized that fact over the winter. Widow Mead wasn't the first to come visit her. She had just been about to take a break when the old woman showed up. Knowing that the widow had made the long walk to see her made Anoria regret the need to stop and rest, especially in the middle of the day.

"Is it just two panes you need for your window?" Anoria asked.

"The clear glass," Widow Mead specified. "Not that greeny stuff. I need the clear, and William has agreed."

"I'll get them finished today," Anoria said. "If you'll tell him that he can pick them up tomorrow, please. They'll be ready tomorrow."

"Good," Widow Mead said, nodding her white-haired head. "Good. Even at the farm this winter, everyone was clustered so close to the windows that I couldn't see to read. The windows are wonderful, they really are."

Widow Mead headed back down the lane, and Anoria sighed again. She was beginning to wish that she'd never heard about glass houses or windows. Everyone for miles around wanted them. So much more could be done in the winter when you had proper light to work by. Anoria felt guilty when she had to stop and rest long enough to clear her mind for more spell preparation. Only small children had to rest in the middle of the day, after all.

"Anoria," Debra called from the house. "Anoria, come to lunch."

"Coming," Anoria shouted. I can squeeze one more in after lunch, she thought. And maybe another before dinner.

Location: Intercessor's Home, Greenshire
Date: 2 Pago, 141 AF

"Yes, sir," Gregory said. High Intercessor Landris was not happy. He was proving that with every word he spoke.

"You did say you would have it ready today," the High Intercessor said stiffly. "I'm not early, I don't think."

"No, sir, you aren't," Gregory said tiredly. "You're right on time. I'm sorry. The parish has been a bit upset that two men were injured in plowing. I've had a lot of counseling to do. I simply haven't had a chance to finish your window. I do have enough of the red and yellow glass to finish it, but I haven't had time."

"You might have sent me a message, Intercessor Gregory," High Intercessor Landris said. "I wouldn't be so upset, if I had only known before I came all the way here from Gent."

"High Intercessor, please feel free to stay with me for a day or two. I can get it finished, if I only have a little more time," Gregory said, motioning the High Intercessor to enter his house and leading the way to the parlor. "Frankly, I could use you. Perhaps having a High Intercessor visit will stop some of the interruptions. Every time I get started on the work for your window, some parish girl stops by with another dish for me to try. I wasn't so well fed at the seminary or even at home."

High Intercessor Landris hid a smile. "Occupational hazard, dear boy, occupational hazard. Intercessors tend to be well thought of, generally. That attracts the girls like bees to flowers. What you need to do is find a dragonish housekeeper. That's what I did, back when I was a single man."

"If only we had a dragon handy, I would." Gregory grinned ruefully, happy that High Intercessor Landris was relaxing a bit. "Unfortunately, we don't. If you'll stay tonight and tomorrow night, I can get that window finished for you. Especially if you'll run interference with the young ladies of the parish."

"Not to worry," High Intercessor Landris said comfortably. "I can do that. Now, about all these dishes they've been bringing. Expect I could use a bit of lunch, anyway."

Location: Cooper Home, Greenshire
Date: 10 Pago, 141 AF

"Yes, Mistress Mason," Joanna agreed. "Yes, I said I'd have the healing salve ready by now. But the comfrey hasn't done well this year, and I've had to go rather far afield to gather more. Also, the lavender is late in blooming. I have a small container that you can have, but it will be another week, I think, before I have the full order made up."

Gena Mason stomped away, shouting, "If I had my windows, this wouldn't have happened. Rupert wouldn't have cut his hand, and I wouldn't need the salve if I'd only had the windows."

"And I'm not responsible for rainy weather," Joanna muttered to herself, turning to go inside. "Honestly, Mother," she steamed as she sat down at the table, "you'd think I'm the person who is responsible for rain. I can't help that the lavender isn't ready yet."

"You and Anoria are working too hard," Debra said. "And so is Gregory, judging from what I've seen. You need to stop accepting so many commitments and learn to pace yourselves."

Location: Cooper Home, Greenshire
Date: 29 Estormany, 141 AF

"Anoria, just what do you think you're doing?" Cordelia asked. She had been stopped dead by what she saw as she entered the workshop.

"Release that spell carefully." Cordelia waited a moment until Anoria had complied. "Now let the magic flow away smoothly." Anoria did as she directed and Cordelia looked her over carefully.

"Gregory says you're worn to an absolute frazzle, and I can see he's right." It was true. Anoria's eyes had dark circles under them, and her hair was more flyaway and duller than ever. Generally, she looked horrid. But that was the least of it. You didn't do spell preparation when you were tired or rushed. Not ever. It was the first lesson of magic use for book wizards. Spell preparation, even more than spell casting, was exacting and even the smallest mistake could turn a useful spell into death for the wizard as soon as it was used.

Cordelia overrode Anoria's protest that she was just fine and popped them to Greenwood. She refused to listen to anything until Anoria had eaten a snack and had a cup of cocoa. She was still angry, an anger fueled by terror at what might have happened. Her eyes flashed fire as she asked, "What are you doing, driving yourself into exhaustion? Don't you realize that it's dangerous? You don't want to adventure, but you're risking your life to make a pane of glass. You're more worn out right now than I ever was, even after turning back an army of orcs."

Anoria was, if the truth were known, relieved by Cordelia's intervention. She was tired and knew it. She was even a bit scared by what she had been doing. "It's just hard to say no, Cordelia," she admitted. "It always seemed I could do just a little bit more. Everyone wants what we can make, and it's not like I'm the only one working hard. I hate to say no to them, so I've pushed myself a bit. Maybe a bit too much. I am tired. Really tired."

Cordelia knew this was true. Anoria was yawning, even after the sweet cocoa that usually woke her up.

"You, young lady, are going to go to bed. And you are going to stay right here for two full weeks. Don't even consider using a spell of any sort."

Anoria smiled a smile that clearly told how much she loved Cordelia, and Cordelia's heart was touched.

"I'm going to go back to Greenshire and establish some limits," Cordelia warned. "You have to know that I'm probably going to scare the pants off some people, and they'll walk on eggshells around you for a while."

"Do you really have to do that, Cordelia?" Anoria asked. "It's my doing, after all. I could have said no, but I didn't. I'm a little tired, but nothing bad happened. Just let me get a little rest and I can go back. I'll be more careful."

"Anoria, think for a moment. Do you realize what could have happened in that workshop of yours? Not only could you have killed yourself, you could have taken the farm with you when you went. Michael, Debra, Joanna, all of them." Cordelia held up her hand with the thumb and forefinger about a half inch apart. "You were this close, Anoria, this close. Yes, I do have to do it. Otherwise, you'll just get overconfident again and do too much."

Anoria's face paled a bit. She hadn't considered that possibility. "You may be right. But the glass really is important, Cordelia. Every winter there are accidents that happen because of the darkness in the cottages. I'm helping to stop those accidents."

"I understand that," Cordelia said. "But people have lived with scraped hide on the windows for centuries. And just because people can get more done in the winter with the light, isn't a reason that you should kill yourself. I'll admit that some of the reasons for wanting the windows are good. But some of them are just people showing off how rich they are. When they really aren't that rich! The south-facing windows—those I can understand. But for some of your customers, the ones who are pushing the hardest, it's purely for status. Windows on the north side of the house, in the dead of winter when the wind is blowing? Does that make any sense?

They'll only wind up putting the hide covers over them, anyway. That's the kind of thing I'm going to stop."

Anoria considered for a moment. Some of the villagers had been pushing hard for windows that they really didn't need. Cordelia had a very good point. "I think you're right. Maybe I do need to maintain a little more distance. If I just concentrate on south-facing windows, that will cut down on the demand a bit."

"Good," Cordelia smiled. "That's one of the reasons I maintain a standoffish attitude. People tend not to realize that wizardry is just as much work as plowing. And it's a lot more dangerous. They don't think about that part. They'll know what could have happened when I'm finished with them, though. Now, you go get some rest. I'll be back later."

CHAPTER 33

Location: Intercessor's House, Greenshire
Date: 29 Estormany, 141 AF

Once Cordelia was sure that Anoria was well asleep and would stay that way for a while, she popped to Gregory's home. "You were right," she said. "The girl was worn out, and that's simply not acceptable. Not at all. You can overstress yourself in this business. And when you do, bang, you're dead. I'll not have this, not any longer."

Gregory nodded. "I've had that experience, sort of. Early this year, when there was that plowing accident. It's lucky for me that the intercessor spells come the way they do, when I pray in the morning. They're fully prepared, ready to go. But my healing spells are more limited than people realize, I think. They expect that because I'm an intercessor given magic by Barra, I can do anything, heal any wound. It just doesn't work that way, I'm afraid."

"I'm going to tell you something I've learned in a long life," Cordelia said. "You, Joanna, and Anoria are young, so you haven't had to learn this yet. Many people, given the opportunity, will take advantage of others. It's just a part of human nature. It pays to develop a . . . call it a disassociation, I guess . . . from others, when you have things they want. If they feel a little fear of you, then they won't approach you for silly stuff, only for what's truly important."

Gregory grinned ironically. "You mean I needn't heal Kegan Chandler's scratched arm? Don't worry. I've figured that out, just in the last month. Mistress Chandler quaked in her shoes when I gave her the 'how dare you' glare I was taught at the seminary. I wondered at the time why I should ever need it."

Cordelia grinned. "I take it you understand that now?"

Gregory nodded. "Oh, yes. I certainly do. And certain over-worried, protective mothers are buying Joanna's healing unguents in an effort to avoid asking me for silly stuff."

"Joanna," Cordelia muttered. "I'm afraid that Mistress Joanna is part of the problem. I believe she and I need to have a bit of a talk."

"Don't be too hard on her," Gregory advised. "Anoria could have said no. Not all of it is Joanna's fault."

Location: Cooper Home, Greenshire
Date: 29 Estormany, 141 AF

"But we've made promises," Joanna protested. "We have agreements."

"That, young lady," Cordelia said severely, "is just too bad. Anoria is worn out. She could have killed herself trying to keep up. And that is not going to happen. She will not be back for at least a month. You, Mistress Joanna, in your never-ending grasping for gold, are largely responsible for that. And you, Mistress Joanna, can just tell people that they'll have to wait."

Michael nodded agreement. "I've told you before, daughter," he said, "that money isn't everything. Had I wanted money, I'd have gone adventuring like my brother James. A good life is a good life, and part of that is time to just live, not work."

Debra, much to Joanna's surprise, agreed readily with Cordelia. "That's all very true, Joanna. I admire your stamina, but I'm afraid I don't really admire some of your traits. Part of it is Anoria's fault. She doesn't like to disappoint you . . . or me, for that matter. But we're going to have to take more care and slow down a good bit. I've always wanted a good life, but that doesn't have to mean being rich. You, just as much as Anoria, need to stop working so hard. I should have noticed how tired you all are before, but it was so gradual that the change just snuck up on me."

Joanna was a bit shocked and a bit wary as well. Cordelia just didn't look like the person she had grown used to. Her face was severe, and she seemed to be very angry. Joanna thought for a few moments. "I understand. I expect I got carried away. I'll try to be a bit less, ah, demanding."

"A good bit," Cordelia said. "A very good bit. I haven't forgotten the Goat spell, you know."

Location: Temple, Greenshire
Date: 1 Barra, 141 AF

On seventh day, the day of temple services, Cordelia made a rare public appearance. In Gregory's temple, during the morning service, she stood before the podium, dressed in full wizard robes that had her rank showing in masses of purple embroidery. They were her most intimidating clothing. Her face remained severe, and she had made sure that the village's leading inhabitants would be at this service.

She stood in front of Gregory's podium. "I'm going to inform you all of something you seem not to understand," she said. "Mistress Anoria is my adopted daughter as well as my student. I've allowed her to take part in the life of the village because she is a very caring person. Perhaps she's a bit too caring, in fact."

Cordelia glared around the temple, letting her gaze rest on the people she knew were the worst offenders for a moment. "In the future," she continued, "Anoria will not be pushed beyond the limits I set. I will not allow any further exploitation of her. Not by you, not by anyone. And the next person who makes the smallest attempt to push her beyond her strength is going to regret it. You don't seem to understand that she could have, quite literally, killed herself from overwork. If she had cast the wrong spell at the wrong time, she could even have taken some of the village with her."

As the parishioners rustled a bit, Cordelia continued to glare around the temple and now her voice went utterly cold and deadly. "I want people to understand that I will not allow this, not any longer. Anyone who would like to argue about it, or attempt to circumvent my restrictions, is welcome to deal with . . . me."

Cordelia disappeared, popping back to Greenwood. She smirked just a tiny bit as she descended the stairs. *That ought to put the cat among the pigeons.*

* * *

Gregory conducted the remainder of the services with a deliberately solemn face. Afterward, as he stood at the door, he made a pretense of agreeing with some of the more vocal villagers. "You do recall the songs and stories about Cordelia Cooper," he reminded a few people. "While I dislike threats to my parishioners, I have to say that Lady Cordelia was actually quite patient. For a dangerous wizard, at any rate."

Certain of the villagers began to remember old tales and passed them onto others. Those stories told of a wizard known more for her great power than for her restraint. Cordelia, if the truth were known, was not an evil wizard. But she was no shining light of goodness either. Part of the reason she quit the heavy-duty adventuring was that it was getting harder and harder to tell whether she was one of the good guys or one of the bad, and not just for her. She could be a very nice lady, but at base she was tough as nails.

When Gregory said things like, "Well, you understand that a mother does tend to protect her children," people drew the conclusion that it just wouldn't be a good idea to press Cordelia or Anoria any further than they already had.

Location: Intercessor's House, Greenshire
Date: 7 Barra, 141 AF

"Intercessor Gregory," Deaconess Willow said.

Gregory smiled. Deaconess Willow had been in the parish for about twenty years and had taught many of the younger adults as well as the current batch of children. "Yes, Deaconess Willow. What can I do for you?"

"Well, it's common to check with the intercessor when you make a change in what you're teaching at the school. I just wanted to make sure I had your approval before I do it," Deaconess Willow explained.

Margaret Willow was about forty, Gregory thought. She was a somewhat spare looking woman who wore her brown hair in a bun at the back of her neck.

Gregory's forehead creased. "What change do you want to make, ma'am?"

"Well, I should have done it earlier, I suppose. I did, in fact, mention this a time or two when Anoria was in school, but I never stressed it. I want to add a bit about wizardry and the difficulty of crafting spells. Since

Anoria will be continuing to live among the villagers, I think it would probably be a good thing for the villagers to understand just how difficult what she does actually is."

Deaconess Willow's face was very earnest. Gregory smiled at her. "I think that would be a very good idea, Deaconess Willow. You teach the children; the children will explain it at home. It should help stop some of the more overbearing individuals, as well." Then Gregory's face broke into a large grin. "You never know, it might even help them understand that, even with the help of Barra, I can't work miracles, either."

"I shall be happy to add that as well," Deaconess Willow agreed.

Location: School, Greenshire
Date: 15 Barra, 141 AF

"All right, children settle down," Deaconess Willow said. "Most of you were in the temple when the wizard Cordelia made her appearance last week. So, today we are going to talk about how magic works."

"Some of you were in school with Anoria Adrian, so you may remember our discussions of the magic she was learning. If you'll think back to those discussions, you may realize why the wizard Cordelia was so upset."

Mason Holland raised his hand. "But that's real wizard magic. The kind that wizards who go on adventures and stuff use. Not the simple things Anoria does." Mason had a romantic view of adventure and the sort of useful, prosaic spells Anoria did simply didn't fit it.

"Magic is magic, Mason," Deaconess Willow said. "Now, to cast a spell it must first be crafted. Crafting a spell is very exacting work and very tiring. It's best done when you're fresh, and there is a limit to how many spells a wizard can have crafted and ready at one time. The problem with it is basically the same as doing any exacting finicky thing when you're tired.

It's easy to make mistakes. Even a little mistake can cause the spell to go wrong. If that happens, it can hurt, or even kill, the wizard and those around him."

Location: Greenwood
Date: 15 Barra, 141 AF

"No, we're not," Cordelia said. "Not yet, at any rate."

Anoria, who had just wondered if they might return to Greenshire, looked a little troubled. "We do have some commitments," she began.

"And Joanna is arranging that they'll be filled when they are filled. And that, my dear, is all there is to it," Cordelia said. "You are going to learn that you can't push yourself that hard, ever again. So we're going to do a bit of traveling and take a break, both from studying and producing products. The glass can wait."

Over the next month Anoria and Cordelia traveled around the world. Anoria couldn't quite overcome her urge to do things, so she still collected unusual plants for Joanna and kept on the lookout for items of interest. But part of the traveling took them to visit people and places that had some horror stories about rushed spell-crafting. The one-eyed wizard, Zentara, an old friend of Cordelia's, explained that she felt lucky to be alive, even with one eye. Anoria's face paled a bit when Zentara told her story of a badly crafted spell. She resolved to be more careful.

"I get the point," she said to Cordelia. "I really do. I promise I will be more careful. Could we please do something that's fun instead of going to hear another horror story?"

Cordelia actually blushed a bit. "Have I been overdoing the warnings?"

"Just a bit." Anoria smiled. "I understand why, though, and I appreciate it. I'll be good, I promise. But if we're taking a break, let's do something that's fun."

"You've never met many elves, have you," Cordelia thought out loud. "I've got an old friend, someone I haven't seen in, oh, thirty years, I guess. He and his tribe aren't woods elves, either. Sea elves are a little less common. Let's go see Louanomannian."

CHAPTER 34

Location: Island of the Sea Elves
Date: 17 Cashi, 141 AF

Louanomannian was happy to see an old friend. His wife appeared to have some reservations, but her concerns eased as she looked at Cordelia. Humans aged much faster than elves, after all. Cordelia knew that and had expected that reaction. The visit was a success.

After two weeks of swimming in the sea, Anoria's looks had improved to the point that Cordelia felt it was safe to go home and let Anoria return to Greenshire if she wanted. The saltwater and sun had lightened Anoria's hair, and she was no longer so pale and ill-looking. She had even gained a bit of weight.

"Tomorrow, then?" Anoria asked. "We'll go back tomorrow?"

"Yes," Cordelia agreed. "I've enjoyed the travel, but I'm ready for home, I think." Cordelia sighed a bit, and Anoria took a good look at her. Cordelia's eyes had a bit of a faraway look to them, perhaps even a little regret.

"Do you miss him so much?" Anoria asked. "You and your friend Lou seem to have a history."

"That's just a little bit personal," Cordelia said. "But yes, we have a history. We were . . . very close at one time. Quite a few years ago. But you see the difference, don't you? He spent much of the last thirty years merged with the coral, as sea elves do. I, on the other hand, have lived every day of that thirty years."

"Stories tell about how that sort of thing can be overcome by love," Anoria ventured. She was nearly seventeen now, and thoughts of marriage and children were beginning to take up some of her time.

"There's a reason they're called stories," Cordelia said. "Bard and minstrel tales are what they are. I've few regrets, you know. I've got Greenwood, my barony, many friends, places to go, and people to see. Lou is the past, and he'll stay there. And, I have you and your training, as well." Cordelia paused a moment and stared out to sea. "I've few regrets," she repeated.

Anoria felt that there was a lot more to this particular story, but kept her thoughts to herself. Cordelia's faraway look had set her to thinking. Perhaps Cordelia was lonelier than she appeared.

Location: Cooper Home, Greenshire
Date: 29 Cashi, 141 AF

"I'm back," Anoria announced. She had sneaked up on the door of the stillroom to catch Joanna by surprise.

Joanna jumped and squeaked. Anoria began to giggle.

"Anoria," Joanna said, after giving her a big hug, "I'm so sorry. I didn't realize . . ."

"It isn't your fault," Anoria interrupted. "I knew better, or I should have. And I won't do it again, either. Catch me up on all the news from the village. Is everyone going to be afraid of me again?"

"I don't think so," Joanna smiled. "It seems to have blown over, at least most of it. I've told everyone that we're not taking any more orders, not until we catch up with our commitments. So, we're not going to do what we did before and push too hard. Right?"

"Yes, Mother." Anoria rolled her eyes. "What else is going on?"

Joanna giggled a bit. "It's a hoot, what's going on. Kind of embarrassing for Gregory, but funny. I swear, every girl in this village, not to mention Brookshire, has set her cap for him. There's not a day that goes by that two or three of them don't show up with some cake or pie. They're all trying to impress him with their cooking and sewing skills. You should have seen Vivela Gellert at the temple! She was wearing the most amazing blouse. It was embroidered so heavily that you could barely see the fabric. All to try and impress Gregory."

Anoria's face creased a bit in puzzlement. "Vivela Gellert? Why would she think a flashy, embroidered blouse would attract Gregory? And why Gregory? She's her father's oldest daughter and ought to be looking for a farmer, not an intercessor."

Joanna smiled a bit to herself. She had come to believe that Gregory and Anoria were meant for one another. Perhaps the news that other young women were showing an interest in Gregory would bring Anoria to that knowledge. "I didn't say it was flashy, Anoria. Just heavily embroidered. She is very good at needlework, you know. And Gregory will need new vestments at some point. For that alone she would be perfect as an intercessor's wife."

Anoria sniffed. "And who else is making a fool of herself, aside from Vivela?"

"Orla March is one of them," Joanna said, stifling a laugh. "She took him a jar of her famous jam."

Anoria looked outraged. "Orla March is only fifteen years old! She's not old enough to be out of short skirts yet, much less old enough to have a 'famous' jam."

Joanna continued mentioning names, and Anoria continued shooting down the hopes of every one of them. By the time they were finished, hardly a single woman under the age of twenty-five had escaped Anoria's assessment as totally unsuitable. And all for very good reasons, of course.

"Well," Joanna said, "if you think all these girls should marry all these other men, you ought to start trying to match them up somehow. Otherwise, one or the other of them is going to latch on to Gregory some day."

"I may just do that." Anoria sniffed.

Location: Mead Cottage, Greeshire
Date: 30 Cashi, 141 AF

It turned out that Anoria was quite good at matchmaking. She enlisted the Widow Mead as well, which gave the widow's son-in-law a break from her meddling. William Hagen was rather grateful to Anoria for that in the coming years.

"I'd say that Vivela Gellert would be much better off with Ahearn Jamison rather than his younger brother," Arabelle Mead said. "She's strong-willed, that one. Cedric Jamison would be a better match for Sorcha Oakes, over at the sawmill. And speaking of the saw mill, well, Sloane Oakes is twenty-four now. But he's already keeping company with Glynis Gellert, so we've nothing to do there. And there's Jonny Cooper, the baker's journeyman. It's past time he married. He'd be a prime match for Rhona Baker in a year or so, when she's ready. That family runs to daughters."

Arabelle Mead had been born and raised in Greenshire. She knew everyone and nearly everything about them. Her little cottage sat on the west side of the village square and had a direct view of Gregory's temple. Now that Anoria was limiting her glass production, she could find time to stop by to chat with Arabelle. At seventy, Arabelle was still sharp as a tack, Anoria found. She also knew who was related to whom, and how far back the connection went.

Arabelle Mead was also well aware of the reason for Anoria's sudden interest in matchmaking. Just like Joanna, she knew that Anoria and Gregory were meant for each other. It only remained to bring them to that realization. "I understand that Gregory's windows are still in demand," she probed. "Isn't he needing some more glass, I heard?"

"He hasn't said," Anoria answered. "What color does he need? I've a little time to hand."

"Ah, well, you'd have to ask him that, I imagine," Arabelle said. "Just go over there and ask him, why don't you?"

"I'll not be making that kind of spectacle of myself," Anoria said, a bit stiffly. "I've been talked about by this village quite enough lately."

"Well, come outside then," Arabelle suggested. "We'll sit in the sun and discuss my flower beds. I expect he'll come over to see you, once he knows you're here."

And sure enough, Gregory did step over when he saw that Anoria was in the village. Arabelle listened to the ensuing conversation with a little smile on her face.

Location: Village Square, Greenshire
Date: 2 Timu's Time, 141 AF

Anoria and Arabelle started their campaign at the festival of Timu. Timu, the god of time, didn't have a month. Instead, he had Timu's Time, a period of five or six days at the end of every year that ended on the shortest day of the year. Ahearn Jamison was standing with his brothers and some other single men on one side of the village hall. Vivela Gellert was holding forth on needlework to a group of her friends on the other side of the hall. Anoria tried to figure out a way to get them together.

"Drat," she muttered to Joanna, who was in on the plans. Anoria couldn't keep secrets from Joanna. "There he stands, with all that brawn. And Vivela just doesn't even look up."

"It would be a bit forward if she did," Joanna pointed out. "And as for him, Ahearn is probably afraid she'd turn him down for a dance, you know. She'll inherit the farm, and he's just a hired hand."

"What did Vivela bring to the dance for her contribution?" Arabelle asked.

"Bread pudding, I think," Joanna said. "I have to admit that she does wonderful bread pudding."

"They say," Arabelle mentioned, "that the way to a man's heart is through his stomach."

"Aha," Anoria and Joanna said, eyes gleaming.

"Mistress Joanna," Anoria said.

"Mistress Anoria?"

"I should think that you and I might acquire a dish of Vivela's famous bread pudding, don't you think? And then we shall sashay around the hall while we enjoy it, shall we not?"

"Methinks thou hast a plan." Joanna giggled. "We can umm and ahh over it, I should imagine."

And they did.

Location: Cooper Home, Greenshire
Date: 8 Wovoro, 142 AF

Sorcha Oakes proved to be an altogether tougher nut to crack, however. She was only eighteen and didn't feel she was ready for marriage. Anoria tried, but Sorcha resisted all attempts to interest her in Cedric. That is, she resisted until her brother Sloane married Glynis Gellert in the sixth month of that year. Sorcha found that Glynis had some of her older sister's rather annoying traits.

"I'll just be . . . be . . ." Sorcha steamed one day after temple. "I don't know what I'll be. But I'll not be sitting over an embroidery frame all day, every day, that's for sure. Glynis has some kind of competition going with Vivela. What are they doing, competing for best needlewoman in Greenshire?"

Sorcha didn't have much use for feminine pursuits like needlework. She liked cooking, a lot. But her chosen vocation, in fact, was woodcarving. Her father had taught her, during the long summer evenings.

"She wants you to give up your carving?" Anoria asked, putting on a shocked face. "But you're very good at it."

"Glynis seems to feel that being married to my brother makes her the boss," Sorcha muttered. "And Mother seems to agree. I've got to get out of that house. They're driving me mad, they are. Constant urging to sew, sew, sew."

"I should imagine that Cedric and Desmond might like a decent meal now and then," Anoria pointed out. "And while it's true that they only rent the Titum house, I've heard a rumor that they want to buy it. Seems to me a woman could be her own mistress, assuming a woman was willing to take a chance."

"Hmmm."

Location: Greenshire
Date: 15 Barra, 142 AF

Through various machinations by Arabelle Mead and Anoria, with Joanna's enthusiastic help, Sorcha Oakes married Cedric Jamison that fall before Anoria left for the winter. It hadn't taken that much. A little shove here and little nudge there. Arabelle was quite convinced that there would be a new crop of infants being baptized at the temple, come the summer.

Arabelle and Anoria's matchmaking did have one rather spectacular failure, however. Deaconess Margaret Willow declined to have anything to do with Ralph Holland. She was quite definite that she was perfectly willing to teach children, but had no desire for any of her own.

Arabelle cackled a bit at this. "I understand," she snickered over a cup of tea one day. "I might have remarried back in the day, myself. Thought about it, I did. Might have done it, too, if it hadn't been for that bed business."

Arabelle and Margaret both laughed at the look on Anoria's face when she had worked that out.

CHAPTER 36

Location: Greenwood
Date: 20 Barra, 142 AF

"What are we going to work on this winter?" Anoria wanted to know.

"I've no real idea," Cordelia answered. "After we got back from our trip, I spent a good bit of time trying to improve Wizard's Mark. It just didn't work, though. I improved it, yes, but it still can't be used to record an entire spell. I did develop another spell that uses a Wizard's Mark as the base. One we'll keep to ourselves, I think. It's called Glow Mark. Once you have Wizard's Mark on something, you can use Glow Mark, and the mark will shine like a torch for weeks, depending on how much power you can put into it. It's a useful enough spell, I guess, if you're going to need light for a while and don't want to be constantly preparing the Light spell. And assuming you don't have a gold coin to glow."

"Have you ever considered making a pen that would always write the correct symbol?" Anoria asked. "I've noticed that I might have the correct symbol in my mind, but even with as much practice as I've had on the runes, they just don't always write down the way I intended them to. And, of course, when that happens, the whole spell is ruined, and you have to start over. In addition, you've wasted a sheet of the paper and all that hideously expensive ink. And for a long spell, if you're on, say, the last few lines, well, there goes even more paper and ink."

"Hmmmm," Cordelia muttered. "I don't know. I never looked at it that way. We'll have to check the reference books at the University of Drakan, I think. It's by far the most extensive library of runes and symbols."

"Good." Anoria smiled. "I loved the food in Drakan. When do we leave?"

Location: Library, University of Drakan, Dragon Lands
Date: 4 Cogainie, 142 AF

Cordelia had to laugh, even if it was a library. Anoria was immersed in books, to the point that a towering stack of them was in danger of toppling on her head. As well, she had a smudge of ink on her nose, and she was sitting with her legs folded in the oddest manner.

Cordelia's laugh rang out, and several scholars looked up, apparently intending to shush her. However, they quickly changed their minds when they recognized her.

"Come along, Anoria," she said. "Enough study. Do you realize we've been in Drakan for three months?

Anoria looked up and grinned, something that made her look about twelve years old to Cordelia. The ink smudge helped in that regard. "Three months? How did three months pass so quickly?"

"The study of magic theory always did that to me too," Cordelia said. "But enough of it. Let's go do something fun. Have you ever met a dragon?"

"I never knew anyone who talked about meeting a dragon," Anoria said. "I didn't know you could actually meet one. I've read about fighting dragons, but not meeting them. And I never, ever, heard that it could be fun."

"Well, it's time then," Cordelia decided. "We'll go meet my friend, Brazla. You need to meet more magical creatures, anyway."

"Brazla?"

"Well," Cordelia admitted, "that's not really her name. She's got one of those mile-long dragon names that no one but a dragon can pronounce properly. I did her a favor once, a long time ago."

Location: Brazla's Home, Dragonlands
Date: 5 Cogainie, 142 AF

Brazla lived in the center of a vast desert. She was quite interested in conversation and proved to be quite interested in Anoria's sorting pot. "Sand has different stuff in it?" she asked, her scales glinting in the sunlight.

"It's rather amazing how much," Cordelia said, reclining in the shade of a large boulder. "I think Anoria has found about thirty different kinds, haven't you, Anoria?"

"Thirty-three, so far," Anoria agreed. "It's strange, I'll tell you that. And the colors never seem to turn out the way we expect them to either. For instance, there's some bluish-green stuff. You'd think the glass would be bluish green, wouldn't you? But it comes out red."

"Red glass," Brazla muttered. "Red glass?"

Anoria nodded. "That's what I do, you know. I make glass with magic. It's very useful. A friend of mine makes colored windows of it, as well. They're very pretty."

Brazla's four-inch-wide eyes squinted in thought. They were small in her great head, which was six feet long from snout to the ridge at the back. "Do you have the pot with you?"

"Oh, no," Cordelia said. "We left it behind at the workshop. I could get it, if you wished."

Brazla displayed a certain amount of the selfishness that brass dragons were known for when she said, "I want to see it work. Bring it . . . please."

The "please" was what cinched the deal. Brazla was not known for human pleasantries, and for her to use one meant great interest. Cordelia agreed to bring the pot, as well as the melting table, just to satisfy Brazla's curiosity. It only took a few moments, and she was back with both items.

Anoria demonstrated the spells, and Brazla watched, fascinated. The red sand of her desert divided into just as many elements as the creek sand at home. "More please," Brazla requested, watching carefully as the different colors poured out in various directions.

Anoria refilled the pot and invoked the spell. "Once more, then I'll have to craft the spell again," she said.

Brazla looked at her with some curiosity. "You need a bigger pot."

"Well, I'm not that strong a wizard," Anoria admitted.

Cordelia flinched a bit at that. In the general rule of things, that was not something you wanted to admit to a dragon, even a brass dragon. Even though brass dragons were generally considered among the nicer ones.

Brazla's look became intense and Cordelia tensed. "Don't worry, Cordelia, I'm only looking." There was a pause. "Still, you could sort more than the pot holds. Half again as much, I would think."

That was true enough, Cordelia realized. The pot had been made for a partially trained wizard, and was big enough to hold most of what that wizard could sort in one batch. Anoria was a bit more skilled now, and a larger pot would take advantage of her increased ability. Furthermore, a larger pot would sort as much as Anoria's ability allowed and just leave the rest in the bottom of the pot. As Anoria got stronger, she could, with a larger pot, sort more sand with each spell. "Drat," she muttered. "Why didn't I think of that?"

"Perhaps because you're human," Brazla smirked. "Let's see if this works. I could cast 'enlarge' on the pot three times, if you liked. It would grow larger with each spell. I always have that one available," Brazla confided. "Sometimes a girl just wants a little more shade. It's quite useful on rocks."

"Let's not, at least not now," Cordelia suggested. Sometimes dragons forgot that humans didn't have their natural resistance to magic. Magical experimentation was more dangerous for humans and needed more care. "I think it would be better, or at least safer, to make a new pot."

Brazla laughed a very draconic laugh and rolled in the sand. "Humans," she said. "Humans. You're so very fragile.

"Another point you have apparently forgotten is that different places have different kinds of sand," Brazla continued. "The sorting pot is nice and makes things easier, but if you were to spend a few weeks in a place that already had white sand, you could do much more for the amount of effort."

CHAPTER 36

Location: Greenwood
Date: 27 Prima, 143 AF

When they got back home, the first thing Cordelia did was to make a much larger sorting pot. And this one had a slightly different design. It was six feet high and had spouts at various levels. When "separate by weight" was used, the heaviest sands or powders exited at the lower spouts and the lighter ones at the higher spouts. "Separate by color" caused the sand or powder to come out at spouts around the top.

Anoria suggested a small refinement, and Cordelia added a wire loop to hold containers under the various spouts. All in all, it was an unusual looking rig. It did work very efficiently, however.

Cordelia was glaring at the melting table, when Anoria walked into the work room. "Please don't," Anoria said. "Please don't."

"Why not?" Cordelia asked. "It might work."

"And it might not," Anoria pointed out. "It might not. Besides, a two-foot square of glass is just about right. There's always a lot of scrap, that's true. But Rob Benedict uses most of it. He's even doing the glass cutting now, which is fine with me. I never got the knack of that. Clarence did, and it was his idea to cut diamond shapes and put them together as a window. Those are very popular and use up most of the scrap."

Cordelia calmed a bit. "I suppose you're right about that. A four-foot square piece of glass would be harder to handle without breaking."

Anoria nodded. "It would. And I've learned my lesson, Cordelia. I won't push myself the way I did before. Having the larger sorting pot is wonderful. I only have to craft one of each sorting spell once a day, which leaves me a lot of room for the Melt spells. What I would really like to be able to do is produce glass bowls and bottles, large and small bottles. The small ones would be wonderful for Joanna's perfumes, and a larger bottle could be used for so much more."

"Why bowls?" Cordelia asked. "People already have wooden and ceramic bowls. Why glass?"

Anoria grinned widely and put her feet up on the desk. "Because they're pretty. I just like the idea. Imagine a clear glass bowl full of peaches sitting on the table in the sunshine from a glass window. It would be a beautiful sight."

Cordelia fell into the spirit. "Hmmm. How about a bowl of walnuts, with their beige shells, sitting in an orange bowl on the same table?"

Anoria countered with, "Bright green apples in a deep red bowl."

Cordelia giggled, which made her look twenty years younger. "We could think those up for days, you know."

Anoria nodded agreement. "And I'm quite sure that other people can think up more combinations, as well. And why not? All of life doesn't have to be a search for work, work, and more work. There just ought to be room for pretty. I'm sure they'll be useful for many things, but mainly, I'd just like to do something pretty. Do you know what I'd like to see?"

"What?"

"A deep green bowl filled with Joanna's pink musk roses. If you put water in the bowl and maybe some rocks to hold them in place, I bet it would last a week or so. And the whole house would smell like roses."

"I bet it would," Cordelia agreed. "Well, let's hit the books, and I'll call on my friendly fire elemental. He's quite fascinated by the uses we put his element to, you know."

Location: Greenwood
Date: 9 Banth, 143 AF

Cordelia took the silver objects from the portable pantry and set them on the work table. They were a set of two sheets of silver, flat around the edges, bowl-shaped depressions in the center. The second sheet was only different in that the bowl-shaped depression in it was a little smaller. The table for the glass panes had been relatively simple; gravity flattened the top of the glass plate. They only needed to handle the bottom surface, and that only had to be flat.

Well, there were the sides of the original table, but the containment part of the spell managed that while keeping the heat from reaching out and burning the table to ash and melted silver. To make a bowl, two silver surfaces were needed to compress the glass into the required shape. The containment field of the silver bowls would be shaped by two curving surfaces, not one flat one. The geometry of the spell and the spell containment vessel—the bowl table—were both more complicated. Then there was the issue of the mass of the sand in the container. In the pane table, any leftover sand was simply left on the top of the new pane of glass. It was more mass than the spell was designed to handle, so it was ignored.

The bowl table, on the other hand, would have to deal with the excess sand in some other way. It couldn't just push the sand out of the way. There was a silver plate with a bowl-shaped depression in the way, which meant the new table would have to have a place to put the excess material, a catch cup or something like that. It might also make it harder to contain the heat and make sure that all the sand was heated evenly.

The original table used a set of magical structures that repelled matter to keep the sand from contact with the silver bottom plate. The shape of those structures had been engraved into the table using magic moss. Thus the table aided in the control of the spell, making it safer for a less trained and practiced wizard to prepare. Most magic containers did that to some extent, which was why a lot of the more old-fashioned wizards, and especially natural wizards, disapproved so strongly of spell containers. Cordelia remembered her master screaming at her that she must know her spells so well that she could prepare and cast them in her sleep. And some of them she did know that well: Stonewall, Translocation, Servant, Wizard Bolt, and Transform. But even for a natural wizard it took years to learn a spell that well. And a lot of book wizards, even very good book wizards, never learned any of their spells that well.

Cordelia smiled as she drew runes on the outer plate. She had been one of those old-fashioned wizards who disapproved of spell containers before Anoria. The problem with learning a spell into your bones, as Master Cartwright taught her she should, was that it vastly limited the number of spells that a wizard could learn. Spell books that you could reference while you were preparing a spell added a great deal to a wizard's flexibility.

That was important, but it still left all the control of the spell in the hands of the spell preparer, and that had seemed to Cordelia right where it was supposed to be.

Before Anoria.

Anoria was a clever child and a quick study, but something like a spell to separate sand by color or to invite enough heat to melt that sand in a controlled way and then cause the heat to leave quickly and evenly . . . that was a very complex spell for a wizard of Anoria's level of training. By using the sorting bucket and the melting table to fine-tune the spell, the spell Anoria prepared and cast into the containers could be simpler and more straightforward. Without the containers, Anoria would have been able to prepare and cast the sorting and melting spells, but they would have been less effective and had more backlash.

For instance, much of the heat that melted the sand into glass would have escaped into the surrounding space, melting or burning anything close. That would also have meant that more heat would have had to be let into the world and less of it would have returned to the fire plane for the same amount of melted sand. It would have been a more dangerous spell even if it worked exactly right, and it would have been much easier to get it wrong. The same was true of the sorting spell that Anoria had adjusted. The pot, with its engravings in magic moss to contain the spell, meant that Anoria's changes were more likely to simply cause the spell to fail than to cause disaster.

Properly made spell containers made magic safer. However, they probably did encourage sloppiness and potentially dangerous experimentation.

Cordelia had consulted with a fire demon of her acquaintance on the design of the first Melt spell, and she thought she'd need to talk to him again about these new tables. She wasn't quite sure how it would work and didn't want any accidents. She made another note on the shaping of the glass and drew another rune on the smaller bowl-shaped plate. This would help even the flow of the glass, she thought. More and more, as she got into the work, it seemed that this was a subtly different kind of magic.

Location: Fireplane
Date: Not Applicable

Balrikan, a fire demon, greeted Cordelia with a burst of heat that would have burned her to a crisp if she hadn't been shielded. He wasn't actually being mean; it was just the way that fire demons greeted each other.

Cordelia politely threw a fireball in return, and then they got down to business.

They discussed the new melt tables and what would actually happen to the sand as it was heated within the containment of the two silver sheets. Cordelia had brought some sand with her, and Balrikan played with it, compressing, heating, cooling it, for his control of temperature was very great.

"The air will have to be removed as it is heating," he told her. "For two reasons. One, air expands greatly and if you don't let it escape, the pressure will blow the top off. The other is, the air will interfere with the structure of the glass."

They continued discussing the processes for another hour, and Cordelia left him with her gift, ten pounds of the little crystals found at the bottom of a manure pile. They were, to Balrikan, a delightful treat. Though how anyone, even a fire demon, could enjoy eating something that came from the bottom of a manure pile was beyond her understanding. Much as how anyone could enjoy eating ice cream was beyond Balrikan's.

Location: Greenwood
Date: 19 Banth, 143 AF

Back home, with the plates modified to allow for the removal of air and excess sand, Cordelia and Anoria got back to work on developing the spells and magical structures for the new products.

"I can see how the bowl table is going to work," Anoria said. "But how on earth are we going to make a bottle? And bottles have to have stoppers of some sort too. Although . . ." She stopped for a moment. "I guess that the stoppers could be wood. Maybe even fancy-carved wood."

"That sounds like the simplest way to do the stoppers," Cordelia said. "Even if we made a third table to make stoppers for the bottles, glass on glass doesn't make a very good seal."

"Are we going to make two bottle tables? One for large and one for small?"

"That would seem to be the way to do it, but I'm not quite sure how we'd accomplish the feat," Cordelia admitted. "With the bowl, it's easy to fit the two plates together. But a jar or a bottle needs a neck."

"Could we do it the way the orcs did it?" Anoria asked. "Blowing melted glass into a form?"

"Well, we could use the table for a form. I'm not sure how we'd blow the melted glass into it, and I'm not sure how we'd get the bottle out after it cooled, either."

"A two-sided form? And we'd put the sides together to make the form and then take the form apart to get the bottle out?"

"Maybe," Cordelia said. "But I keep thinking that we're looking at this wrong. We may be copying the orcs too much. After all, they do it without magic, and we're wizards. Let me give it some thought and look through my books."

Cordelia did give it thought, and she did look through her books. She looked through her reference books and she looked through her spell books, and she found a spell for shaping stone. It had never been one of her favorites, and she'd learned it after she had made the house for her nephew. But it used the principle of similarity. You shaped the form you wanted the stone to take in miniature out of clay or mud, then cast the spell, and the stone copied the form of the model, but it was much larger.

That spell, though, was much too complicated for Anoria. But when Cordelia got to looking at it, she realized that much of the complexity was to allow the spell to copy any form that the model took and to adjust for the difference in size between the miniature and the stone to be re-formed. If a wizard already knew the shape and size she wanted, she could simplify the spell quite a bit. She could use the model of a bottle as a spell containment vessel then, as the spell was cast into the containment vessel, its shape could be refined by the structure of the runes applied to the model.

It was a different way of making bottles, and it started with an already formed pane of glass, not with sand. So it meant that producing the bottles would require extra spells. But it would get things simple enough that if it worked, Anoria could learn the spells.

Cordelia set about crafting the simplest bottle-shaping spell she could manage. And when she got that done, she popped to Kronisburg to the same shop where she often bought her magical supplies and arranged to have two silver bottles crafted. When they were ready, she would take them home, engrave the necessary runes onto them, and Anoria would be able to use them and the new spells to make several bottles from a pane of glass.

CHAPTER 37

Location: Cooper Home, Greenshire
Date: 6 Pago, 143 AF

Anoria had developed a routine for production this summer. Ten panes of glass on first day. Ten small bottles on second. Five panes of the truly clear glass on third day, because there wasn't as much demand for glass that couldn't be cut to fit. Seven large bottles on fourth day. On fifth day, she splurged a bit. She could usually produce eight bowls of various colors, as well as two panes of colored glass. It took a little time for the coloring agents to accumulate. When William Hagen needed it, she could produce ten sheets of steel on sixth day, but she limited that to every other week.

She almost always had seventh day free of chores. And she began looking around at the younger people of the village. "Who do you think we ought to get together this year?" she asked Arabelle. "There must be someone."

Arabelle Mead grinned openly. Yes, there was one match that she wanted to see happen but it could wait. Anoria was only twenty, in spite of her accomplishments. Gregory was showing no signs of interest in any of the village girls, and the spate of food gifts had gradually petered off. Yes, that one could wait.

"Drake Aden," Arabelle said. "He's getting on toward thirty. Past time he married. I make it that Seda Perrin would be a good match for him. She's quiet and he's loud, but his strengths will play to her weaknesses and vice versa. And that brother of hers, Armin—he's twenty-five if he's a day. I don't understand this putting off marriage, I really don't. I'm thinking that Jakinda Aden is a good match for him."

"Jakinda," Anoria said. "Jakinda? She's just about the smartest person in the village. And Armin, well, you just can't call him especially . . . ah . . . smart."

"Just as well," Arabelle said. "Again, her pluses will make up for his minuses. Sharp as a tack, that one is. Sharp enough to see that she'll wind up in charge, just as she should be. And Armin, well, he won't mind. Boy doesn't want to put the effort in, wants to be told what to do. That match will work, I'm sure."

Anoria shrugged a bit. "If you say so," she said doubtfully. "What about Franz Gellert? He's been alone in that farmhouse since he inherited it from his Uncle Max. And he's got a bit of a feud going on with his other uncle, Jasper. Now that Ahern is in charge it's not so bad, but things were a little hot for a while." Anoria settled back in the sun, confident that Arabelle couldn't make a match with the very difficult Franz.

"Got that figured as well," Arabelle cackled. "Alice Aden. Poor girl is allergic to wool and lives on a sheep farm. Makes her sneeze all day and all night. Franz doesn't have sheep, after all, only chickens and the farm. It will be a relief to her, that match will."

So, through a number of maneuvers, a few hints, and some downright pushing, the matches were made. The most surprising, however, turned out to be Deaconess Willow. On her own, with no help from the notorious duo of matchmakers, Margaret Willow decided that Fred Bade needed a second wife. He didn't get along with anyone, much less his son or daughter-in-law. Deaconess Willow had him wrapped around her little finger inside of a week.

Anoria barely recognized Margaret Willow. From a rather severe, spare woman, she had blossomed into something quite different. She gained a bit of weight and loosened the tight knot of her hair. Suddenly she was one of the happiest matrons in the village.

Location: Cooper Home, Greenshire
Date: 13 Pago, 143 AF

While Anoria and Arabelle were making matches, with little to no consultation with the people being matched, the villagers of Greenshire, Brookshire, and even Copriceshire were getting used to the new products. Joanna was selling her perfume in the tiny bottles. The larger bottles were sold independently for all sorts of uses, as were the bowls.

Anoria mostly wanted to make the bowls, well, for pretty. They required one less spell than the bottles, which made her life easier, and she liked seeing the sun shining through the various colors. It was a surprise to her when a woman came in wanting a plain, clear glass bowl. She didn't think the clear ones were all that attractive and hadn't made a lot of them.

"Why do you want a clear one?" she finally asked a woman from Copriceshire. "The colors are so pretty."

"For baking," the woman said. "Put a little pig fat and flour in it, then put your bread dough in it, and it bakes up fine. I want the clear one so I can see the color of the crust when the bread is ready."

"You can cook in them?" Anoria was startled. That certainly wasn't the reason she'd started making them.

"Oh, yes. I found that out when my daughter put one on a hot stove. It didn't break, so I thought I'd try baking in it. It worked out fine, so I want another. That way I can bake bread in one and a meat pie in the other."

As Joanna often said, the customer is always right. So Anoria made the woman another clear bowl.

The next day, thanks to that woman's gossiping at the Chandler's, two Greenshire women brought in broken bowls, complaining that they had broken when all they'd done was put them in the oven.

It was very confusing, this situation. Anoria didn't know why the colored glass bowls were breaking or why the clear ones weren't. But she thought the reason might be related to the fact that they could cut the colored glass panes, but not the ones made from just the pure white sand.

She went ahead and replaced the colored bowls with clear ones, but she also put out the word that the colored bowls and colored bottles were not suitable for baking or cooking. She had to replace a few more before the word got out, but eventually the various villages' women stopped breaking bowls in their stoves.

She had Joanna put a notice up in the family's market stall, too. It said: Not responsible for misuse of colored bowls for cooking.

CHAPTER 38

Location: Intercessor's House, Greenshire
Date: 6 Cogaine, 143 AF

As a rule, the area around Greenshire was very sedate and safe. Deep in the heart of Fornteroy Province, in farming and grazing country, the local inhabitants rarely saw a soldier. When one came walking north from Gent on an early spring market day, he collected stares all the way to the intercessor's home. He looked sort of familiar to the inhabitants, but no one could really place him. He also looked tired and had a rather vague, faraway look in his eyes.

When the soldier knocked on the door, Gregory was taken aback when he answered. It took a few moments to recognize the red hair and the lock of it that always fell into Laurence Firebird's face. "Laurence, Laurence," Gregory said. "It's you, isn't it?"

Laurence's face creased a bit as he tried to place the man in front of him. "Gregory. When did you move in with my father?"

Gregory grew more worried as he looked into Laurence's eyes. "Come in, Laurence," he said, noticing that the villagers were staring. "Come in and let's talk."

Gregory ushered Laurence into the kitchen and had him sit at the table. He made some of the cocoa that Cordelia had given him and cut a piece of Leanna Mason's recently delivered cake. The gifts of food had tapered off a bit, but a new group of girls came of an age to marry every year. "Eat and drink," Gregory urged. "You look tired."

Laurence drank the cocoa in one gulp and sat, staring into the cup. In a few moments, he took a bite of the cake. Gregory made another cup of cocoa, feeling that Laurence was beginning to revive a bit. He waited until Laurence was ready to talk. With the food and the sweet drink, the faraway look in Laurence's eyes began to fade a bit. "Where's my father?" he asked.

"He was transferred to Gent," Gregory said. "Two years ago, now. I took the parish shortly after he left."

"He's happy there?"

"I understand he's doing quite well," Gregory answered. "Didn't you stop in Gent at all?"

Laurence shook his head. The faraway look was back in his eyes. He began to talk. "No. I never thought to stop there. When I left the army, all I could think of was coming back to Greenshire. I was happier here than I was anywhere else. I just assumed that Father would be here and that he and I might, finally, be able to talk, instead of yelling at one another."

Gregory had been looking at Laurence carefully. His uniform was clean, but patched. Laurence himself was thin and had finished the slice of cake in mere moments. Gregory stood, went to the larder and cut a slice of ham and another of cheese. He placed these on two slices of buttered bread and set it in front of Laurence. "Eat," he directed. "I can tell you've had a bad time. Just eat. Then you can rest for a while. We'll figure something out after you've rested."

Laurence visibly restrained himself from falling on the food like a starving child. He ate slowly, chewing every bite. He drank the tea Gregory made him, as well. When he had finished, he slumped in the chair and looked around. "Windows," he muttered. "We never had windows."

Gregory urged Laurence to stand up and took him to the spare room. "Lie down," he said. "Sleep. When you wake up, it will be time to talk. You look too tired to think."

Gregory pulled Laurence's battered boots off and covered him with a blanket. "Sleep," he urged and reinforced the command with a spell. Laurence fell into a deep sleep, and Gregory felt it was safe to leave him alone for a while. He left the house and headed for the Cooper place.

Location: Cooper Home, Greenshire
Date: 6 Cogaine, 143 AF

"I don't know what he's been through," Gregory told Debra and Michael. "He didn't have the energy to talk, not for long. But I think we need a familiar face or two around him when he wakes. And I remembered that he and Joanna and Anoria were friends."

"Anoria won't be back for a few weeks," Debra mused. "She and Cordelia are off on one of their research projects. But Joanna and Laurence were very friendly at one time. He used to help her compound lotions and perfumes. Let me get Joanna. She can sit with him."

* * *

Debra bustled into the stillroom to speak to Joanna. "Dear," she said, "I have some news."

Joanna looked up from grinding rosemary into a powder. "What news, Mother?"

"Laurence Firebird is at Gregory's house. He's not in good sh—" Debra didn't get to finish her statement, as Joanna had taken off running.

Location: Intercessor's House, Greenshire
Date: 6 Cogaine, 143 AF

"What happened to him?" Joanna asked during the walk to Gregory's. "Why would he be in such bad shape?"

Gregory shook his head. "I don't know. He's in the king's uniform, so it's likely he was involved in one of the border wars between us and the Servile States. All I can be sure of is that he's been to faraway places and he's tired. I think he may have seen some things he didn't expect to see. He looks very worn."

"We'll fix that," Joanna said. "I always liked him, you know. And I always felt his father was wrong to try and push him into the intercessorhood when he didn't want to go."

* * *

Laurence woke several hours later, to find Joanna sitting in a chair beside the bed he was sleeping on. She was immersed in a book and didn't notice he was awake. He lay and watched her for a while, remembering the days he had spent working with her and her herbs and flowers. They were good memories.

Finally, he said, "Roses."

Joanna looked up from her book and smiled. "Roses, Laurence?"

"You always smell like roses. I always loved that."

Joanna rose from the chair and stepped nearer to the bed. "It's my favorite too."

Laurence motioned her to come nearer, which she did. She perched on the edge of the bed. Laurence took a deep breath and closed his eyes before letting it out. "Rosemary, too. And a bit of lavender."

"You always were good at figuring out scents," Joanna said. "How are you?"

"Better," he answered. "It was a long trip. I'd finally found the words to speak with Father, and I hurried. Too fast, I guess. In a day or two, I'll hurry back to Gent. I need to speak to him and explain."

Joanna raised her hand and brushed Laurence's wayward lock of hair out of his face. "Explain what?"

"That I understand now. On the battlefield, I prayed, something I swore I'd never do. I prayed to Zagrod, asked him to please tell me why we were fighting. And he did. I need to tell Father that I've found the understanding that I never had before. The gods, at least some of the gods, really do care about us. But there are limits on what they can do, and I can understand that better now. You have to see what the Servile States have turned into, the suffering and the cruelty. And we were cruel too, in fighting them. And I wondered what we were doing this for, what good could come out of it. And then Zagrod showed me. It's hard to explain."

Joanna's eyes were soft as she looked at him. "I always knew you would come to understand the gods' goodness. It just took a while."

Laurence shifted a bit, and Joanna fluffed the pillows for him to lean against. "Are you hungry? Thirsty?"

Laurence shook his head, the errant lock falling back down. "Just tired, still. I don't know why I woke. I think it was the roses. That smell always brings memories of you. Did you know that I took some of the petals, when I ran away?"

"Yes. I knew. I saw you that night. I couldn't sleep for worrying about what your father would do. He was so angry. I saw you in the garden, in the moonlight. But you left before I could get downstairs."

"He just yelled. He always just yelled. I was so embarrassed. Him grabbing me by the ear and pulling me away like that. He was going to send me to Gent the next day. Said he was going to pull strings and force me to attend the seminary. I couldn't bear that thought. I can't stand the city, even now. I want to be here, in the village, with fields and woods around."

Gregory, from the bedroom door, asked, "You said Zagrod answered you? What else did he say?"

"Go home."

Location: Intercessor's House, Greenshire
Date: 10 Cogaine, 143 AF

Laurence's story came out over the next few days as he rested. Gregory sent a message to Larendo Firebird to tell him that his son was home. Larendo arrived on the fourth day after Laurence.

Larendo and Laurence were closeted in the study for several hours. They both had reddened eyes when they came out and joined Gregory in the kitchen.

"You still refuse to attend the seminary?" Larendo asked.

"I don't need to be in cities, Father," Laurence answered. "I need to be here. And finding understanding doesn't make me the proper material for an intercessor either. I'll get work here in Greenshire. As a farmhand, perhaps."

"If that's what you want," Larendo answered. "I'll not try and drive you in my direction, not again. But I need to return to Gent. I'm happy there, and I never was cut out to be a village intercessor."

Gregory felt a certain amount of relief at that. He'd worried for a bit that Larendo would want to resume his duties in Greenshire. "I'm sure that Laurence can get work," he said. "Farms always need more hands to work them."

Larendo and Laurence spent a few days together at Gregory's house. It was a pleasant time for them all. Larendo remarked that he hadn't been given such a surplus of cakes and pies when he had been the intercessor.

"You weren't single and marriage bait. And even after Mother died, you weren't approachable," Laurence remarked. "Gregory is."

"Gregory is going to get fat," Gregory said. "Gregory can't seem to convince the young ladies of the village that he is not in the market for a wife just now. Eat, please. Usually by the middle of summer the gifts taper off, and I can go back to being the intercessor and stop fending off the girls."

"An intercessor should marry," Larendo announced pompously. "How can you counsel a married couple if you have no knowledge of the state yourself?"

"Rather carefully, I expect," Laurence said, grinning a bit. "Rather carefully."

* * *

Larendo left the next morning, and Laurence decided that he would look for work that day. "Come have breakfast first," Gregory suggested. "We'll try to figure out which farm is most likely to need the help."

"Catch me up on who's doing what," Laurence said as Gregory rustled up a meal. He was sitting at the table with his back to the open door. The springtime air wafted in through it. "And tell me where all the glass came from. I've never seen a village that had so many glass windows. And I don't recall them being here when I left."

"That was Anoria's doing," Gregory explained. He stopped for a moment and decided to ask the question that had been on his mind for several days. "I understood you and Anoria were close. Are you back here to try and marry her?"

Joanna Cooper was walking up the path when she heard Laurence answer. "Anoria was my friend, Gregory. But I never felt a romantic attachment to her. I love Joanna. Always have."

"It's about time," Joanna said from the doorway. "I've been waiting six years for that."

CHAPTER 39

Location: Cooper Home, Greenshire
Date: 14 Banth, 144 AF

"We'll wait for Anoria and Cordelia to get back," Joanna insisted. She and Debra were planning her wedding. They were in the greenhouse, soaking up the warm light from the sun. "I'm in no hurry and neither is Laurence. We'll wait."

"Very well," Debra said. "I've waited this long to see you married, another week or so won't hurt, I suppose." Michael and Laurence were planting the fields together. Clarence was in school and it was just the two of them in the house. The hired girls were in the stillroom, which was now a separate building, alongside Anoria's glass workshop. "I will be glad to see her back as well. When she's away, it's like part of the family is missing. And Cordelia, as well. I never thought I'd ever feel that way about Cordelia."

"Cordelia and Anoria are pleased to hear it," Cordelia said from the front door. "I suppose we should have come to the greenhouse in the first place." She grinned when Joanna and Debra jumped a bit. "But we came in the back door."

Anoria peered around Cordelia and asked, "What's going on? Why are you being so lazy, Mistress Joanna? The middle of the morning it is, and here you are, not doing the least amount of work. What happened to my driven friend?"

"She's learned better," Debra said, wryly. "And about time too. Come out you two. Hugs all around, and I'll make us some tea. We've got a lot of catching up to do."

Location: Town Square , Greenshire
Date: 22 Banth, 144 AF

The wedding was held the next seventh day. The village declared it a day for a spring festival, and, fortunately, the erratic springtime weather cooperated. Joanna wore a dark blue gown and carried some of the flowers she grew. The roses weren't in bloom yet, but she had some spicy smelling pink flowers in her hands as she walked to the temple.

Anoria accompanied her as her attendant, dressed in a becoming shade of lighter blue. She carried more of the flowers, as well. Gregory performed the ceremony on the temple steps so that all could see and hear the vows. Afterward, every table in the village was brought to the square, and everyone celebrated for several hours.

Arabelle Mead cornered Gregory as he was on his way to the drinks table to get a cup of cider. "When are you going to take the plunge?" she wanted to know. "I've seen your eyes following Anoria around the square. Why don't you just ask her?"

Gregory looked around to make sure no one was close enough to hear his reply. He leaned down a bit to answer. "Anoria has it in her to be a great wizard, I believe. What would a great wizard want with a simple village intercessor? She'll go adventuring one day, just like her foster mother."

"You're wrong, boy," Arabelle said. "Wrong, wrong, wrong. This village is her home, and she never wants to leave it for long." Arabelle and Anoria had talked quite a bit about what Anoria really wanted in life.

"But she's going to be very powerful," Gregory objected.

"Powerful doesn't have to mean dangerous," Arabelle pointed out. "I know her quite well, you know. She'll not go adventuring, not that one. Pay some attention, why don't you? Have you ever heard her say anything about it?"

"I suppose not," Gregory said. "I just assumed . . ."

"Wrong," Arabelle said. "You assumed wrong. You know she's the girl for you. I know she's the girl for you. Just ask her."

"In my own time," Gregory said. "You can't have us all dancing to your tune, Mistress Mead."

Location: Intercessor''s House, Greenshire
Date: 25 Noron, 144 AF

"No, Gregory. Anoria will never be a really powerful wizard. She has the talent and the training but not the . . ." Laurence paused, looking for the right phrase. "Desire for action, I guess. I don't really have it either, in spite of some of the battles I've seen. It's hard to explain. There is a kind of intensity in combat or other very risky things. One of the effects of that intensity is to make wizards, or intercessors for that matter, gain magical ability faster. I've known a couple of adventuring wizards, not in Cordelia Cooper's class, but fairly decent ones. They lust after action. They need it to feel alive."

"Cordelia Cooper doesn't seem to have that," Gregory pointed out.

"Don't let her fool you," Laurence said. "She holds it in check, but has the bug. When she was becoming the wizard Cordelia, she didn't hold it in check at all, not from the stories I've heard. She'd go up against anything, the riskier the better. Seriously, Gregory, you can expect Anoria to get better. She will; much the same as you will. But it won't be at the rate of an adventuring wizard."

CHAPTER 40

Location: Cooper Home, Greenshire
Date: 25 Cashi, 144 AF

Gregory considered what Arabelle and Laurence had told him for most of the summer. Tess and Armand Factor, his parents, came to visit for part of that summer, and he was busy. There were babies to welcome, funerals to officiate, and weddings to perform. And through all of them, he found himself listening for Anoria's voice.

Finally, one day in the late fall he decided to speak. As she could usually be found in her workshop, he decided to speak to her there. And, as was usual on fifth day, Anoria was producing bowls and colored panes of glass.

She had just lifted a sparkling dark blue bowl from the table and was holding it up to the light. "Beautiful," Gregory said.

Anoria jumped nearly out of her skin and dropped the bowl. Gregory dived to catch it and barely made it in time. Unfortunately, he had managed to knock Anoria off her feet in the process. She landed on her bottom with a thump. And then she glared at him through the curtain of her hair.

He almost decided not to say anything, but felt laughter bubbling up. She was a sight. Her hair had come loose when the pins fell out and was straggling over her face. He couldn't stop the snicker.

She brushed the hair away with one hand and tried to keep glaring, but started giggling. "You should see yourself, Intercessor Gregory. Here you are, lying on the floor, covered in dust, clutching a bowl in your hands. I agree it's beautiful, but you needn't have thrown yourself on the floor. I could make another."

Gregory started laughing as well. He stood up and set the bowl down, before helping Anoria to her feet. "Ah, but we can't have that, Mistress Anoria. You still drive yourself too hard, I think." Gregory began dusting himself off a bit and, with his face turned away, said, "But it wasn't the bowl I was calling beautiful."

Anoria stopped giggling. "It wasn't?"

Gregory stopped brushing at his pants and looked her in the eyes. "It wasn't. It was you. I know I've been slow to speak, but I think I've loved you for years. I came to ask you to be my wife, Anoria."

"You never said." Anoria's voice sounded a bit choked. "Why didn't you say?"

"Because I'm a little slow, sometimes," Gregory ventured, hoping she would smile again. "It seems everyone knew you were the woman for me, except me. Will you marry me? Soon?"

Anoria's face glowed. "I will. But it won't be that soon. Cordelia will be here tomorrow, and we're going to Drakan for research again. I'm committed to it, and I won't let her down. Will you wait the winter for me? Or, now that you've spoken, will you decide to speak to someone else?" Anoria was smiling as she spoke, and Gregory's heart warmed to see it.

"As long as it took me to speak to you," Gregory said, "I don't think you have to worry. Shall we tell the others?"

"I'd rather tell Cordelia first," Anoria admitted. "I want to tell her in my own time. While we're on the trip, I think. She's like a mother to me, you know. And I don't like the thought of leaving her alone in the forest either." Anoria had noticed that Cordelia was no longer quite the reclusive person she had been in the past.

"She lived alone in the forest before you came along," Gregory pointed out. He put his arms around Anoria and held her close. Her hair smelled wonderful.

"Not so much anymore," Anoria said into his shoulder. "She's in and out of the farm almost weekly, nowadays. I'll need a little time to speak to her. And you'd best be prepared. If we marry, I expect she'll be in and out of the parsonage as well. Will that cause you problems with your High Intercessor? And what about marrying a wizard? Have you considered what the temple will say?"

Even though the villages of Greenshire and Brookshire had come to accept Anoria, there was still a certain fear of wizards and their works in most places.

"I'll speak to High Intercessor Landris this winter. I doubt there will be a problem, but I'd have to speak to him anyway. If there is a problem, perhaps Barra can help me solve it."

Anoria snuggled into Gregory's arms. Somehow this all felt very right. "Until the spring then?"

"Until the spring."

CHAPTER 41

Location: Greenwood
Date: 25 Coganie, 144 AF

"I thought you said you couldn't produce a pen," Anoria said, staring at the pen Cordelia was holding.

"I said I'd look into it," Cordelia corrected. "And I did. The problem with a pen of Wizard's Marking is that the basic Wizard's Mark spell is really more a stamp than a pen. You don't draw the Wizard's Mark with your finger; you just touch the object, and the mark appears. You have to set the mark you're going to use when you're preparing the spell. That's the real difference in Improved Wizard's Mark. It acts more like a pen, and you actually put your fingers together like you're using a pen and draw with it."

"Improved Wizard's Mark" was the spell that Cordelia used to help guide the magic in the spare rooms and the pots of sorting and table of melting. "The process for making an enchanted item that casts a spell over and over again, or one that continually produces a magical effect, is well established. So I based it on Improved Wizard's Mark and this"—Cordelia waved the pen—"is the result." The pen was made of ivory and had a tip that was platinum. There were lots of runes inscribed on it in very small script.

"And how does it work?" Anoria asked. "Will it write down any spell you want? Can I say 'Write me a spell of invisibility? ' "

"No, that won't work," Cordelia answered. "What it's good for is inscribing not quite magical items like the table of melting, the spare room, the pantry, or the cold room."

The pantry was a spell Cordelia had developed after Anoria had moved in. It created a room like the spare room, except this one was full of food. It was the parent of the Portable Pantry spell and of the Cold Room spell. The cold room was like the pantry, except it was always cold and you had to put the food in it. That was one of Anoria's jobs now that she could use spells. She had to use Cold Room on the specially inscribed false door every few days to keep the cold room going. If she didn't, the room would disappear, and whatever was in it would make a mess in the hallway.

The Spare Room spell, the Pantry spell, the Cold Room spell, and even the Portable Pantry all used a variation of Wizard's Mark that let you draw magically on a surface. The drawings around and in the false doors of the various room spells helped control the flow of magic in those spells, making them easier to recharge.

"It's not like a regular pen that can blob or make a line too dark or too thin," Cordelia said. "As long as you know what you want to write, the pen will write it. I have tried using it for recording spells, but for some reason it gets the colors wrong. So you still have to write your spell book with the special colored ink."

"Cordelia, making magical items this powerful takes life force or many, many years," Anoria said, obviously concerned.

"Don't start worrying about that now," Cordelia chided. "It took no more than I could spare, and it will work for simply practicing runes."

"That alone will save a bundle on paper and ink," Anoria agreed hesitantly. She was well aware that Cordelia didn't like discussing the life force cost of enchanting items. "Even now that I can use spells, I still waste some ink. I can't tell you the number of runes I knew how to write that were spoiled by the pen making a blob just where I didn't need one."

"Same here," Cordelia said. "Bottle after bottle of ink. That won't happen again, though."

"Wonderful."

Location: University of Drakan, Dragon Lands
Date: 27 Prima, 145 AF

The scholars at the University of Drakan were very helpful, as they always were. Cordelia was continuing her research on the "Pen of Wizard's Marking." It still had a few quirks, but she and Anoria were learning to work around them. Still, after two months of academia, they were both tired of research. "What shall we do with the rest of the winter?" Cordelia asked.

"Do you remember Brazla's suggestion?" Anoria asked. "Are there really places that have white sand? And black sand?"

"There are," Cordelia answered.

"Can we go collect sand?"

"Why not?" Cordelia grinned. "There's an island, I know. The people all wear clothing made of grass, when they wear clothing at all. We'll go visit. The beach there is as black as coal."

Anoria blushed at the thought of grass clothing. Cordelia laughed.

Location: Black Beach, Spice Islands
Date: 28 Prima, 145 AF

Anoria and Cordelia walked by the water's edge on the black beach. The waves made a wooosh sound and the breeze was very pleasant. Anoira decided that it was time to talk.

"Cordelia?"

"Yes?"

"Gregory has asked me to marry him."

Cordelia broke into a wide smile. "It's about time."

Anoria gaped. "You don't mind? You don't?"

Cordelia stopped walking and took Anoria in her arms. "Of course not, silly. I've known for several years that the two of you would make a good match. I'd have been a little more worried if it had been someone else, but Gregory is just as much of a stay-at-home as you are. I believe you'll be very happy." Marrying another magic user would also make for a more equal partnership, Cordelia believed.

Anoria had tears in her eyes. "I was afraid you'd object. You've never married. And I always had the feeling that you'd rather I followed in your footsteps and went adventuring."

"Pah! That's not for everyone," Cordelia said. "Yes, it was for me. I still miss it now and then, even. But what you do is different. True, you won't gain the power I gained. But you won't face death every other week either. You'll have the knowledge, though, and you'll pass it on. That's really what's most important to me. And I've come to believe in the last few years that more wizards ought to concentrate on making life better for everyone, rather than killing things. Anoria, I've done a lot of things in my life, some good, some bad. Mostly, I think, necessary. But the truth is that the greatest good for the world I've done with my magic is that silly road

I'm making for Count Whitehall. Just because it will let people move their goods to market faster and easier."

Cordelia paused for a moment. "Not that killing orcs is a bad thing, you understand. It's just that not everyone needs to do it. I was very good at it in my day. And in spite of the songs and tales, I didn't deliberately kill anyone who wasn't trying to kill me, I'll have you understand. But over the last few years, since you've come to me, I've realized that we—wizards, I mean—could be doing more than fighting battles. The glass, for instance. I'd never have had that idea on my own. And it's done quite a bit of good."

"You're really a village girl at heart, aren't you?" Anoria teased. "You can take the girl out of the village, but you can't take the village out of the girl." In spite of her fearsome reputation, Cordelia had returned to the vicinity of her home village, after all.

"Well . . ." Cordelia sniffed. "In some ways, I suppose. But you'll note that I'm very much in favor of all children receiving the same opportunities. I'll guarantee you this—any father who wants to educate his sons and not educate his daughters will get to deal with . . . me."

Anoria believed it.

Location: Seminary, Gent
Date: 28 Prima, 145 AF

"And that's what I'm going to do," Gregory finished his prepared speech and looked High Intercessor Landris in the eye. His face was defiant.

"And you expect me to object?" High Intercessor Landris asked.

"I don't know, sir," Gregory admitted. "But I'm going to marry her, objections or not. I thought you ought to know that."

The High Intercessor nodded. "Some might. Those who are a little more conservative at any rate. But, like you, Barra grants me spells. So I understand. And it's my opinion, which is not shared by everyone, that there's no reason a wizard and an intercessor shouldn't marry. I'd think, although it's not proven by any means, that the children you produce would be more likely to inherit the magical ability." High Intercessor Landris was a rather portly man now. He hadn't always been. Gregory had even heard a rumor that Landris had been an adventuring intercessor in his younger days.

"Don't worry, my boy," High Intercessor Landris said, rising from his ornate chair. "You'll get no objections from me. In fact, I'd be pleased to perform the ceremony. And, since I'm your High Intercessor, I doubt anyone else will have an objection. Of course, if they do, well, they can just deal with . . . me."

CHAPTER 42

Location: Yellow Desert, Dragon Lands
Date: 8 Banth, 145 AF

Anoria squinted from the glare. "Brazla wasn't exaggerating, was she?"

Cordelia was also squinting from the glare. "Doesn't look it. Miles and miles of pale yellow sand. Miles of it."

Anoria pulled the sorting pot from the portable pantry. "I've got to see what happens here. I've got to."

"I have to admit I'm a bit curious myself," Cordelia said. "There doesn't seem to be any color but yellow. It can't be gold, I don't imagine."

"Probably not," Anora said. "Watch this separation. I'll bet we get just as many different kinds of stuff as we do from the stream at home."

And they did. True, there was a much larger percentage of transparent sand, which would come in handy. But there were also a number of the other colors as well.

"Strange," Cordelia muttered. "Let's try a mountain stream or something. I'm tired of hot." Beads of sweat were running into her eyes and making them sting. She dusted the fine sand off her hands and sneezed.

"Works for me," Anoria agreed, wiping sweat from her face. "I'm a little tired of hot, too."

Location: Forest of Areadel Elflands
Date: 9 Banth, 145 AF

The cool was a relief. "I guess I'm not cut out for those island climates," Anoria said. "They're so hot and wet. And the deserts are so hot and dry."

"You might have tried the local fashions," Cordelia remarked. "I'll admit they aren't very modest, but they do suit the climate."

"I didn't see you climbing into a grass skirt," Anoria countered.

"True," Cordelia conceded. "Very true." She changed the subject, rather rapidly in Anoria's opinion. "What will we find here, do you suppose?"

"No idea." Anoria grinned. "Dirt, I expect. What else would be in a mountain stream?"

Anoria was quite surprised to discover a much larger percentage of gold in this area. "That's just strange," she muttered. "We went to a place that had the color gold all over it. We didn't find gold. We come to a place that doesn't have any of that color and what do we find? Strange."

Cordelia said, "The natural world has many surprises."

Anoria laughed. "Gregory said that to me once." She lifted the sorting pot and heard a strange rattle. "Shouldn't this be empty?"

"I would have thought so," Cordelia agreed. "Tip it out. What do we have?"

Anoria complied. "Looks like rocks."

"Hmmm," Cordelia said. "It does indeed. But just in case, throw them in the bag. I'll have them looked at."

"Will do," Anoria agreed. "But what use are dull, flat-looking, greenish, bluish, reddish rocks?

"What use is clear sand?"

"Well," Anoria admitted, "I suppose you have a point."

Location: Greenshire
Date: 24 Pago, 145 AF

Anoria and Gregory were married on Midsummer's Day. The entire village attended, as did Cordelia. High Intercessor Landris officiated. He performed the ceremony on the temple steps, just as Gregory had done for Joanna and Laurence, as well as for many other couples.

Anoria and Gregory were sitting at the head table for the Midsummer feast when the most surprising thing happened. Cordelia, who was sitting on Anoria's right hand, froze for a moment when the High Intercessor's laugh rang out. High Intercessor Landris boomed at his secretary for a moment and then returned his attention to the feast.

"Bernie," Cordelia asked. "Is that you? I thought you looked familiar, but I didn't recognize you until you laughed."

"Good Barra! I haven't heard that name in years," High Intercessor Landris said. "Cordelia? You're the wizard they talk about here? I didn't realize they meant you."

Anoria and Gregory watched in bemusement as Cordelia and High Intercessor Landris stood and embraced one another. Through the babble of words that ensued, they realized that the two had known one another quite well at one time.

But that's another story.

The End

AFTERWORD AND NOTES

The magic of Anoria and Cordelia's world is the same as the magic in the Merged World series of stories and books. The 'orrible truth is I used it because I had it handy. (Paula leaves the magic to me, since she is a sane and rational person, and when creating magic, it helps to be a little crazy.) Well, there is another reason but that book hasn't been written yet.

So here is how magic works in Anoria's world.

Magic is an energy field that originates in neighboring universes called "planes." The planes, like the Plane of Fire or the Plane of Ice, have different laws and the creatures and beings that live in them are based on different structures. So the salamander that the orcs use to heat the glass moved to the Material Plane for stuff to eat. Stuff that burns, which is hard to come by in the Plane of Fire, because most things that will burn are already burned up there.

Anyway, magic moves from these other planes through the Material Plane (the universe that Anoria and Cordelia live in), and as it moves through, it interacts with the people, animals, plants, and stuff that are in the Material Plane. Different sorts of things affect the magic in different ways. Crystals, since they have a very orderly structure, affect it one way; living things, since they are very complicated, affect it in very complicated ways. Mostly, the more complicated something is, the more it affects the magic. People are pretty complicated, so they affect it a lot. What they call Magic Moss is more akin to lichen or fungi than moss, between a plant and an animal. It lives mostly off magic, and to do that it has to capture a lot of magic. So it has evolved to do that. That is why it's so useful in making magic Items.

Spells are magic tied up in knots, then released in a certain way. When a person thinks or speaks or moves, it affects the magic flow, twists it or ripples it or the like. The same thing happens when a cow moos or a duck flaps its wings, even when a mouse sniffs cheese. Almost all the time this has no effect on the world that anyone not a god could measure. But if a person learns to think the right things in the right way and the right order, that person can tie the magic flow into knots like you use to tie your shoes. Then, when they let the magic untie the right way, stuff happens.

People can make simple but powerful spells. The gods, being much smarter than people, can make very, very complicated spells. Starting a fire isn't very complicated, but healing a wound . . . ? That is *very* complicated, so mostly only spells granted by gods can heal.

Just like it's easier to tie a knot if you have something to hold the string in place, it's easier to craft a spell if you have a magical item to craft it into. That was one of the reasons that Anoria's glass melting table worked. Because Cordelia helped her make it, and once it was made it was much easier to craft the melting spell into it than it would have been to craft that spell without it. Cordelia could have designed a spell that wouldn't have needed the magic table, but then Cordelia is a very skilled and powerful wizard.

Weekdays

People don't name days on Anoria's world, instead they number them. First day through Seventh day. Anoria's world has a moon like ours and that moon has a twenty-eight-day orbit like ours.

Months

There are twelve thirty-day months plus Timu's Time, in the calendar of Anoria's world. Each month is named for a god of the pantheon of the people keeping the calendar. For Anoria and most of human culture on Anoria's world, the months are as follows:

1 Justain, god of law and justice,

2 Prima, goddess of healing,

3 Banth, god of travelers and crossroads,

4 Noron, god of war and contests,

5 Zagrod, god of knowledge,

6 Pago, god of natural magic,

7 Wovoro, god of the sea,

8 Estormany, goddess of the sky and weather,

9 Barra, goddess of the harvest,

10 Cashi, goddess of trade and bargains,

11 Dugon, dwarven god of making and craftsmanship,

12 Coganie, goddess of Death.

Twelve months of thirty days gives you three hundred and sixty days. With around five and a quarter days left. Those five and a quarter days are Timu's Time. The last day of Timu's Time is the shortest day of the year in the northern hemisphere and the day after that is the first day of Justain.

Year

When your calendar starts depends on who you are and where you live. In Anoria's case, she lives in Whitehall County. And Whitehall County was founded and given to the first Count Whitehall one hundred and thirty-four years before this story starts. The elves who lived there before were not consulted. Other places count from different events but for convenience we have used the dating system Anoria uses.

About the books

Anoria is the first book in a series of about three (maybe more) books. The Family of Wizards stories will be about Anoria and her family and the people of the village of Greenshire, which, over the years, is probably going to grow quite a bit. And about how they and others like them will affect the larger world and be affected by it.

The Cordelia stories, Born in Magic, Schooled in Magic and so on, are about how Aunt Cordelia got to be Aunt Cordelia. The truth is Cordelia's life was much harder and less pleasant than Anoria's. It was downright adventurous.

The Merge stories, some of which have been written but only a few have been published so far (depending on when you read this), are about a world very much like ours except that, very suddenly, magic starts working in it and the people that have played a certain role-playing game called WarSpell have gained the memories and abilities of a character that they played in the game. Those stories tie in with these books.

Made in the USA
Las Vegas, NV
18 February 2022